BOOKS BY HELENA NEWBURY

Helena Newbury is the *New York Times* and *USA Today* bestselling author of sixteen romantic suspenses, all available where you bought this book. Find out more at helenanewbury.com.

HOLD ME IN THE DARK

HELENA NEWBURY

regular job, I'd worked with a few feds and he didn't sound like any of them. They'd all had sticks up their asses, their voices smarmy and smoothly clinical. This guy *growled,* a low, throaty rumble that vibrated right through me. A blue collar voice, rough as denim and fiery as whiskey. It wasn't refined or polite. But it was a voice that would never, ever bullshit you.

My thumb lifted slightly from the button and I switched on the security camera in the hallway outside. The guy looked like a dockworker someone had forced into a suit at gunpoint. He was tall: the camera was mounted level with the top of the door, but his head was scarily close to it and his frame seemed too big, too animal, for a suit. His white shirt was stretched tight across broad, curving pecs and his jacket hung from shoulders more suited to a quarterback. His tie was loose and askew, like he was halfway through tearing it off. And his dark hair was tousled, as if someone had been running her hands through it, or he'd been in a fight, or both. I'd never seen someone suit an outfit less.

*And yet...*the shirt hugged those hard pecs in a way that made you want to run your palms over them. The cut of the suit showed off the glorious X-shape of him, wide shoulders, narrow waist and muscled quads. It had molded to him until it fit him like a favorite pair of jeans and the smartness of it set off his roughness perfectly. I'd never seen someone suit an outfit *more.*

I tilted the camera for a better angle and he must have heard it move because his head snapped up and he glared right into the lens, right at *me.*

His stare was so strong, I actually jerked back from the screen. His eyes were the pale blue of the sky on a crisp, clear morning, when there's not a hint of pollution or cloud and you can see for miles and miles. They caught me, held me, *pinned* me. They sought out every little secret, made me want to confess *now* because if he caught me in a lie it would be so much worse: they were half cop, half priest. I couldn't look away from that gaze and when I did, when I managed to tear my eyes away for just a second, I slammed up against a brutally hard jaw, roughly stubbled. A jaw that took punches and stayed there, unswayed, demanding *is that the best you got?* Lips that curled and pressed tight as he scowled at me: so angry and yet so hard and perfect in their shape. Like he might just lunge forward and—

I swallowed and flushed, my own lips suddenly tingling.

"I'm Special Agent Samuel Calahan," the man told me. "And I need your help."

He was gorgeous. Rough and rumpled and moodily gorgeous. I could feel the flush soaking down from my cheeks and all the way through my body. I wanted to mold myself to him and rub up against that roughness like a goddamn cat.

And then I remembered. And glanced down at my legs.

I wanted to have met him a year ago. *Before.* I wanted to run to the door and fling it wide. I wanted to tell my brother all about him.

I took my thumb away from the red button and instead pressed the button for the intercom. "Go away," I told him. "Leave me alone."

BOOM. This time, the door shook on its hinges. I stared at it in disbelief.

"*Now you listen to me, goddammit!*" the man yelled. "There's a woman in trouble. She's with a guy who's going to hurt her and the only shot I have at finding her in time is *you.* So whatever your problem is, get over it because I need you and I'm not leaving here until you help!"

I tugged on the wheels, sending me coasting backwards across the room. I came to a stop next to my desk and stared at the monitor. The man—Calahan—was glaring back at me from the camera. But there was something in those pale blue eyes, something beneath the anger, and it was powerful enough to make me catch my breath. A sadness like I'd never seen, soul-deep, *aching.*

The anger was just frustration. He couldn't bear to let something bad happen to a woman.

I looked towards the door. I wanted to keep him out there. As long as the world was safely out there, there were no stares, no questions. It was as if the accident never happened. But the second I opened the door, the illusion would be shattered. I didn't want to see his reaction, that reaction all men have, that *disappointment*—

"Her name is Jennifer Schuller. She's a dental nurse from New Jersey. She was on a date with a guy she met online, but when it ended, the guy started getting weird. Wouldn't let her out of the car. She called her friend in a panic, said they were heading for the Catskills, then the call was cut off. Cops found her phone broken by the side of the road—he must have tossed it out the window. We figure he's taking her somewhere in the mountains, but it's too big an area." I could feel my throat go tight with worry. "We'll never find them in time."

I saw those amazing green eyes soften, her own fear forgotten for a second. "What can I do?" she asked.

"The guy lives here in New York. That's why the local cops called the FBI. An hour ago, we raided his apartment. We found..."—I closed my eyes for a second and sighed, trying not to remember— "There were photos of some *bad shit*. Bad enough that we're really worried about Jennifer. It's looking like the guy had all this planned. I'm betting he has a cabin somewhere up in the Catskills. And I'm hoping the location's somewhere on *this*." I showed her the laptop. "It's encrypted. We can't get in. I called Lily, but she said you're the expert, when it comes to encryption."

She looked at the laptop, then back at me. She didn't come out from behind the desk. I could see the battle all over her face. She wanted to help, but.... *Is she scared of* me? I know I'm a big guy and I nearly knocked her door down, but I wasn't being intimidating *now*. Or at least, I wasn't trying to be. I could feel my heart hammering, but I tried to make my voice gentle. "Yolanda... you're the only chance we've got. And we're running out of time."

She held my gaze for a second longer and then nodded to herself. She turned side-on to me but instead of standing up, she coasted forwards and I figured she must be pushing herself along on an office chair. I sidestepped around the desk to meet her as she came out and—

Oh.

I blinked stupidly at the wheelchair. That was the last thing I'd been expecting.

I looked down into her eyes... and my stomach fell through the floor. She looked wounded. Wounded by the shock on my face. I tried to rearrange my expression, but it was too late. Those beautiful dark green eyes blinked, suddenly liquid. *No! Wait! I didn't mean—*

She looked away, lips tightening, and stuck her hand out for the laptop.

I've never wanted to undo a moment so much. I extended my arm and she snatched the laptop and—

I'm not the most sensitive guy. Most of the time I have no clue what a woman's thinking. But even I could see she'd got shields around her a foot thick and thanks to me they'd just slammed shut. Someone—some man—had seen her like this, and his reaction had torn her damn heart out. And now she thought I was the same.

But I wasn't, I'd just been surprised. The wheelchair didn't bother me. All I felt was anger, that something had hurt her. But now she was going to hate me forever—

The laptop was just sliding out of my fingers. I lunged forward and grabbed my end of it again. Because *no,* dammit, I wasn't going to leave things that way. It wasn't right and when something's not right, I can be a stubborn son of a bitch.

She tugged again, still looking determinedly away from me. But I held on. I held on until she *had* to look at me. And then I met her gaze and just looked at her, honest and open. I lowered my head fractionally. *I'm sorry.*

And I saw her shoulders loosen, just a little. Her shields inched down.

I kept looking at her. I drank in those eyes, that face. Her lips were blush-pink and her lower lip had this beautiful, delicate pout to it that made me imagine crushing it under mine. I looked because I couldn't *stop* looking. And whatever was on my face, it did what I couldn't do with words. It told her that I didn't care about the damn chair.

Her shoulders relaxed a little more. She looked away and I thought I saw her cheeks color. She looked back at me and nodded.

That would have to do. I let go of the laptop. She wheeled herself back behind the desk and went to work.

me that I'd said "Call *us* back," not "Call *me* back." Like we were partners. And it *did* feel like that. She'd become part of this.

I pushed the idea away and stood up. I was way, way too attracted to this woman. If I stayed around her, I was going to do something dumb. "Thank you. I'll get out of your hair."

I reached for the laptop, but she slapped a hand down on it. "That's *it?* No! I need to know what happens!"

My stomach knotted. I knew the look in her eyes because I saw it in the mirror every day. She'd become involved. She'd felt the fear, knowing she was the woman's only hope. Then the high of cracking the case, the one that can become so dangerously addictive. Now she needed closure. But I didn't want her getting any more involved... with my work or with me. I knew what that did to people.

"What you did was amazing," I told her sincerely. She blinked at me and looked away as if she didn't know how to process that. As if no one ever told her that. "But I can take it from here." I unplugged the laptop and gently slid it from under her hand. Tucked it under my arm and headed for the door.

I got three steps before there was a hiss of wheels and she slewed in front of me, making me pull up short. She stared up at me, determined. "I need to know if she's okay!"

I felt this *pull.* Deep and powerful, it went way beyond her looks. She was a firework of a woman, brilliant and quick, enigmatic and exciting. I didn't just want her, I *liked* her. And I knew that's exactly why I should get the hell out of there.

I looked down into her eyes. New York tipped under my feet and I was falling out of concrete and traffic and crappy air and towards lush green, misty forest.

What if we need to get something else from the laptop? The location could be wrong. Or the cops could get there and the cabin's empty. Maybe there's more than one cabin.

I told myself that was the reason. The truth was... something important had entered my life. In a matter of minutes, it would leave again and I'd never get it back. I wanted to hold onto it just a little longer.

"I guess I could wait here," I heard myself say. "Until they call back."

She nodded. Then I looked away, because I couldn't look into her eyes any longer without saying something I'd regret. And out of the corner of my eye, I saw *her* look away, too. So I thought it was safe and I looked at her again, but then *she* looked at *me* again and that was it: we were trapped. I couldn't look away from those damn eyes. I was *fascinated* by this woman. And every second we stared at each other, the tension was ratcheting higher. She'd started to breathe faster and I had, too. We were breathing in rhythm: when had *that* started?

This is bad. I couldn't let myself get close to her. She deserved much better than a bastard like me. If she knew what I'd done, the secret that ate at me every day.... But I still couldn't look away. *I am out of my depth.*

She broke our gaze and I thought I saw her flush. "Coffee?" she asked.

I grabbed for something, anything, familiar. "Hell yes, coffee."

She went over to the kitchen counter and I followed, watching as she brewed it. I glanced around the apartment. Over in one corner was an exercise bike. *What's that for? I thought her legs didn't work.*

I looked back to Yolanda. I tried to think of something smart to say, but watching her do something as normal as making coffee, sitting instead of standing, all I could think about was—

"You're wondering what happened to me," she said without looking up.

"What? No!" I lied.

"Good," she said, in a tone that said *I don't believe that for a second.* She passed me a coffee and offered me milk, but we both took it the same way: black, no sugar.

I glanced at the chalkboards. "So why math?"

"Why justice?" she asked immediately.

I frowned at her, curious. She hadn't just put up shields to protect herself, she'd wrapped thorns over them to keep everyone away. And it probably worked, with most people. They'd say she was *difficult. Grumpy. Not a team player.*

talking quietly, he changed completely. The volume dropped, the voice softened and that bass growl became a magical harmonic that made my whole body buzz and throb, the energy pooling in my groin.

And. That. Ass. Every time he'd turned away from me, my eyes had swiveled to look at it like they were magnets and it was a hunk of sculpted, rock-hard iron. You could write poetry about that ass. I'd never seen one so hard and perfectly shaped and I've spent enough time sitting, while men around me are standing, that I think I qualify as an authority.

He didn't look disappointed.

Crazy. Maybe he would have wanted the Before me, the one who could jog and ice skate and dance—badly—and one day maybe push a baby stroller. Not this After version.

You're assigned a therapist, after something like this happens. Almost a year on, he's still telling me that I'm adapting badly. I point to my lowered kitchen units and customized desk and how fast I can get around in my chair, but I know that's not what he means. He uses words like *acceptance* and *reaching an understanding with my situation.*

But I can't.

Every morning, I *forget.*

I get up how I've always gotten up: a bad-tempered groan, eyes still shut, then a twist and roll towards the edge of the bed. Except now, nothing happens. My upper body twists and my legs just sit there, holding me in place. And the reality of it crashes down on me: that cold gray blanket, suffocating and inescapable. My therapist tells me that I'm not really forgetting. How could I forget, after 427 mornings? What's really happening is that I haven't fully accepted it.

And he's right. I still want it to be undone. I want to turn back the clock to the day it happened. I want to tell my brother that I *don't* want to go out for a run, and keep him home and safe. I want a time machine or a brand new medical treatment or, hell, I'd take a magic lamp at this stage. I just want to be back how I was.

I'm from Beaverton, Oregon, right on the other side of the country. Greener, wetter, *slower* than New York. My mom is a midwife, my dad a history teacher. When she gave birth to twins, no one was expecting us to be anything special. But my brother Josh and I had a weird, quiet manner. Both of us were obsessed with building blocks: sorting them and stacking them and taking pleasure in how four blocks could become one big block, and four of *those* could become one even bigger block, and, magically, that bigger one contained *just the right number* of blocks, when you put them all in a line. We didn't have a name for what we were doing because we didn't have numbers yet. But we understood the satisfaction, deep in our hearts, when things added up.

It wasn't long after we started school that someone first used the G word. Josh and I found that funny because neither of us felt like geniuses. Maybe that's why the bond between us was so tight: to each other, we were normal. Numbers just made sense to us. They split apart in my mind: I see 12384 as twelve 1032s the same way most people see the word *moonlight* as a combination of *moon* and *light.*

Our parents encouraged us and we loved them but my brother and I needed each other. We both knew what it was like to get into a problem and go *deep,* sitting silently as our minds bathed in quiet, mathematical calm. Once, I did it for sixteen hours and that got me in trouble. A child psychologist came to the house and interviewed me and then talked to my parents. Listening at the door, my brother and I heard, *"Minds like theirs can be fragile. There's always a danger of them... snapping."*

I don't know if my parents knew that I had overheard this conversation. Certainly they never mentioned it. But for the rest of my life, the psychologist's words stuck with me, and I started to visualize my mind as this hugely complex, hugely delicate glass structure that was placed atop a high ledge... and could fall and shatter into a million pieces at any time.

After the conversation with the psychologist, our parents made a big push to get us outdoors more, to play with other kids, to ground us. Josh and I reluctantly took up running. Neither of us really liked it but, as long as we were together, it was okay.

Inseparable, we both applied to Princeton and got in on math

4

CALAHAN

Three Weeks Later

THE WORSE the mood I'm in, the more I slouch. Everyone in the New York FBI office knows this. If I've just pulled an all-nighter on a stakeout, I'll sit low in my seat, wincing at the sunlight. If I've had a case thrown out of court and some scumbag I caught is back on the streets, I'll go further: slumped down, legs kicked out under my desk, almost hidden behind my monitor.

Today, I was close to horizontal. Chair reclined all the way, head barely above the level of the desk, only my hand moving as I scowled at my screen. As people approached, they saw my expression and quickly changed course.

I was meant to be reading through a report on organized crime in the city. A year ago, we'd scored a victory when we'd prevented a gang war erupting. But part of the fallout had been that Hailey, an agent I'd worked side-by-side with for years, had left the FBI because...well, because she'd met a guy.

And I know what you're thinking because it's just what lots of other people in the department were whispering. *Hailey found someone and now Calahan's pissed off. Were the two of them....*

The answer is *no*. Sure, I was attracted to her and sure, there were moments when we both wanted to. But I never let anything happen. We were just friends.

But I miss her. I don't have many friends and she was the closest. It's okay when I'm on a case but when I'm spinning my wheels, like right now, I wind up thinking too much. The memories start waking, the pain and guilt starts and I find myself in a bar, unsure if I'm drinking to forget or to work up the courage to do what needs to be done.

And these last three weeks had been harder than usual because there was something new in my head, something iridescent and vivid, impossible to ignore. Her.

I kept seeing her face, hearing that gentle accent. The essence of her was in my head and it wouldn't leave me alone. She was the soft to my hard. Soft skin, soft lips, soft shining hair. She was pine fronds brushing your bare arms, rain on your face, nature. I was concrete and busy streets and shoving people out of my way.

Her mind was incredible. She was smart in a way I could never be and yet she didn't lord it over people the way some of the eggheads at the FBI did. I suspected they weren't half as clever as her. And that moment when we'd looked at each other and neither of us could look away....

I wasn't just attracted, I was fascinated. I felt like a huge, lumbering dinosaur, hypnotized by a fluttering butterfly. Someone once told me there are air people and earth people. They said I was definitely an earth person and thinking about how I used to pile into someone in a tackle in high school, or how I only really trusted stuff I could touch and feel, that sounded about right.

But air people...they were the creatives, the thinkers. They didn't really belong to our clumsy, physical world—that's why they always felt a little out of place. Their minds were off in a place that the rest of us couldn't see or reach and they brought glimpses of it back to us through art and music... and math.

Yolanda was the most *air* person I'd ever met.

And I didn't even know her real name. I could probably do some digging and find out who was paying rent on her penthouse, but this was a woman who had to hide her tracks from the crime bosses she hacked: her friend Gabriella had already had a hitman sent after her. I was pretty sure I'd find that the penthouse was owned by a company in the Cayman Islands and that would be the end of that. I could call Lily, but even if she knew Yolanda's real name, she wouldn't share it. Even if she would, it would feel wrong, like invading her privacy.

"Sit up, Calahan," said my boss right in my ear.

I nearly fell out of my chair. I hadn't even heard her approach. I struggled up to something approaching sitting while Carrie perched herself on the corner of my desk.

"I'm still waiting for your report on the Catskill kidnapping," she said.

"Yeah," I mumbled. "Just working on that now. Writing you a report. An email. I'll email you a report."

Carrie pinned me with a look. She has long silver-blonde hair, a sharp suit, and she can do a good impression of a school principal when she wants to. Not a week goes by without her calling me up to her office to bawl me out for breaking the rules and I've been *this* close to being fired more times than I can count. But she's stuck her neck out for me more than once because we both want the same thing: to get the job done.

"You look like hell, Sam," she said.

"Thanks."

"You sleeping?" Her face softened a little. "It's October."

That wouldn't mean anything to most people, but Carrie knows. An anniversary was coming up. A really bad one.

"I'm fine," I told her.

She passed me a slip of paper. "Well, go be fine somewhere else. NYPD wants us to take over a case."

I snatched the paper from her hand, feeling my heart soar. *Finally.* Something to lose myself in. With luck, it would keep me busy till the end of the month. No more thinking about Yolanda, no more feeling sorry for myself. "What is it? Mafia? Drugs?"

"Murder. Happened less than an hour ago."

I frowned at her and rubbed at my stubble. Police work has a strong vein of pride running through it. Once a case is yours, you don't give it up without solving it. Usually, it's a whole screaming match to get the cops to let us take over, even when it's obviously an FBI matter. I couldn't imagine the NYPD arriving at a crime scene and just straightaway calling us in.

Not unless....

My stomach tightened into a cold, hard knot. Not unless it was something really bad.

The crime scene was in Harlem and as I drove over there, I shook off my worries. The city was enjoying an unseasonably warm day, probably the last we'd get before winter took hold. The sky was blue and it was pleasantly warm.

The address was an old but classy apartment building. Three patrol cars were parked in its shadow and a couple of cops were mooching around, along with one guy not in uniform. I showed my badge as I walked over. "Detective Giggs?"

He nodded.

As I stepped out of the sun and into the building's shadow, the temperature dropped enough to make me shiver. Maybe that's why Giggs looked so pale. "What've we got?" I asked.

The detective shook his head. Not like he was being an ass. Like he had no words to describe it.

That bad feeling I'd had came back.

"What floor?" I asked.

Giggs looked over his shoulder at the apartment building and his face paled a little more. He swallowed. Swallowed again. "Fourth." He said it quick and quiet, like he was trying not to disturb his stomach. But it didn't work. As I walked towards the building, I could hear him throwing up behind me. *Not a good sign.*

On the fourth floor, there was an officer standing guard, a big guy with black hair. His uniform said *Kowalski.* He looked queasy, too, but he was holding up better than Giggs. I noticed he'd taken up position just far enough down the hall that he couldn't see inside the apartment. Another bad sign.

"Anyone go in or out since it happened?"

"Just me, Sir. I was first on the scene. Went in to check the victim was dead, then locked it down and called Detective Giggs. He had a look at the scene and called the FBI. No one else."

"Good." I took a step down the hallway.

"Sir?" blurted Kowalski.

I turned back to him. Kowalski was at least as big as me but in that second, he looked like a scared kid. He stood there, big-eyed and open-mouthed, unable to find the words. But I got it. He was trying to warn me. On some primal, instinctual level, he didn't want me to go in there.

I nodded that I understood and carried on down the hall. My stomach was churning, the hairs on the back of my neck rising. I swore it was getting colder.

The apartment door was wide open, crime scene tape across it like it was trying to hold the badness in.

I looked.

—

Now I knew why Detective Giggs had called us in. God, to think I'd actually been glad to get this case.

All I wanted was to turn around and walk out of there. Tell Giggs tough, we were busy, he could handle it himself. No, wait: I wanted to do one more thing. I wanted to slam that apartment's door tight shut, lock it and never let anyone go inside again.

"Sir?" asked Kowalski from down the hall. "Did you ever see anything like that before?"

"No," I said quietly. "I didn't."

But I couldn't walk away. Because Giggs had been right to call us. The NYPD were way out of their depth. And if I didn't take this, no one would. And the person responsible would go free.

"You said you went in to check the victim," I said. "And Giggs, too. But the floor looks undisturbed."

"We figured out a way, sir." Kowalski picked up a plank of wood and some bricks. "They're doing some construction, one street over. I borrowed these." He put the bricks just outside the apartment's door, then rested the plank on them so it extended into the room, hanging in mid air like a diving board. Finally, he stood on the hallway end of the plank to counterbalance me. Now I could go inside without touching the floor.

"That's pretty smart, Kowalski," I said. "Got a feeling you'll make detective one day."

Kowalski glanced inside the room and quickly looked away. "Not sure I want to, sir."

I took another look inside. "Yeah," I said. "I don't blame you."

I walked slowly down the plank and into the room. I didn't look at anything else but what was in front of me. I've never lost it at a crime scene, but I had to be careful because I could feel it starting: that cold that sinks into your skin and soaks into your brain, building up and up until it comes out as throwing up or pissing yourself or just running, bolting down the hallway and not stopping until you feel the sun on your face again. I'd seen all those things happen, over the years, but I couldn't let any of them happen to me because if I lost it, I still had to come back and carry on. I wouldn't pass this one on to anyone else. I wouldn't wish it on anyone.

Just focus on the body.

It was in the center of the room. A black guy in a suit, sprawled on his back on the floor, his eyes closed as if asleep. I could see why Kowalski had had to check he was dead. But looking closer, I could see the gray tint of the skin. I knew what that was.

The body had been completely drained of blood.

At any other crime scene, the next logical question would be, *what did they do with all the blood?* But not at this one.

Don't freak out, Calahan. Don't you fucking freak out.

I took a deep, slow breath and finally allowed myself to look around.

Every single square inch of the walls, the ceiling, even the floor, was covered in a pattern, intricate and incredibly complex. And so disturbing, you'd go crazy if you looked at it too long.

It was a thing that didn't live in nature, that had no place in our world. It was made up of things like tentacles, dark and slender, some twenty feet long, so knotted and tangled together that they were difficult to trace back: I couldn't see where the center or body was, if there even was one.

There was no one place you could say looked like eyes, and yet it felt like you were being watched. There was nothing that looked exactly like a mouth, but you felt you were about to be devoured. When you looked closely, the entire thing was made up of writing, the letters packed so close they formed solid lines.

And the whole thing was written in bright red blood.

The last place I looked was straight up. *JESUS!*

I did something I hadn't done in a very long time: I crossed myself.

Directly above me, as if waiting to drop from the ceiling, was the heart of the thing. I could feel myself starting to panic-breathe. It was spidery, but it didn't have enough legs: only seven. And the legs were too long, curling and winding, reaching out for me. It made me think of something that lived at the bottom of the sea and never sees sunlight.

The room was *wrong*. Wrong on some deep, primal level. I could feel sweat soaking my shirt and I felt twitchy and unstable, eyes darting around the room too fast. *Fight or flight.* My body wanted me out of there, *now,* and only my stubborn brain was refusing. I looked down at my hands. *Jesus, I'm shaking.*

I crouched on the plank so that I could see the words that made up the thing up close. I squinted. Turned my head. But I couldn't make sense of it. The letters weren't right, there were too many *S*s and *I*s—

And then my brain realigned and I realized I wasn't looking at letters at all. All those *S*s and *I*s were fives and ones. I was looking at numbers. And the words weren't words. They were little groups of numbers, symbols and Greek letters. Equations.

The whole thing was made up of equations.

I've been around. I've seen more murder scenes than I can count. But this killer was like nothing I'd ever seen. He hadn't panicked and run, or tried to cover things up. He'd stayed at the scene for what must have been hours, writing all this, just to send us a message. That took nerves: the guy was ice cold. And, given that I couldn't make head or tail of the equations, he was smart—a hell of a lot smarter than me. And given the blood, and the patterns, he was batshit crazy.

Cold, smart and crazy. A really bad combination. I didn't want to jump to any conclusions, but I knew the type and these guys never kill just once.

A feeling washed over me, one I'd had many times before. I was suddenly dog-tired and ahead of me was a long swim through an ocean of cold black tar. I didn't want this case. I never even wanted to be a cop.

But if I didn't stop this guy, who would?

I started making phone calls. Kowalski helped me fetch more planks from the construction site and we got the crime scene photographer in and meticulously photographed every inch of the pattern. But I knew flat pictures weren't going to do the job of capturing it. Nothing could. To get the feel for how it arched overhead, how it spread like a dark cancer around corners and up door frames, you had to be there.

I checked around for other clues. The killer had been careful: we couldn't find a print anywhere. The only thing I did find was a fragment of a cherry-red plastic wrapper, sucked tight against the intake of the air conditioner. It was a triangle, as if someone had torn open a packet and discarded the corner. I bagged it and shoved it in my pocket to go into evidence.

The coroner came and took the body away. I stumbled outside and stood there in the sunlight, trying to get some warmth back into my bones. The light was turning gold and red: another hour and the sun would be down. I'd spent the entire day working the scene, lunchtime forgotten. I told myself that's why I felt like death.

I got a text from one of the eggheads in the FBI's tech division. I'd sent her a couple of photos of the equations, just to see what she thought. The text said, *Way out of my league. I passed them around, but no one here has any idea what they mean.*

The killer had sent us a message, knowing we wouldn't be smart enough to read it. *He's out there, laughing at us.*

There'd been a thought trying to surface in my head all day, ever since I'd first seen the equations, but until now, I'd been mercilessly holding it down. I knew someone. Someone even smarter than the killer. Someone who *could* read the equations.

No. No way was I bringing her into this. I wouldn't wish that scene on another FBI agent, let alone a civilian. And especially not *her*. Not someone I... liked.

And there was a bigger problem. I was too damn attracted to her and that would make being around her hell. I couldn't get involved with anyone. Not after what I'd done. The last thing I deserved was happiness and the last thing she deserved was a screw-up like me.

I couldn't call her. For both our sakes.

5

YOLANDA

I WAS ON the bike, sweat pouring off me as I pedaled for my life. The muscles in my legs are just fine and the bones have healed: it's the nerves that no longer work. Without nerves, I can't make the muscles do anything. And if muscles sit around doing nothing, they atrophy, and you get matchstick legs.

The bike prevents that. I stick electrodes to my legs, little electric shocks stimulate the muscles, my legs pedal and my muscles get a workout. Having your lower body working away with no conscious control is about as disconcerting as it sounds and it doesn't make it any less exhausting. But it works and anything that helps me feel a little more normal is a win, so I do it every day.

The problem is that it leaves my brain free to wander. And it kept coming back to one thing, as it had done for weeks.

Sam Calahan was like a big, heavy rock that sat right at the center of my mind. He just had so much rugged, muscled mass, so much gravity, that every other thought got captured and sucked in until it slapped up against that hard roughness. *Should I make coffee after this? I wonder how Calahan takes his. I need to get some new workout pants. Pants... damn, his ass looks good in those suit pants. God, I'm so sweaty. He looks like he works out. I bet he does it topless, all tanned and glistening—*

Every time I closed my eyes, he was close to me again, his stubbled jaw inches from rasping against my cheek. I could feel his hand brushing my bare wrist, the hot heaviness of him heating my skin. I could smell vanilla and cinnamon—

A timer beeped and I lifted myself off the bike and into my chair, then took a shower in the wet room. Thin white lines gleamed on my thighs and calves as they caught the light: my legs are a mess of scars from the accident.

But hey, it's not like anyone's ever going to see them.

I pulled on some fresh clothes and rolled over to the chalkboards. But as soon as I started working, I could hear his voice, deep and rough and vibrating all the way down my spine. Math was impossible. *Dammit!*

Fine. I'd get him out of my system. I'd find out about him. That would demystify him and then I could forget about him.

I shot over to my computer and rattled his name off on the keyboard, running a deep search on all the databases I'm plugged into. I blushed at just how urgently I did it, how breathless I went when the first picture appeared.

There was a group shot of him in his police academy graduating class. Another of him in a newspaper after a court case that had put some big mafia don in jail. He'd looked rumpled even then. But he looked happy. Up until....

The change seemed to come four years ago. In all the photos after that, his eyes had that sadness they had today. *What happened?*

There wasn't much publicly accessible, so I did what anyone would do: I hacked the FBI. That isn't as big of a deal as it sounds. They rely on a flawed encryption algorithm I broke years ago, so I just breezed in.

I dug through Calahan's record. A whole slew of commendations but an even bigger list of reprimands. He must be wearing out the carpet between his desk and his boss's office.

He seemed to be working on a new case. There was a folder called *SoC Photos.* Curious, I opened it and brought up the first one—

A man in a suit lay on the floor. His black skin had turned a sickly gray and there was something about the way his limbs lay, too loose, too slack—

SoC. Scene of Crime.

I let out a moan of horror and grabbed for the mouse to close the picture, but nudged the scroll wheel by accident. Another picture appeared and I flinched, bracing myself.

But it wasn't another body. It was math.

Equations, but not written in an order I could make sense of. They were arranged in a sweeping, curving path and I had to rotate the image to follow them. They were written in some weird, red ink—

I realized what it was and my stomach lurched. But I couldn't look away. The math had a rhythm to it, a shape. It was like discordant music, rasping and jangling against my nerves... and yet, at the same time, it was expertly composed. I went back to the folder of photos: God, there were hundreds. I opened another and another. Some elements made sense: *that* was to do with probabilities within a population, *that* was to do with time, measured over centuries and—

I leaned forward, transfixed. *That's for calculating the routes of wormholes in space.* The math was amazing in complexity and scale. My brain itched to see the whole thing, to dive in and begin solving it. For a moment, I felt a little drunk, like a crossword fiend who's just been handed a crossword puzzle the size of a football field. And yet there was a wrongness to it that made my skin crawl. Math had always been beautifully pure, in my mind, beyond love or hate or politics. But this math felt *evil*.

And then I saw it. A giant, starfish-like thing with seven legs that stretched out to the corners of my screen. I went rigid in my chair, my skin going cold. There was something deeply disturbing about it. I'd been using the mouse pointer to keep my place, but when I brought it close to the starfish thing....

I didn't want to touch it, in case—

You're being stupid.

In case it moved.

How could someone create this? How could someone be both so

brilliant that they could handle these sorts of equations, but so disturbed that they could forge them into... *that?*

I zoomed in until the equations that made up the thing filled my screen and went to work. An hour passed. Two. The equations were repetitive, but a little different each time....

I drew in a strangled gasp, grabbed my phone and dug Calahan's number from his FBI file. Three rings and then I heard that gravelly, no-bullshit voice. "Calahan."

I wasn't ready for the effect his voice had on me, my entire body singing like a tuning fork. "It's a countdown," I blurted.

There was a second's pause. When he spoke again, his voice was different. Gentler. "*Yolanda?!*"

"It's a countdown," I said again.

"What are you—*What's* a countdown?"

I live so much in my own head, I sometimes forget that other people aren't in here with me. "I saw the crime scene photos," I told him. "The equations. I hacked the FBI."

"You—" It started as a yell, but became a hard whisper. I imagined him furtively cradling his phone. "You did *what?!*"

Now he said it like that, hacking the FBI *did* sound kind of bad. "That doesn't matter," I told him. "I saw the equations. I can help you."

Silence for a few seconds as he debated. I could feel my heart thumping.

"We're fine," Calahan said at last. "We've got our own people."

"Have they solved it yet?"

"Not all of it," He sounded defensive. *Not any of it.* "But they'll get there."

"You don't have time," I told him. "That black spidery, starfish thing—you know the part I'm talking about?"

A second's pause. "Yeah," he muttered, and I could hear the unease in his voice. *He feels it, too, when he looks at that thing.*

"The equations count time. It's cyclic, but it reduces each time, until it disappears completely. I can't tell when without seeing the whole thing, but… it's a countdown, Calahan!" I swallowed. "Until he does it again."

Silence.

"I can help," I said desperately. "Let me help."

I could hear him breathing. I didn't understand: *what is there to debate?*

Then, "No."

And before I could argue, he ended the call.

6

CALAHAN

I STEPPED BACK from the board. In the center, photos of the apartment building together with a map. Then photos of the victim and details of his family. And around that in a huge, red cloud, the photos of the equations we'd still made no progress in solving.

The idea of the board is, it helps you think in new ways and see connections you'd missed. But however hard I looked, there was nothing. It had been two days since I took the case and I was no closer to a suspect.

The door opened behind me and someone approached. I didn't need to turn around: I recognized the heels. A moment later, a paper cup of coffee was pressed into my hand.

"Security said you'd been here all night," said Carrie. She looked at the board. "Want to talk me through it?"

I grimaced, then took a deep breath. "Daniel Grier. Dentist. 44, divorced—amicably, four years ago—no criminal record, two children who live with their mom."

"Dentists see a lot of patients," said Carrie. "A lot of young moms with kids. Affair with one of his patients, jealous spouse?"

This is what I hate about murders. Every inch of the victim's life gets picked apart, looking for a motive. As if it's *their* fault. But in

Grier's case, I'd found nothing. He was as clean as they come. "I checked his computer and his phone," I said. "He wasn't having an affair. He'd started seeing a woman from his church choir a few months ago. She's devastated."

"Family?"

"Live in South Carolina and were all there at the time of the murder. They're flying out today."

"Debts? A gambling problem no one knew about? A drug problem no one saw?"

"Healthy bank balance. No drugs at his place." I crossed my arms and glowered at the board. Most of the people I come across in this job, even the victims, aren't people you'd choose to meet. It's mostly gangsters killing gangsters, thugs killing thugs. But I'd spent the last forty-eight hours immersed in the life of Daniel Grier: I knew him now better than I know most of my neighbors and he was *good*. He was a guy you'd borrow a lawnmower from and forget to return it and he wouldn't give you a hard time about it. A friendly, peaceable guy who did his job, paid his taxes and was in the process of falling in love again. A good man. A hell of a lot better than me. And we'd utterly failed to protect him. "Want to know what's *really* weird? Grier didn't live at the apartment in Harlem. It's vacant. He lived over in Morningside Heights. There are signs of a struggle there."

"Wait," said Carrie. "You're telling me someone kidnapped Grier and drove him ten blocks across town just to kill him? Why not kill him in his own home?"

"Beats me," I muttered. "Security cameras at both places were offline. We think someone hacked them. No prints—our killer wore gloves."

Carrie cursed. "No motive, no leads." She nodded at the equations. "Except *this*. A message?"

"That's my theory. He's toying with us. Showing how clever he is."

"The tech guys any closer to solving it?"

"Nope."

She cursed again, shaking her head.

I didn't mean to say it, but I was exhausted and it just came out. "I think he's going to kill again."

"What makes you say that?"

I looked at my feet. I'm not good at lying to Carrie, despite all the practice I've had. "Just a hunch."

She studied me, waiting to see if I'd crack. But I lifted my head and stared back at her. She sighed. "A serial killer. Just what this city needs. If you're right then we need to get this math deciphered *now*."

I grunted my agreement. Carrie gave me a friendly pat on the arm and started to walk away.

The killer was out there, laughing at the dumbass police who couldn't solve his riddles....

Except he didn't know we had a secret weapon.

I can't. This stuff freaked even *me* out. I didn't want it anywhere near her.

But if I didn't ask for her help, someone else was going to die.

"I might know someone," I blurted.

Carrie stopped, turned around and walked back to me. "Who?"

"She's a mathematician."

Carrie's eyebrows shot up at the *she*. She tilted her head to one side: *tell me everything.*

I looked away.

Carrie sighed and stabbed a finger towards the board. Other people were starting to arrive for work and she lowered her voice so that only I could hear. "Sam, I'm going to say something and you might want to pay attention because I've been doing this a while. I've seen murders. I've seen serial killers. I once took down a man who carved up an entire family and scattered the pieces across four states. But I have never, ever, seen anything like this. If you have someone who can tell us what these numbers mean, *call her! Now!*"

She stared at me until I reluctantly nodded. Then she marched off towards the elevator.

Why did I tell her? But I knew why: I'd told her because I knew she'd talk some sense into me.

I looked at the board. Daniel Grier's gray skin. The swirls of bloody numbers. *I can't bring Yolanda into this.* Cases like this took their toll on you. I didn't want to look into those green eyes and see they'd lost their innocence forever.

But it was more than that. I was drawn to her, fascinated by her. But I couldn't be with her. I didn't deserve that peace, didn't deserve even a second's release from the guilt burning inside me. And Yolanda... she didn't deserve the risks that would come with being with me.

I'd have to keep my distance. But fighting that pull, every second we were together... that would be agony.

I can't....

Then I growled, mad at myself. *Yes I can.* The hell with my feelings. I wasn't going to let someone else die. I grabbed my coat.

8

CALAHAN

IT WAS THE fourth time I'd walked through Yolanda's apartment building, but the first time I'd actually had time to look around. The place was beautiful but *old*, probably built back in the 1930s. I could see elaborate balconies and gargoyles through the windows and inside it was all white marble and big art deco mirrors. The private elevator, which ran directly to the penthouse and skipped all the other floors, was so old that it had a metal gate instead of a door. Yolanda rattled it closed as soon as we were inside.

"I'm parked across the street," I told her, and reached for the button for the first floor.

Before I could push it, her hand slid under mine, the back of it cool against my palm. Her finger stabbed the button for the parking garage. "We'll take *my* car," she said firmly.

She turned her head, flicking her black hair out of her eyes, and looked up at me, those green eyes daring me to argue.

But I didn't argue. The prickliness, I realized, was a defense mechanism. She'd gotten so used to having to prove herself....

I stared right back at her. *You don't have to prove anything to me.*

And her eyes changed. They softened as her shields dropped just a little. And as soon as they softened, it was like I was falling into them again: lush green forest, the air cool and wet. I could feel her hand under mine, my heat soaking into her, and I had this urge to just close my fingers around it—

The elevator shook as it began its descent and we both looked away, drawing our hands back. The inner wall of the elevator was mirrored and I glared at myself. *Idiot! What the hell are you doing?* God, she'd been on the case less than a minute and already, I was acting crazy. *Just get her to the scene. Let her do her thing with the math, then you can go your separate ways.*

When we reached the parking garage, Yolanda slammed back the gate and was halfway across the dark concrete vastness before I'd registered that we'd stopped. I was still amazed at how fast she could shoot around. It was like all that excess brain power had to be burned off as movement when she wasn't thinking.

She skidded to a stop by her car. I don't know what I'd expected: something boxy and practical, maybe. Not *that.*

It was a sports car that looked like it had arrived from the twenty-second century. It was low and sleek, full of graceful curves and, as we approached, the doors opened upwards like an eagle preparing for take-off. The dashboard came alive with symbols and a woman's voice greeted us in Japanese. Yolanda grabbed an overhead handle, lifted herself and swung into the driver's seat. Then she folded the wheelchair and pushed it up a ramp and into a slot behind her seat, where it clicked into place.

I realized I was standing there like a dumbass, so I quickly climbed into the passenger seat. The doors closed. Yolanda pulled a thing like a trigger on the back of the steering wheel and we surged forward silently. *Electric.*

We reached the exit of the parking garage and she stopped for a second. "What's the address?" she asked.

I told her and she pressed a button and repeated it for the GPS. And the cop in me noticed something.

The GPS had a list of all the places you visit regularly, to save you having to re-enter them. Except in Yolanda's case, there was just one place in the list: a physiotherapy center across town. That was literally the only place she'd ever driven this car.

I thought of the grocery store delivery bags in her apartment. My stomach lurched as I put it all together. *She never leaves her apartment except for that one appointment. And even that, she's honed to minimize contact with the outside world. She goes elevator - car - physiotherapy - car - elevator - apartment. The car's electric so she doesn't even have to stop for gas.*

I looked across at Yolanda. The GPS had worked out the route and it was asking her to confirm. But she was sitting there frozen. The car was still in the shadowy parking garage, but the light from the outside world was just brushing her face through the windshield. I could see how big her eyes had gone: she was so scared it made my chest ache. I almost told her to stop. *We'll go back upstairs. We'll do this another way.*

But before I could, her finger stabbed decisively at the screen. She pulled the trigger on the steering wheel and we shot forward onto the street.

9

YOLANDA

W E SPED silently through the city. I kept my eyes on the road and tried not to think about how far I was from home, how every turn of the wheels took me further from my apartment.

We pulled up at an intersection and the guy next to us looked admiringly at my car. That's the main reason I went to the trouble of importing it from Japan: it draws attention and that means they're looking at it, not me. There are other reasons, though. It has an insane amount of power and I love to go fast. The lowness of it makes climbing in and out from a chair easy: swinging myself up into an SUV is a pain in the ass. And finally, they designed it with hand controls instead of pedals so it fits me without any alteration.

With a chime and a singsong message in Japanese, the GPS announced that we'd arrived. I pulled up behind a patrol car.

You can do this.

There was a cop guarding the building and he watched as I got out. I have the process *slick* and it takes less than ten seconds, but doing it under his gaze felt like putting on a Broadway show. The entire time, my brain was taunting me that one slip, one tiny misjudgment of balance, and the chair would be on its side and I'd be in a red-faced heap on the ground with people running to help—

I dropped lightly into the chair. *Exhale.*

We passed through a front yard that had been carefully tended, with planters full of pink and purple flowers and a maple tree casting shade. The place looked so normal... until you saw the crime scene tape. Calahan lifted it up so I could duck underneath. We rode the elevator up to the fourth floor in silence and we were halfway down the hallway to the apartment when Calahan's hand on my shoulder stopped me.

"Just—" he started, but he couldn't finish. When I looked up at him, he was looking ahead of us, towards the open door, his lips pressed tight together. Then he glanced down, met my gaze, and just shook his head. A warning. *Just brace yourself.*

I could feel it too, a *wrongness* that the photos had only hinted at. It was as if everything that was good and clean and bright ended halfway down the hallway. Inside that apartment was something else, something that sucked those things in like a black hole.

I gave the wheels a determined shove and coasted forward towards the door. But a few feet from it, I suddenly jerked to a stop. I looked down at myself: without consciously willing it, my hands had gripped the wheels. The wrongness got stronger, the nearer I got, and it was as if my body was reacting on instinct to what was inside. All the little hairs on my arms were standing up and I could feel sweat breaking out along my spine. My right arm tensed: I was a split-second away from spinning the chair in a 180 and getting the hell out of there.

Calahan came up beside me. "It's okay," he murmured. His voice, so deep and throaty, could be surprisingly gentle. "You don't have to."

I thought of the countdown. Someone else was going to die.

I took a deep breath. "Yes I do," I told him. And pushed myself inside.

On the drive over, I'd wondered about how I was even going to get inside the room without damaging the writing on the floor. But Calahan had thought of that. Big sheets of transparent Perspex had been laid down like flagstones, covering the entire floor. I rolled in....

And saw.

It was so *dense!* The blood had turned black as it dried and the numbers covered the walls so thickly, what had been a bright, airy room now ate up the light. And the patterns... they flowed and morphed, twisting from floor to wall to ceiling, forcing you to turn and turn and turn to follow them until you went dizzy. There was something animal about them. They flexed and bent in a way that made me think of snakes and eels, slimy dark forms sliding through oily water. And there was no way to look away because it was everywhere you looked. A strange sort of claustrophobia came over me. It felt like the lights were dimming. It felt like being swallowed. *You could go mad, in here.*

My hands had gone slack on the wheels. I coasted to a stop right at the center of the room and looked down. There was a gap in the equations there, which should have been a blessed relief. But the gap was exactly man-sized. I swallowed. I knew what—who—had been lying there.

Calahan approached from behind me and somehow managed not to make me jump. I was shocked by how slowly and silently he could move, given his size. "You okay?"

I managed to nod. "You were right. I had to see this."

"Our killer's a man," said Calahan. "Or at least, tall." He pointed to part way up the wall. "We figure he used an old-style fountain pen filled with blood and the pen strokes change, about here. They go from pushing *up* against the wall—because that's the highest he could comfortably reach, standing on the floor—to pushing *down* against the wall—because that's when he switched to standing on a box, or a step ladder, or something. I got a few guys of different height to try it and I figure he must be six feet or a little over."

I stared at him, amazed. *He got all that from pen marks?* I quickly looked away before he turned around and saw I was staring. I looked down at the gap on the floor again. "You think Daniel Grier knew his killer?" I asked quietly.

"Usually that's the way," said Calahan. His voice was almost apologetic. "Usually it's a spouse or a friend or someone at work."

I stared at him. *Jesus. That's the world he lives in?* No wonder he was gruff.

Calahan rubbed his chin, the rasping sound loud in the silent room. "But there's another possibility. If you're right and he's going to kill again, if we're dealing with a serial killer... then it may be he's got no relationship with the victim. He could have seen Daniel at a train station or at a coffee shop. If that's the case..."—he turned and looked at me—"You may be our only chance at catching him."

I swallowed. Nodded. Tied my hair back in a ponytail to keep it out of the way and went to work.

Usually, I follow an equation from start to finish, breaking it down along the way. But here, I had to physically *follow* it, as it crept across the floor and then up the wall like ivy. The math was amazing. Beautiful, in a way I'd find difficult to explain to Calahan. When I approach a problem, I'm tentative, nibbling at the edges until it cracks open. But this person was bold. He knew exactly where he was going and to get there, he'd brought together everything from theories of time and space to what seemed to be equations for genetics and probability. All of it merging into something that felt weirdly functional, in the same way as the encryption equations I work with. This stuff wasn't purely theoretical. It *did* something.

I could feel my brain coming alive—maybe the first time it had been completely alive since college. Encryption is one very specific sort of math and it worked my mind the way doing one exercise over and over would work one muscle. But this... this was like a full body workout, stretching me in every direction. As I rolled inch by inch across the Perspex, staring down at the equations, it felt as if I was gliding over a frozen lake. It was scary, as if the ice might crack under me and I'd fall straight into that dark writing. But at the same time....

At the same time, it was weirdly enticing. I couldn't figure out why, but a tiny, secret part of me actually *wanted* to fall. It wanted to sink into those dark spirals and never surface again. I kept almost going *deep* and then, just as I was about to lose myself in the math, I'd jerk out of it, heart thumping, as if some survival mechanism had kicked in.

10

CALAHAN

S HE LOOKED so determined, as she wheeled herself back across the yard. Shoulders squared, jaw set... *ready*.

But ahead of us was the cop who was guarding the place. He'd been watching from the doorway the whole time we'd been out there. He smirked and rolled his eyes as she approached. Just because she'd lost it a little at a crime scene, just because she'd needed to get some air. The cop turned to me, smirking wider. *These civilians, huh?*

Yolanda saw it and faltered.

And suddenly I felt anger boil up out of my belly like lava, filling my chest, making my arms tense and my fists clench. I strode right up to the cop and glared at him from a distance of three inches. He went instantly pale. My eyes flicked down to his badge. *Officer Davison.* He wilted. He didn't know whether I was going to report him or punch him. Neither did I. I was actually shaking with rage.

I grabbed the crime scene tape and held it up for Yolanda to pass under. Then I stalked beside her to the elevator and slammed the button. *What was that?* I could still feel the rage thrumming through my veins, fiery and—

Protective.

I pushed that thought away and we rode the elevator up in silence.

Back in the apartment, Yolanda focused on that unsettling starfish thing on the ceiling. At first, she was just reading: I watched, fascinated, as her eyes jumped between symbols that meant nothing to me. But then her eyes closed and she became very still. It was like what had happened at her apartment, but even more intense. Her hands skimmed through her hair and freed it from its ponytail. She started to twist her fingers in it, gathering it and then gradually dropping it, as if each strand was a possibility she was discarding. She brought it all together in one thick rope and twisted and twisted, her movements getting slower and slower....

And then she stopped. There was no outward movement at all. I couldn't even see her eyes moving under her closed lids. At first, I waited. But it went on for minutes.

I stepped closer. "Yolanda?"

No response.

I squatted next to her. "Yolanda?" I asked, worried.

Nothing. I stared at her. My face was less than a foot from hers and it was a rare opportunity to just gaze at her, to drink in that fragile, otherworldly beauty. But seeing her like this scared me. She was completely still and unresponsive. It was as if every single bit of her energy was being redirected to that incredible brain. *Is that safe?!* "Yo—"

Her eyes opened and the first thing she saw was me. And I saw those green eyes soften, saw her swallow.

She feels it too. Something in my chest lifted, before I could crush it down. *Ah, hell.* What the hell was I going to do about this woman?

"Three days," she said.

I blinked. "What?"

"We have three days," she said. "Before he kills again."

at Grier's apartment, injects Grier with something to knock him out fast, then zip ties him. Puts him in the trunk of his car, takes him across town to the apartment in Harlem, doses him with anti-clotting agents and muscle relaxant and finally bleeds him."

Hearing it all laid out like that made me worse. The thought of all the blood draining from him, clear tubes filling with red…. My vision went dark at the edges.

"Which side of the neck is the needle mark?" asked Calahan suddenly.

"Right side," said Doctor Liedner. So matter of fact, as if she was talking about which tail light was busted on her car. "So your killer's likely right-handed. Look—" And she—

Daniel Grier was a little overweight and he had rolls of fat around his neck. And Doctor Liedner was prying those rolls apart with her gloved fingers, the flesh gray and lifeless and cold—

The room went dark.

12

CALAHAN

I RAN OVER to her, but she was gone, slumped in her chair in a dead faint.

Idiot! I knew better than this. I knew this almost always happened on a first autopsy. Hell, it happened to me! And Yolanda wasn't even a cop. *Why did I drag her down here?*

Because I hadn't wanted to say goodbye. I cursed. What the hell was wrong with me?

I thanked Doctor Liedner, grabbed Yolanda's chair and pushed it through the hallways and outside. Only when we were out in the sunlight and the breeze did I kneel down beside her and gently cradle her cheek with my hand. I tried not to think about how soft her skin was, how good it felt against my palm.

"Yolanda?" I asked gently. "Yolanda?"

Her eyes stayed shut, but her lips parted a little. I couldn't stop staring at them. Blush-pink and silken. If I just extended my thumb a little, I could brush it across them—

I gritted my teeth and kept my thumb where it damn well was. *"Yolanda?"*

Her eyes opened. I looked down into all that beautiful forest green and had to swallow before I could speak. Christ, I was like a teenager around this woman. "*Hey!*" I said lamely.

She looked confused. Then she went red. "Did I faint?"

"Just... lightly," I told her. I was trying to speak through a huge surge of relief. I hadn't realized how worried I'd been. "Happens to everyone, their first time. It's my fault. Should have been watching for it."

"Everyone?" she asked. "Even you?"

"I went down like a felled tree. Broke my nose on the exam table."

She was still blushing, but she laughed. And that drew her attention to my palm, still pressed against her cheek.

I stared at her.

She stared at me.

I forced myself to draw my hand away. But I swore that, for half a second, she followed it with her cheek, pressing against it as if *she* was reluctant, too.

Now that we were out of the morgue and back above ground, my phone started to buzz with all the messages I'd missed. One was from Carrie, wanting an update on the case before the end of the day. I sighed. "I've got to go brief my boss on how we're doing," I told her. "You should come along."

"Me?!" Yolanda's eyes went wide.

"If she has questions about the equations, I'm not going to be able to answer them." Yolanda still looked horrified. "Look, I know hackers don't like the FBI, but no one's going to arrest you. It'll be fine. You can meet the people I work with." Now she looked physically ill. "Yolanda, what's the matter? They're good people, you'll like them."

"Nothing's the matter. I'm sure they're great." She sighed. "Fine."

I frowned. Why was she so reluctant? "Okay. Thanks." I nodded towards Central Park. "We can cut through the park. And you should grab something to eat, you haven't eaten all day."

She wheeled herself in silence for a few minutes. Her eyes were everywhere, suspicious and wary. She didn't like it out here on the street and I felt lousy for bringing her out here. But I liked the idea of her trapped in that penthouse even less.

"Do I get to know your real name, now?" I asked.

She shook her head.

"I can't just keep calling you *Yolanda.*"

"Everyone calls me Yolanda."

"Online. What about offline?"

She frowned at me, then looked away. My chest contracted. *There is no offline.* I was the first person she'd spoken to face-to-face in... weeks? Months?

When we got into the park, with its wide paths and greenery, she seemed to relax a little. The sun was going down, but it was still comfortably warm. We picked up a couple of burgers and cokes from one of the cafes and stopped to eat them. The burgers were amazing, the meat hot and juicy and the cheese melted into gooey perfection. A string quartet was playing nearby and it was blissfully peaceful.

And then Yolanda took this enormous bite of her burger. I mean huge, like a third of the burger just vanished. And it was just such a surprise, to see someone so delicate wolf down—

"What?" mumbled Yolanda.

I shook my head. *Nothing.*

She swallowed. "You're grinning at me," she said reproachfully.

I realized I was, but I couldn't help it. She'd just looked so cute. And being there with her just made me—

Happy.

The warm glow had crept up on me, but as soon as I realized what it was, it was like a freezing gray ocean thundered down, sluicing it away, drowning me. *Happy?* After what I did, I thought I deserved to be *happy?!* I shouldn't even be here! *She* should be here, laughing and singing and lighting up the world, and I should be—

I turned away from Yolanda, unable to speak. I wanted to yell, to smash, to destroy. And the thing I wanted to destroy most was myself. I took three shuddering breaths, forcing myself calm.

"We should get going," I muttered.

When I turned around, those beautiful green eyes were full of concern. But she nodded.

We finished our food and moved on, not talking. We were almost across the park when a group of female joggers passed us going the other way, pushing baby strollers. Yolanda's hands went loose on the wheels and she slowed to a stop, her eyes following them, her face forlorn. My chest ached. *This is why she doesn't go outside. Everyone's a reminder that she'll never stand or walk or run....*

And then the last woman in the group ran past, and her kid looked towards us and gurgled happily... and Yolanda suddenly pressed her lips together, sucked in a big gulp of air and looked away. And then she was gone, racing off ahead of me towards the exit of the park.

I was a moron. It hadn't been about the running. Is that what she thought, that she could never...?

I had to run to catch up. God, she could really move in that thing. By the time I caught her, she was waiting at the crosswalk that led across to the FBI building. I arrived beside her breathless and worried. "Yolanda!"

Her head snapped around and she glared at me. "What?" she snapped.

I stopped. There were no words. And even if there were, even if I knew them, she didn't want to hear them. The last thing she wanted was my sympathy. "You got mustard," I said at last. "There." And I pointed to the corner of my mouth.

She glared at me... and then nodded. "Thanks," she muttered. And wiped at the mustard we both knew wasn't there.

As we crossed the street, my sadness turned to anger. I wasn't angry at her, I was *pissed* at whatever had happened to her, to take away her brother and leave her like this.

I was still scowling when we reached the FBI building. But when I pushed through the doors, I felt myself calm. Stepping into the lobby always feels like coming home. Even when I have a shitty day at work, I wouldn't want to be anywhere else. I held the doors for Yolanda. "Welcome to the FBI."

I realized something: I'm proud of what I do. I just don't usually have anyone to share it with.

She rolled slowly in, looking down at the big FBI seal on the floor and then up at the flag hanging overhead. I took her up in the elevator to my floor, eager to introduce her to everyone. As soon as the doors opened, I saw Stan Hooney. Hooney's a great guy. "Hey!" I called.

Hooney turned and beamed. "Hey! You want a coffee? I'm heading to the break room."

"Always. You know how I take it. Thanks."

Hooney kept his eyes on me. "Does, uh... does *she* want one?" And he jerked his head towards Yolanda as if she wasn't capable of speech.

I just stared at Hooney. *Wait, did he really just—*

Yolanda spoke up. "Yes, thank you. Black, no sugar, please."

Hooney blinked as if surprised and hurried off.

Okay, that was weird. I didn't know what to say to Yolanda. But before I could do anything, other people were surrounding us, wanting to say hi. I introduced Yolanda but it was like they couldn't make eye contact with her. The guys, who would normally be all over any woman as hot as her, went awkward and embarrassed. And the women.... They all know I've been single for a long time. If I walk into the office with an attractive woman, immediately they're either warning her off me or saying what a cute couple we'd make. But with Yolanda, that didn't happen. It was as if she was sexless, as if making the normal jokes would somehow be in bad taste.

I got more and more angry. This was my home, my family. *How did I never see this before?*

I looked at Yolanda. She didn't look mad, so much as tired. It slowly sank in. *She knew it would be like this.* This was normal, for her. No wonder she stayed in the safety of her apartment. *And then I went and dragged her out of it.* I wanted to apologize, but I had no idea what to say.

"*Calahan!*" The yell filled the room: hell, they probably heard it in the lobby. Carrie Blake, my boss. Everyone froze, then scuttled off to their work, glad it wasn't them she was summoning.

I hurried over to where Carrie was standing and Yolanda hurried alongside me. *She* wasn't in trouble, but Carrie's voice has that effect on people.

Carrie was brandishing a piece of paper. "That kidnapping case you worked, up in the Catskills? According to the NYPD, they found an encrypted laptop when they raided the kidnapper's home. You left with it and less than an hour later, it's miraculously decrypted. Please tell me there's an explanation that doesn't involve you breaking the law!"

Dammit, I knew that was going to come back to haunt me. All three of us stared at each other in silence. Seconds ticked by. I opened my mouth to admit it, knowing that Carrie might finally fire me, this time—

"It was me," said Yolanda. She looked Carrie straight in the eye without flinching. "Agent Calahan visited me on another matter and he had the laptop with him. I took it without his knowledge and got past the decryption for... fun. Because I like a challenge. I assumed it was Agent Calahan's laptop, I had no idea it was a piece of evidence."

I stared at Yolanda in horror. Carrie crossed her arms and glared at her.

Yolanda just stared back, refusing to buckle. So Carrie turned her frown on me.

"Happened just like she said," I told her.

"So it was all a happy accident," said Carrie sarcastically. "Nobody broke the law. How convenient." She studied Yolanda, Then she looked at me. And suddenly, her eyes softened,

I felt my face going hot. Carrie doesn't miss much.

Carrie moved a little closer to Yolanda. "I take it you're the mathematician who's going to help us with the Grier murder?"

Yolanda nodded.

"Thank you," said Carrie. "We appreciate it." She asked Yolanda what she'd learned about the equations so far, nodding soberly as she listened to the answers. When they'd finished, she turned to me. "Agent Calahan? A word?"

She took me a few paces away, our backs turned to Yolanda. "I like her," Carrie whispered, trying not to smile. "Don't fuck it up." And she walked off.

I turned back to Yolanda. "You didn't have to do that," I told her.

"She was ready to fire you."

"She's *always* ready to fire me." But Yolanda was right. I'd been breaking the rules more and more, recently. I *was* on thin ice. I took a deep breath. "Thanks. Thanks for covering for me. And... I'm sorry. About how people treated you."

She looked away and nodded, embarrassed. Then she looked towards Carrie's retreating back. "I like her," she said.

Alison Brooks, one of my fellow field agents, emerged from an interview room. A stout black guy in a suit followed her out and I saw the family resemblance even before Alison introduced us. "Mr. Grier," she said, "this is Special Agent Calahan. He's leading the investigation into your brother's death."

I saw Yolanda's face fall. It was the first time she'd met grieving relatives and I knew exactly how she felt because I still remembered my first time. Suddenly, it all becomes *real*. You understand the gaping hole the death has torn in their lives.

I shook hands with the man. "I'm sorry for your loss."

He clasped my hand in both of his. "Danny was a good man, Never hurt nobody his whole life." His voice was a rich South Carolina bass but I could hear the tremble underneath: the poor guy was close to losing it. "You going to find out who did this?"

Out of the corner of my eye, I could see Yolanda lean forward a little in her chair, her eyes fierce. Meeting this guy had made it personal for her. She wanted my answer, too.

I nodded firmly. "Yes. Yes I am."

He gave a quick nod and turned towards the exit, tears in his eyes. Another guy followed him out of the room: a brother, from the age. Then another. And another. I was just turning to talk to Alison when another two emerged. I looked at Alison, amazed.

"Daniel was the youngest of seven brothers," she told me. "I know, right? They all flew in together so we could interview them. It's a close-knit family, they're in pieces."

The best way I can describe Alison is: she's like a cat. Not the playing-with-yarn, curl up on your lap kind. The stalking panther kind, graceful and deadly. She's younger than me, and I sort of mentored her a little when she was getting started.

"Did you get anything useful from them?" Yolanda asked her.

"The sum total of jack shit," said Alison. "Daniel Grier was a good, honest man. Everybody liked him. No debts, no drugs, no mistresses... and it sure as hell wasn't one of his brothers, there's not one of them that wasn't close to crying, in there."

I gestured towards a map of New York on the far side of the room: *follow me.* Yolanda arrived first, overtaking me and skidding to a halt beside the map. I arrived next. Alison took her time, not so much walking as *prowling,* and her eyes were on Yolanda the whole time. Appraising her. Assessing her. What was *that* all about? Alison can be a little cold with strangers but she's usually friendly towards people I know.

Yolanda looked up and caught the tail end of Alison's stare, and she shrank back a little in her chair. *Dammit! What's going on?* I needed these two to work together!

I quickly pointed to a red pin on the map. "Grier was abducted here, in Morningside Heights." I swept an angry line across the map with my finger. "Then the killer drove him ten blocks, to Harlem, just so he could kill him there. *Why?* Why not just kill him where he was?" I rubbed at my stubble and glanced at Yolanda. "And I've been thinking about what you said, about the death being painless. This doesn't feel like a normal murder. There's no... *hate.*"

Alison and Yolanda both shook their heads, as confused as I was.

I sighed. "Let's get you home, so you can get to work," I said to Yolanda. "Because if there's any way this makes sense... it's locked up inside those equations."

13

YOLANDA

I ROLLED THROUGH the door of my apartment, pushed it closed behind me and let out a very long sigh. It was past seven and between Harlem, the morgue and then the FBI, I'd been on the go all day. My brain ached from solving equations, my arms throbbed from wheeling myself around and I was pissed off and grouchy from what had happened at the FBI. It wasn't Calahan's fault, but... I could have predicted how they'd treat me. It had been exactly the same at my old job.

There were a few of them at the FBI who were okay. Calahan, of course. And Carrie seemed harsh but fair. They'd treated me like I was a person. But there were other reasons I'd felt uncomfortable. Part of it was being a hacker in a room filled with federal agents. Part of it was feeling like an outsider. They all belonged there, they were so...*professional*. It hadn't helped that I'd been in sneakers and jeans.

And then there was Alison. That appraising look she'd given me.

I'd asked Calahan about her on the journey home, trying to sound casual. He'd told me she was one of their best agents, always on some undercover operation or another. He swore he had no idea why she'd seemed cold towards me. But I was pretty sure I knew the reason.

She had a thing for Calahan, and she was worried I was going to steal him. Which was ridiculous. She looked like some FBI recruitment poster, with her shining, sleek hair, and crisp suit. And Calahan had told me how she'd won the FBI's martial arts tournament three years running, beating guys twice her size. *She's basically a ninja.* How could I ever compete with her?

I ordered pizza from my favorite pizza place. When I finished, I found myself gazing across the room at my computer. I could hear the photos of the equations calling me. It was too late to start any real work: by now, it was after eight. But it was too early to go to bed.

Maybe just a quick look.

...

I surfaced, briefly, because my mouth was too dry. I glanced at the clock in the corner of the screen and froze in disbelief. It was after two. *What?* How had six hours gone by?

I straightened up and the pain that shot down my neck made me want to weep. I'd been hunched over without moving for far too long. And it felt like I'd been *deep* for a good portion of the time.

It was the equations. They'd drawn me in.

I looked at the numbers on the glowing screen and an involuntary shudder went down my spine. Even now, when they were reduced to just photos, there was a dark power to them, something that ran like cold, glistening oil between the coral-like folds of my brain. Reading it actually made me feel ill, my head pounding and my stomach somersaulting. And yet I couldn't look away.

I'd assumed that the feeling of wrongness was to do with the apartment in Harlem, that it was about it being a murder scene, about all that blood. But somehow, that wrongness was here, in the writing itself. How was that possible?

At least I'd made a lot of progress during my marathon session. Visiting the crime scene had shaken me up, but Calahan had been right, it had let me understand how all the photos fitted together and now I could follow the equations much more easily. And I'd been busy figuring out what they did. Math textbooks and research papers were piled high on my desk, a rainbow waterfall of sticky notes cascading from them.

I'd been right: some of the math related to wormholes and other really advanced stuff. I was awed, but I'd also found myself getting excited. Ever since I lost my brother, I'd been lonely. It was intoxicating to learn there was someone else out there who was like me.

But now I thought about it, that idea made me go cold inside. *Like me?* Did that mean I wasn't so different to the killer? Was it just that his mind had cracked and mine hadn't... yet?

And I wasn't convinced by Calahan's theory that the equations formed a message, that the killer was taunting us. It felt like they had a purpose.

With a last shudder, I closed the photos. Enough for one night. I poured a big glass of water and glugged it down. That solved my dry mouth, but I still felt shaky and unsettled. I was exhausted but if I crashed now, I was going to have nightmares of oily black, twisting tentacles. I'd keep waking up and lie there, scared to go back to sleep and—

Then the pain would break through.

I don't have feeling in my legs, but the damaged nerves still misfire, sometimes, like a broken wire shorting out. Muscles tense and cramp painfully and there's no way to stop it. During the day, when I'm thinking, I manage to block it out. But at night, if I'm lying there awake, there's nothing to distract me.

What I needed was to think about something pleasant before I slept, something that would help me relax and give me *good* dreams. Something like—

I felt Calahan's big, warm hands wrapping around mine, squeezing them. And I stopped shaking.

I closed my eyes and remembered him leaning close and looking into my eyes. And I felt a little more settled.

He was a good guy, however much he tried to hide it under all that gruffness. He'd take on all the problems of the world, if he could. But who helped him with *his* problems? Why was he so closed off?

I knew something had changed, four years ago, to make him like this. I had to know what. So I hacked his smartphone.

His location history showed that he went to bars late at night. I checked his cab booking app. He was calling cabs from the bars to residential addresses: never the same one twice. Then another cab in the early hours of the morning, from that address back to his home address.

So he went to a bar, drank, met a woman and got a cab to her place, but he never stayed the night and he never saw them again. One night stands. I was proud of my detective work. And oddly, irrationally, jealous.

It didn't occur to me that what I was doing might be wrong: hacking was just how I found stuff out.

I started to go through his messaging history. There was nothing interesting until I got back to four years ago. That's when I started seeing messages from someone called Becky.

I picked one at random. She was asking what he wanted to do for his birthday. I read his reply and... it was like I was hearing his words, feeling his lips vibrate against the soft skin of my neck as he stood with his arms wrapped around me. He was telling her how all he wanted for his birthday was her, how she was the spirit of the city and she made it come alive for him. It was a totally different Calahan, romantic and open and *free*. I should have felt jealous again, but I didn't: the two of them were so obviously in love that I just went mushy.

I went back to when the messages started. They'd both realized, very quickly, that this was something special, something that should be grabbed with both hands. Within days, they were spending every spare moment together, just... *doting* on each other. It was hard to imagine Calahan doting. But with this woman, I could.

I read about Becky being devastated when her mom suddenly died, after they'd left things on bad terms, and Calahan comforting her. I read about Calahan getting bawled out by his boss, and Becky comforting him. I read about long romantic walks, and movie trips, and that time Calahan burned dinner, and Becky's bad jokes, and their plans for the future. They weren't wondering if they'd be together. They already knew.

And then... nothing. They met, they fell in love and then after only three weeks, the messages just stopped.

There was no explanation, no sign of a problem. Why had they suddenly broken up? Is that why Calahan was the way he was, because he'd fallen in love and Becky had broken his heart?

I thought of his big, clumpy footsteps and the way he filled a room when he was pacing. The way his blue eyes pinned me, interrogated me, the way he could get right down into my deepest thoughts and secrets with just a look. I wanted to blurt all my fears and insecurities out to him. I liked him. I trusted him.

And I wanted to help him.

I closed my eyes for a second and was shocked at how hard it was to open them again. I'd been pushing my brain to its limits all day, only the adrenaline keeping me going. Thinking of Calahan had let me relax and now sleep was crashing down on me like a warm tidal wave. I was half-awake as I rolled to my bedroom, stripped off and got into bed. I tugged the comforter over me as darkness descended.

I slept.

And I dreamed.

14

YOLANDA

I FELT HIS GAZE. That's how I knew he was there. I felt those blue eyes tracing every contour of my face as if he was caressing it. Gliding gently over my cheekbones. Brushing over my closed lids, smoothing my eyelashes, lingering on my lips....

I opened my eyes and he was standing just inside the doorway of my bedroom. Calahan is *big*, but with me lying down, he seemed even bigger. I used my arms to push myself up and back, wriggling up to sitting. I could feel the comforter slithering down my body, but I didn't have a hand free to catch it. And too late, I remembered that I'd been too tired to pull on a nightshirt—

The comforter fell to my waist. We stared at each other, frozen... and then his eyes fell to my breasts and he just *ate me up*. A flush rolled down my body and my hands found the edge of the comforter... but I didn't pull it up. There was something about the way he was feasting his eyes on me: I was still self-conscious, but it was overpowered by a pride that rippled down me in deep, hot waves. When he lifted his eyes to meet mine, I drew in my breath. The sadness was still there, but something even stronger was pushing it aside: molten, animal lust.

He stepped forward, gripped the comforter and then paused for a second. Not in hesitation. So that I had time to consider what he was about to do.

I gulped.

He pulled and the comforter slid down my stomach, down over my panties, down my legs, and onto the floor. I sat there almost naked, every inch of me throbbing, *aching,* reacting to his gaze.

He climbed onto the bed, still fully dressed. One knee came down between my ankles. The mattress sank with his weight and my legs slid inward to brush the hard muscles of his thigh.

The other knee came down, and he straddled me, and then—

I yelped as he took my ankles, gently but firmly, and pulled. In a half-second, I was lying flat again, staring up at him.

He moved up the bed, each press of his hand and knee making the mattress sink and rock. And then we were face to face.

I started to speak, but he brushed his thumb across my lips. My soft mumblings caressed him and suddenly I couldn't remember what I wanted to say. He leaned down and—

The first kiss was soft, careful. Not hesitant—he knew *exactly* what he wanted. Careful like the first footstep on untouched snow, savoring the moment. That gorgeous hard upper lip opening me, spreading me in a way that made me arch my back off the bed, the soft lower one stroking over mine, teasing and toying. But even before it had finished, I could feel the tension building in his body. Inflamed, addicted, just as I was. One kiss wasn't nearly enough.

He drew back. We looked at each other. And then we lunged, desperate, and met in midair, him leaning down and me reaching up. I moaned as we kissed again, hungry and deep, my hands running over his stubbled jaw and then sweeping through his hair. His tongue touched the tip of mine and then they were dancing together. I grabbed hold of his shoulders to support myself because there was no way, *no way* I was stopping kissing him. I dangled there from his big, solid form for long minutes as we went at each other, open-mouthed and frantic. Both of us were panting, now, the kisses falling not just on my lips, but on my cheeks, my throat, the lobes of my ears.

At last, I had to reluctantly let go and fall back to the bed. He followed me down, cradled my face in his hands, and kissed me long and deep.

And then he worked his way down. My breasts first, filling his hands, rolling and squeezing them while his tongue flicked and bathed my nipples to aching hardness. Then lower, over my stomach and on down, the heat of his breath soaking through my panties—

His fingers hooked into the top of them and in one quick move, he whipped them down my legs and off. I was totally bared to him. And then, before I could even recover from *that,* he took one leg in each big, warm hand and—

I drew in my breath as my legs were spread. I was completely exposed to him, my lips parting a little, already slickly moist—

And he knelt there at the foot of the bed and just gazed at me, his eyes like a flame licking across my skin. Any self-consciousness I'd had was burned away in a second. He took in all of me, from the flush of my cheeks to the soft, dark curls between my thighs, and I've never felt so completely, ferociously *wanted.*

Our eyes met. And in one quick move, he was full-length on top of me, his hips between my thighs. We worked together, me pulling off his tie and hurling it aside while he worked at his belt. I unbuttoned his shirt, getting halfway down his chest before I couldn't resist any longer and plunged my hands into the open neck. I ran my palms over the hard slabs of his pecs and then slid them over the muscles of his back. He shoved his pants and boxers down his thighs and I caught my breath as I felt the first hot touch of him: the shock, the thrill. *Oh God, this is actually happening.* My eyes closed as he pressed forward, so *big,* filling me—

There was a *bang.*

My eyes opened to blackness. *What happened? A blackout?*

Another *bang.* I reached for Calahan but he was gone. Had he jumped off the bed to protect me from whatever *that* was? The comforter was on me again. Had he put it back?

Bang.

And slowly, reality crept in. I'd been dreaming. A dream real enough that I'd woken up panting, real enough that I was stickily wet beneath my panties.

Bang bang bang.

And someone was banging on my door.

I searched around for a nightshirt and pulled it on, then lifted myself into the chair. I wheeled myself down the hall, the taste of him still on my lips, the glorious, heavy stretch of him still aching between my legs.

I opened the door.

And stared at a face I'd seen just moments ago. My face went scalding hot and my pussy throbbed and tightened.

"Get dressed," said Calahan. "There's been another killing."

15

CALAHAN

S HE SAT THERE staring up at me, her face turning red. Was she pissed, because I'd woken her? Then her eyes flicked to the side, towards the end of the apartment I hadn't seen, yet. Towards the bedroom, maybe. *Does she have someone else here?* Was there some guy waiting for her? I was shocked by how that idea affected me. The jealousy rippled through my chest and my breathing went tight with anger.

Yolanda seemed to shake herself and dropped her eyes... and then she wouldn't look at me. She waved me in and shot off to the kitchen area. I walked slowly after her, watching as she started to brew coffee with quick, precise movements. I was worried I'd annoyed her... but that didn't stop me drinking in the sight of her.

She wore a faded, dark red nightshirt made of that soft cotton you can't stop touching. It was too big for her, covering her down to the knees like a dress, but its softness meant that it clung to her breasts and... well, she wasn't wearing a bra. Every time she twisted to grab something, things swung and bounced in a way that was hypnotic and every time she took a deep breath or stretched her back.... I forced my gaze to the floor. "Sorry to wake you," I grunted.

"It's fine," she said. She didn't sound pissed off. But then why wouldn't she look at me? The coffee machine came alive with whirrs and gurgles. "Tell me."

"It's over in Norwood," I began. She shot off down the hall and disappeared into her bedroom. *Does she have some guy in there?* I strained my ears but I couldn't hear her talking to anyone. "Definitely our killer," I continued, taking a quiet step forward. "Equations on the walls."

I'd nearly reached the bedroom when she shot out, a pile of folded clothes on her knees. I dodged out of the way and she disappeared into the bathroom, slamming the door behind her. "That makes no sense," she called. "We still have two more days!"

I took two stealthy steps across the hallway and put my head right next to the bedroom door, listening. No sound of breathing, no creaking as someone moved in the bed. I peeked around the doorframe. A big cozy-looking wooden bed with a green comforter. No man. I relaxed, ashamed at how relieved I was.

I moved closer to the bathroom door. It was 4am and at that time, even New York goes quiet. Every time I stopped speaking, I could hear her moving inside. "The body's been there a while," I told her. There was a whisper of soft cotton as it was drawn over skin. "We think this predates the killing in Harlem." A soft *whump* as fabric hit the floor. I imagined her topless, breasts swaying. God, I was hard in my pants. *Move away. Just move further away so you can't hear.* But I didn't. "We haven't IDed the victim, yet."

I heard a faint stretch of elastic and the hiss of fabric being pushed along skin. Her panties coming off. I turned my back to the door, but I couldn't make myself move away. I was drawn to this woman, even though I knew I couldn't have her. "They'll take photos again, but I want you to see it," I told her. The shower came on: a steady sound at first, then changing as she moved around under the spray. I tried not to think about her body shining slickly with water. "From the sound of it, it's the same as the Grier murder, but... different."

The shower shut off. There was the sound of toweling off, as quick and efficient as everything else she did. I took a few steps away from the door and turned towards the kitchen as if I wasn't the slightest bit interested in what had been going on in the bathroom.

Seconds later, she shot past me, head down and eyes forward. She still didn't want to make eye contact. She was in jeans and an old Princeton sweatshirt, her hair still damp. The coffee was brewed and she slid a cup along the counter towards me, cowboy saloon style, and I had to hurry forward to catch it before it went off the edge. We both drained our cups in three quick gulps because we knew we had to move, but her coffee was so good—dark and rich and smooth as caramel—rushing it felt like a crime. I closed my eyes for a second in appreciation, giving a low groan as the caffeine hit my system. I'd gone to bed at two and only managed an hour's sleep before the phone call had come in. And I had a feeling this was going to be a long night.

Yolanda started the coffee machine going again, then shot off across the kitchen. She opened a metal tin, snatched a couple of *somethings* from inside, then raced towards her desk, eyes straight ahead. Why wouldn't she look me in the eye?

She threw something over her shoulder and I caught it on instinct. "Thought you probably needed food," she called without looking back.

I looked at what I was holding. A homemade granola bar, wrapped in plastic wrap. I glanced at the kitchen area. There are two sorts of kitchen: ones for people who like to cook, with lots of pans, fresh ingredients and well-used surfaces, and ones like Yolanda's, where the coffee machine and the microwave were center stage. I couldn't imagine her baking. So who made these? "Thanks," I said.

She grabbed her laptop, notebook and a pen, threw them all in a bag along with her granola bar and shot back towards the kitchen, eyes still avoiding mine. I couldn't take it anymore. The idea that she was pissed with me really bothered me. At the last second, I sidestepped in front of her. "Hey!" I said, holding up my hand to stop her.

She pulled up just before her knees would have hit my legs.

"You okay?" I asked. "Are *we* okay? You mad at me?"

"No," she said quickly. "It's fine. We're fine. It's all fine." And then, when I didn't move out of her way, she sighed and finally looked up at me, just for a split second.

And her face turned scarlet again. She wasn't pissed. She was *embarrassed*. Why would she be embarrassed? I stepped out of the way, confused but relieved.

The coffee machine had brewed another two cups and she dumped both of them into a travel cup and screwed on the lid. She showed me it apologetically. "Sorry. I only have one."

"We can share," I deadpanned. "I don't have cooties."

I saw a tiny smile pull at her lips as she rolled towards the door. "Come on, then," she said. "Let's go."

She drove. It was a little after four and her sports car shot through the empty streets at a speed that made me furtively grip my seat in the darkness. We hit green light after green light—at first, I thought we were just getting lucky. Then I saw Yolanda's eyes flicking between the lights and the speedo. She'd worked out the damn rhythm. She'd *calculated* when the next set of lights would go green and the exact speed we needed to go to pass through them in time.

"Anyone ever tell you your mind's kind of incredible?" I asked, passing her the coffee.

She glanced across at me, then quickly looked away, shrugged and drank some coffee. Her embarrassment seemed to be easing a little, but she still went awkward and shy whenever she looked at me. I would have given a million dollars to know what was going through her head.

"Wish I had your brain," I said. "I have trouble just filling out my tax return."

Silence. I thought that was all I was going to get but a few intersections later, she said, "You don't want to be like me."

I turned to her and waited patiently. She didn't look at me, but I knew she could feel me watching.

"We were never normal, my brother and me," she said at last. "We wanted to do math puzzles instead of play Little League. We went to college at *sixteen,* so when everyone else was out partying, we had to stay home. We didn't really learn to talk to people." She threw me a guilty glance. "That's why I can be a little...difficult."

Our eyes met for a second. I saw her flush and I felt my face going hot. Both of us looked away.

"You're not so difficult," I muttered.

There was a long, warm silence. I had to break it, before something happened.

"And your brain *is* incredible," I said.

She stared hard at the road ahead. "My brain does one thing well. And it's...delicate."

I frowned. I didn't like the sound of that.

"They had to call a psychologist in, when we were kids," she mumbled. "They were worried about us. Minds like ours can... break." Then she gave a little snort of anger and glared down at her legs. "Wasn't my mind they should have worried about."

I nodded sadly. Opened my mouth... and then closed it again.

"What?" she asked, glancing at me for a split second.

"Nothing."

She shook her head. "I know that expression. You want to ask something."

Now *I* shrugged. "I know questions piss you off."

"They don't piss me off, I just—" She sighed. "Do you know how often people ask the same things?"

I shook my head. "Forget it."

She drove in silence for three more intersections. Then, "New rule, Calahan. You get to ask me one question per day about..." She nodded down at her legs. "*One.*" She passed the coffee back to me.

"No matter how dumb?" I asked, my voice a little teasing.

The faintest hint of a smile. "No matter how dumb."

"Okay," I said, pleased. I settled back in my seat, drank and thought. "Why do you live on the fortieth floor of a skyscraper? What if there's a fire? What if the elevator breaks down?"

Silence for a few seconds. Then, "I like being high up." She shot a look at me and her eyes were big and scared. Scared that I'd laugh.

But I just nodded solemnly. That made complete sense.

She relaxed a little. Then, "We're here."

We pulled up between two patrol cars and climbed out. It was still at least an hour before the sun would be up. When I saw the place, I wished we'd driven slower.

The house was old enough that the roof visibly sagged. The clapboard that covered the walls had been blue, once, but the paint had long since flaked away and the exposed wood had been sun-bleached to the color of bones. Every window was boarded up. I've never seen a less inviting place.

The creepiest thing was the darkness. No lights were on because the power had long since been disconnected. But there must be officers with flashlights inside and yet I couldn't see even a faint glow between the boards on the windows. It was as if the house sucked in light. Just like the apartment in Harlem, there was something...*wrong* in this place.

I showed my badge to one of the officers. "First floor or second floor?"

"First," he said. He glanced over his shoulder at the house and brushed his arm with his hand, as if brushing something off it. "First floor."

I cursed. I'd been hoping he'd say *second* because no way was there a working elevator in that place and so Yolanda would have had to stay here. I was the one who'd brought her, but suddenly, looking at the place, I didn't want her going inside. "Okay," I muttered to her. "Let's be careful."

As we neared the house, my flashlight seemed to do less and less. It was as if the darkness was just swallowing the beam. *Maybe the batteries are dying.*

Inside, it was even worse. Anything outside of the flashlight beam was just *black*. The first room we came to was empty. The furniture had long since been stolen and all my flashlight revealed were a few broken bottles, some used needles—

And the cracks.

The walls and floor were made of wood and the planks had shrunk and warped with age, opening up dark spaces between them in which anything could lurk.

Yolanda was using the flashlight on her phone. When I caught her eye, she looked as shaken as me. I looked questioningly at her. *You okay?*

She nodded quickly and rolled down the hall towards the next room. I hurried to get ahead of her, but the hallway was narrow: there wasn't room for me to squeeze around her. Having two flashlight beams merged together was disorienting and confusing, so I switched mine off, but that made the darkness press in even more. "Yolanda," I warned. "Wait, maybe I should—"

Too late. She gave a little moan of fear as her flashlight lit up the room.

It had been the kitchen, once. Now, you could only tell by the checkered linoleum on the floor, brittle curls of it reaching up to brush our ankles. And in the center of the floor—

Like Daniel Grier, the body was fully clothed. Like him, it had been drained of blood. But—

Yolanda looked up at me, her face pale and stricken. "I wasn't expecting it to be a woman."

I put a hand on her shoulder and gently squeezed. The guilt was tearing at me: I'd forgotten that she wasn't used to seeing bodies. And there was something especially disturbing about this one. The woman was about Yolanda's age and build and she had dark hair. Her clothes were neat and perfect: she'd been something young and bright, but someone had snuffed her out and just dumped her here, one leg awkwardly bent under her like an abandoned doll.

"How...how long?" Yolanda's voice had a quaver to it I didn't like. She was one or two steps from panic.

I tried to keep my voice level and calm. "I'd say a week, maybe ten days."

Yolanda said nothing. Both of us just stared at the body and I knew we were thinking the same thing. It was terrifying that someone could just be plucked out of their life, away from friends and family and their job, and left to lie there in the darkness for all that time and *no one found them.*

I reached down and found Yolanda's hand in the darkness. It had gone cold as ice. I took it in mine, listening to her breathing, waiting to see if it would speed up into a panic. But it gradually slowed as she got herself under control. *God,* she was brave. There was something about this place that would make even hardened cops turn and run, but she was still here.

When she looked up at me, her jaw was set, resolute. My chest went tight because I knew what was happening and I knew how dangerous it was: the case was becoming personal. But I nodded that I understood. *We have to stop this guy.*

Yolanda moved her flashlight off the body and started searching the floor. Immediately, I understood what they'd told me on the phone. This scene was different: at the apartment, we hadn't had to search for the equations at all. They'd covered every square inch. But here, the flashlight revealed just smooth, dusty floorboards.

"Maybe they're—" She swung the circle of light onto the wall: nothing. She tried a patch of ceiling: just bare plaster.

Yolanda cursed and rolled towards one corner, sweeping her flashlight back and forth like a searchlight.

What the hell is going on, I wondered. *Where are they?*

Yolanda screamed, dropped her phone and shot backwards, all at the same time. Her phone clattered to the floor, and the room went black.

16

CALAHAN

YOLANDA'S SCREAM rang in my ears. I had time to blink once at the sudden, suffocating blackness and then her wheelchair slammed into me. One wheel rolled over my foot, a handle hit me right in the stomach and something metal scraped my shin. I bent almost double, leaning over the back of it. "It's okay," I wheezed. My face was close to Yolanda's: I couldn't see her, but I could hear her taking huge panic breaths in the darkness. "It's okay, it's okay."

I tried to push the chair off my foot, but Yolanda's hands were rigid on the wheels. Wincing, I grabbed the handles and lifted the whole thing, freed my foot and then put it down. I groped my way to the side of the chair. Yolanda's breathing was out of control: she was full-on hyperventilating, now. *Shit.*

I did the only thing I could do: I knelt down in the blackness, leaned in close and put my arms around her, cradling her head on my shoulder. "Shh," I told her. "*Shh.* It's okay. I'm here."

Her breath was hot against my neck. Wetness plopped against my forearm: something had scared her so bad, she was crying with fear. "*Shh,*" I said again.

There was a whisper of sensation on the back of my outstretched leg, as if something had brushed against it for a second. I ignored it, too focused on Yolanda. "*Shh.*"

At last, she began to calm. Very gently, I unwound myself from her and looked around. Across the room, I could see a faint glow: her phone, lying flashlight-side down on the floor. I stood and took a hesitant step towards it.

"*No!*" Yolanda grabbed my arm and hung on with a death-grip. Her voice wasn't her own: it was shrill and almost childlike. My stomach knotted. She was so logical, so rational... for something to unsettle her this much, it must be—

"It's okay," I said with confidence I didn't feel. I patted her hand, but she still wouldn't let go and I had to gently coax her fingers loose. I swallowed and took a step into the almost total darkness. Another one. Another. I could feel my heart racing out of control. I couldn't ever remember being so scared.

I bent and felt for the phone. As I lifted it, its flashlight lit up a patch of floor and—

The blood had dried, so the equations were matt black. They were written much, much smaller than before, the numbers packed so tightly together that they formed a solid, ovoid body. Branching out from that were eight thick legs made up of more equations, and the whole thing was edged in individual lines of equations so delicate they looked like coarse, dark hairs.

It was a spider the size of my head. And—I moved the flashlight around—there were others, lurking on the walls, in the corners, swelling up out of the cracks between the floorboards. That's why the equations didn't cover the room. The killer had written smaller and tighter, squeezing the same amount of writing into—I scanned around—twenty, thirty, maybe a hundred of these *things*. They were all around us and—

I saw something move, just at the edge of the flashlight beam, and jerked in fear. Yolanda saw it too, and cried out.

There were real spiders in here, too. I remembered the brush on the back of my leg, and the cop outside, unconsciously trying to brush things from his uniform. My throat closed up.

No wonder Yolanda was terrified. She knew that to solve the equations, she'd have to stay here in the blackness for hours, going slowly mad with fear as she searched out every one of the killer's drawings, while real spiders crawled up onto her from the floor and dropped into her hair from the ceiling, scuttling out of the cracks and running over her hands as she followed the equations on the walls.

The killer had planned it this way. *Want to decipher my work? I'll make sure you go mad trying.*

No way. No *fucking* way. Not Yolanda, not her incredible, fragile mind. I marched back to her, grabbed the handles of her wheelchair and *went*. I rushed her out of the room, down the hall and outside, not stopping until we were well away from the house. Dawn was still some way off but after the blackness, the dark blue sky felt like noonday sun.

I moved my hand to Yolanda's shoulder and I could feel her trembling. The fear went beyond just the murder scene or the dark or the spiders. It was an instinctive reaction to something deeply, deeply wrong. Something evil.

I moved around in front of her and squatted down. Her eyes were darting around the ground as if worried that the spiders had followed us outside. "Hey," I said. She didn't respond. I put my thumb under her chin and gently lifted her head. "Hey."

Those lush green eyes looked at me from a face gone even paler than usual. She was breathing too fast and I could see tears welling at the corners of her eyes. The guilt felt like a punch to my guts. *I did this to her. Me.* I'd dragged her out of her apartment. Sure, she'd been trapped there, but she'd been *safe*.

I pulled her to me and wrapped my arms around her.

And something unexpected happened.

I was trying to calm her, but when I pressed close to her, when I felt her soft cheek against mine and buried my nose in her hair... I felt her calming me.

Becky used to say that I came home from work dirty and at first I thought she meant the layers of grime and grease New York leaves on your skin. But she meant a different kind of dirt, the kind that coats you at crime scenes and grinds itself into your soul in interrogation rooms. All cops have it. It's the dirt we try to wash away with alcohol, the stuff that makes us yell at our kids and fight with our wives.

Yolanda took it away. Maybe it was those eyes, like cool, misty forests. Maybe it was her amazing mind, sharp and methodical and clear of hate. Maybe it was the feel of her, the softness of her curves and the sweet little hollow of her collarbone, where my chin fitted so well. The calmness, the *peace* of her... it felt so good I wanted to weep. And never, ever let her go.

No. No, goddamn it. I didn't deserve peace. And she deserved a hell of a lot better than me.

I slowly unwound from her and pushed her gently back. I had to look off to the side, so she didn't see how much I wanted her. *Needed* her. The sense of loss, as the cool air rushed in and filled the space between us, was gut-wrenching.

I forced my feelings down deep, where they belonged. She was still twitchy and tearful, still throwing terrified glances over her shoulder at the house. *My fault.* I'd forced her way out of her comfort zone.

Maybe I had to put her back into it. Get her talking about what she loved. "I got a confession to make," I said. "I basically failed math in high school."

She frowned, her eyes still shining with tears. "They wouldn't have let you join the FBI." And she glanced at the house again, still panicked. I had to fix this.

"Oh, I *passed.* But only because I copied off Johnny Timms. I didn't know what the hell it meant."

She took another look at the house. She couldn't stop looking at it. This wasn't working. "Like, ten-to-the-whatever," I said desperately.

That made her look at me. She sniffed and then frowned, as if she thought maybe she'd misheard. "Like ten to the five? Six to the power of four?"

"Yeah."

She cocked her head to one side suspiciously. But it was working. Her breathing was slowing. "Everyone knows that."

"I don't!" I was overjoyed that she'd stopped looking at the house. But then, when she looked aghast, I felt all the blood rush to my face. I was the dumb kid in high school again, praying the teacher wouldn't call on me. "I actually don't," I admitted, and looked at the ground.

I felt her staring at me for a moment. I think she knew it was a ploy, but she could also see I was telling the truth. She crossed her arms. Uncrossed them. Then, finally, "Let me explain it."

She'd blinked away her tears and those green eyes were the most beautiful thing I'd ever seen. She could have explained the life cycle of goddamn turnips and I'd have listened.

"*To the power of* just means multiplying something by itself," she said. "Three to the power of one is just three. Three to the power of two—which we call *squaring* it—is just three times three, which is nine. Three to the power of three—*cubing* something—is just three times three *times three,* which is twenty-seven."

I screwed up my forehead. "So when they said *eight to the power fourteen,* that was just—"

We said it together. "Eight times eight times eight times eight...."

"...until you have fourteen eights written down, total," she finished.

We stared at each other, her now placid and my brain going at a million miles an hour, fast-forwarding through all the years that had confused the hell out of me. "Why did no one just tell me that?" I mumbled at last. A swell of anger joined the embarrassment. *Because I was just the big dumb jock.* No one had thought I was worth it.

But Yolanda...*she* thought I was worth it.

All of those feelings I'd crushed down inside me escaped and expanded, filling me until I couldn't speak, couldn't breathe. *Goddamn it!*

If I kept looking into her eyes, I was going to do something stupid. I forced myself to stand and I put my hand on her shoulder. Just a quick squeeze, like *thanks,* like *we're friends,* like—

I couldn't let go. She looked up at me and I looked down at her. My thumb wanted to stroke across her collarbone, my fingers wanted to draw her gently forward so I could lean down and—

No! I caught myself just in time. I didn't deserve her. Not after Becky. And besides, she needed someone smart, not a big lunk like me.

I let go of her shoulder.

We had to catch this bastard. But as soon as the case was done, we needed to go our separate ways. Until then, what I could do, what I *had* to do, was protect her. I wasn't going to let my work destroy her, the way it destroyed Becky. No way was I letting Yolanda back into that house, not until I made some changes.

I marched over to the officers manning the scene and started barking orders.

~

While the coroner removed the body, I helped set up big, portable lights, three times the number we'd normally use. With them blasting at full power, the house turned as stark and bright as a laboratory. It was overkill, but not a single cop complained or suggested we turn them down. Everyone could feel the dark horror of the place pressing in around us, waiting to swallow the light: every time the generator stuttered for a second and the lights flickered, everyone would freeze and glance around uneasily.

We laid Perspex sheets on the floor and up against the walls, sealing away anything that crawled out of the cracks. Only then did I let Yolanda back in.

She looked around. Looked at me and nodded. *Thank you.*

And she went to work.

It took hours. For most of that, she was constantly moving, shooting around the room from one spider to another, rocking on the wheels and twirling her pen absently around her fingers as she thought. Even in the light and sealed behind Perspex, the spiders were deeply unsettling to look at. Yolanda traced the equations with her finger to keep her place and when she brushed a spider's curving fangs, I felt physically sick. It was everything I could do not to grab her wrist and pull her hand away.

Occasionally, she'd hit some dense knot of math that challenged even her, and she'd slow down as that incredible brain soaked up all of her energy. She'd become more and more still and then, sometimes, she'd stop. She'd sit there, eyes closed, lips moving, and I knew she was *deep*. I'd seen it before, at the first crime scene, but this time was more unsettling. She stayed down longer: not just a few minutes, but ten or fifteen each time. And when she did resurface, she looked confused and disoriented. As if she hadn't just gone deep into her own head, but had been dragged off somewhere else. I knew that made no sense, but it felt bad. Dangerous. And I couldn't stand the idea that I might be putting her in danger.

I cared about this woman more than I wanted to admit.

I scowled and forced myself to think of something else. This place was the ideal place to kill someone: a quiet street, an abandoned house... no wonder the body hadn't been found for a while. So why the hell hadn't the killer brought Daniel Grier here, too? It made no sense.

Behind me, Yolanda gave a sigh of satisfaction. I spun around as she slumped back in her chair. "Okay," she said, pointing to one of the spiders. "This part is the countdown to the next killing and the date and time works out as *this*." She passed me a piece of paper.

"That's when Daniel Grier was killed." That proved she'd been right: the equations at each killing told you where and when the next one was going to happen. This killing predicted Daniel Grier's. Daniel Grier's would predict the next one, the one happening in two days' time. "Anything else you can tell me?"

"Five of the spiders contain pairs of letters that aren't part of the equations. Initials, maybe?" She showed me and I went to write them down, then realized I'd left my notebook in her car. So I scrawled them on my hand, instead: *AV ES AT AN AS*. I had no clue what they meant. When I glanced up, I was looking right into Yolanda's eyes and what I saw there made my stomach knot. She was as beautiful as ever, but something had changed since that first day I'd met her. She looked paler and those lush green eyes were haunted. The case was taking its toll on her. *What am I doing, getting her involved in this? She's not a cop!*

But if I wanted to catch this guy, I needed her.

My phone bleeped and I checked the message. "Come on," I muttered. "Autopsy's ready."

17

YOLANDA

W HEN WE EMERGED from the house, I froze in shock at the bright sun. It was noon: I'd been immersed in the equations for over *five hours!* By the time I'd driven us to the hospital, I felt almost jet-lagged: a four a.m. start, then the dark house, then the bright artificial light all morning and next we'd be underground in the morgue. "How do you do this?" I mumbled to Calahan.

He stopped at the hospital's coffee stand, bought two coffees, and pushed one into my hand. *Oh.*

Doctor Liedner was waiting for us. "Calahan!" she said warmly. She grinned at me. "And Yolanda." She gave Calahan a sly smile. "*Again.*"

I saw the flush climb Calahan's neck and turn his ears red. My face was going red, too, because even just a harmless quip took me straight back to the night before and my dream, the feel of him as he filled me—

I focused *very hard* on calculating how many rivets there were on the stainless steel walls.

"Okay," said Doctor Liedner. She stopped beside a table and pulled back the sheet. The woman—I couldn't think of her as a *body* —from the spider house lay there, her clothes gone. It felt wrong, that she was just lying there naked, as if her dignity didn't matter, anymore. "Same muscle relaxant in the blood, same anti-clotting agent, same needle mark in the neck, same zip tie marks on the wrists and ankles. No question, it's the same killer."

"They ID her, yet?"

Doctor Liedner passed him a file. "Sharon Kubiak, worked at a grocery store, disappeared eight days ago, which fits with my estimated time of death."

Without being asked, Calahan squatted down so I could look over his shoulder as he read. When we'd finished, we frowned at each other, confused. Daniel Grier was a well-off, African-American man in his forties. Sharon Kubiak was a blue-collar Caucasian woman in her twenties. *What's the connection?*

Calahan sighed. "Anything else?"

"Just one thing." Doctor Liedner beckoned us over to Sharon's head. Then she carefully lifted the left eyelid. I felt my stomach churn for a second, but when I focused on Sharon's eye, I forgot my nausea. There was a diagonal slash of black across the iris, as if the pupil extended through it. "Coloboma," said Doctor Liedner, awed. "Maybe one in ten thousand people have it, but an extreme case like this is very rare. They used to think it was the mark of a witch. Literally, the Evil Eye."

I felt myself pout. Superstitions and me don't really get on. Especially ones that lead to people being singled out because they look different. There used to be all sorts of that crap, people had weird ideas about what made someone a—

"Oh my God," I said aloud.

I whipped out my phone. No signal, because we were underground. I rushed off towards the surface, yelling goodbye to Doctor Liedner over my shoulder.

18

CALAHAN

I HAD TO RUN to catch up with Yolanda. Just as she reached the main doors, she heard me coming and spun around, crashing through the doors backwards. "Do you have the number for Daniel Grier's brother?" she asked breathlessly.

I found it and read it to her as we moved out into the sunlight. "What are you doing?"

"Checking a theory," she muttered, and put her phone to her ear. "Mr. Grier? I'm sorry to bother you, but I'm working with the FBI, investigating your brother's death. I need to know: how many brothers did your father have?" She waited. "And he was the youngest?" She drew in a deep breath. "Thank you, Mr. Grier."

She ended the call and looked up at me, but it was several seconds before she spoke. "I have a theory," she said at last. "But it's kind of out there."

I crossed my arms. "This whole case is kind of out there. Spill it."

She leaned forward and I squatted down to listen. "Daniel Grier had six brothers, all older than him," she said. "And his father *also* had six older brothers. That makes Daniel the seventh son of a seventh son. That's in the bible. It's meant to be a sign of a person of great power, or in some cultures a mystic or a healer. And Sharon Kubiak had coloboma, which used to be a sign you were a witch."

I stared at her, stunned. "You think our killer is hunting witches?"

"I think that's what he thinks he's doing, yes."

It made sense. It explained why the two victims had nothing in common. "But why does he leave the cops messages written in math? That doesn't fit with folklore at all."

We frowned at each other as we thought. We were doing that more and more, figuring things out together. I knew that was dangerous. I had to keep my distance. But we worked so well together....

The silence was broken by Yolanda's stomach giving a loud, long rumble. She flushed and looked away.

"C'mon," I told her, standing up. "I'm buying you the best dog in town."

About twenty yards down the street was a hot dog stand, run by an old Italian-American guy called Petey. He has shaggy, silver curls and skin almost as leathery as his Hush Puppies, and he serves up the best dogs in the city. I go to his stand a lot, because it's right outside the morgue.

I bought two dogs and handed one to Yolanda. I didn't have to ask her what she wanted on it because, honestly, to mess with one of Petey's dogs in any way would be sacrilege. You take it as it comes or not at all.

"Oh God," said Yolanda after one bite. "This is amazing."

And it was. The bun was lusciously soft and chewy, the sausage was properly salty and meaty, the onions melted on your tongue and then you got that hit of mustard and the tang of ketchup. We took our time eating, not talking, just people watching in companionable silence. When we finished, and threw the paper in a trash bin, I caught Yolanda looking around wistfully. "What?" I asked.

"Just... I can't remember the last time I ate a hot dog. Or...." She looked at the street, the people. At New York. *The last time she was a part of this.* I nodded sadly.

We headed back down the street and we were almost back to the car when it happened. One second, she was rolling along beside me, chatting away, and then she cried out and suddenly the chair was on its side and she was sprawled on the sidewalk like a rag doll.

I stood there stupidly for a second. *What the hell happened?* Everyone stopped and turned to look, saying things like *oh dear* and *ooh* and *is she okay* and meanwhile Yolanda was dragging herself along the sidewalk on her arms, her legs just a dead weight behind her. I saw now what had happened: she'd clipped a wheel on the edge of a concrete planter, hooked to one side and tipped.

For the first time, I really understood why she never left the apartment. Out here, one mistake, one tiny slip, and she was helpless.

She'd reached the chair, now. Her face was red with humiliation as she tried to get it onto its wheels without it rolling off the sidewalk into traffic—

Why the hell am I just standing here, watching? I started forward, mad at myself, my hands going down to grab her under the arms.

"*Don't pick me up!*" she snapped, glaring at me.

I froze. "Why not?"

There were tears in her eyes. "Because I'm not a fucking child!"

She finally got the chair back onto its wheels and got the brakes on. Then she hauled herself up hand over hand, the muscles in her upper arms standing out, and finally swung around and dropped into the seat, panting and sweating. She took the brakes off and I saw that her palms were scraped raw where they'd hit the sidewalk. But she didn't even hesitate, she just wheeled herself off towards the car and I had to hurry to keep up.

We climbed into the car and she tried to slide the chair into its slot behind the seat, but it refused to go, bouncing back each time she shoved it in. She finally slammed it home with a yell of frustration, then sat there, hands nursing the steering wheel. "Sorry," she muttered, not looking at me. "I shouldn't have yelled at you."

"No," I said, my voice thick with emotion. "It's okay. I get it."

She shot me a suspicious look, but she must have seen in my expression that I meant it because her face softened and she nodded. Then she started the car. "Come on," she said. "I've got a plan."

19

YOLANDA

W E WERE BACK in my apartment, nursing mugs of coffee as we looked at my computer monitor. "Here's what I'm thinking," I said. "I hack the big search engines and look for people who've been searching for both advanced mathematical formulae and myths and superstitions around identifying witches and other people of power. That's a pretty unusual combination, especially if I limit it to New York IP addresses. I bet we'd only get one or two matches. And one of them would likely be our guy."

I finished, breathless and excited, and looked across at Calahan. He was staring at me, open-mouthed. "What?" I asked, bemused. Then I sighed. "Calahan, this is what I do! I won't get caught!"

"It's not that! It's—" He looked at me, like: *you know.*

But I didn't. "What?"

"We don't have a warrant for anything like that!"

"Oh no," I put a hand to my mouth in mock horror. "And I *never* break the law."

"It's not just the law, it's *wrong!* It's people's search history, it's private!"

"You're *always* breaking the rules!"

"There's a difference between breaking the rules and—" He sighed. "It's *wrong.*"

I blinked at him. He was serious. He actually believed in doing the right thing, some sense of justice and fairness that went beyond the law. I felt myself warm to him in a new and totally unexpected way, one I didn't know how to deal with. So I pushed back from the desk and wheeled myself over to the chalkboards instead. "We have less than two days to figure out where the next killing's going to be," I said gently. "And I'm no closer to understanding the location part." I pointed to the equations. "Maybe I'll get it in time, but maybe I won't. Even if I do get it and we can swoop in and catch him red-handed, wouldn't it be much safer to track him down *now* and arrest him, before he gets close to another victim?"

Calahan cursed under his breath. He got up and paced for a while, eventually coming to a stop in front of the windows. "You won't get caught?" he asked, staring out over the city.

"No."

"And you'll delete everything, right afterwards?"

I rolled my eyes. "Of course. I promise." And then I frowned because saying that felt *weird.*

He sighed. "Okay. Do it."

I rolled over to my desk and went to work. Hacking can be fiddly but it doesn't consume my whole brain the way math does. So I had plenty of time to think: why had it felt so strange, when I'd said *I promise?* I'd only said it to humor him, but the words had felt big and weighty as they left my lips. They mattered.

And that made me think of how he'd stared at me in horror, when I'd suggested the hack. He hadn't wanted me to do something bad. He wanted to protect me, in some way, keep me clean: or at least, stop me getting any dirtier. That should have seemed silly, but it didn't. It felt good. And it made me wonder whether he had a point. Had I been hacking for so long that my moral compass had drifted?

I was one step away from completing the hack when I hit a problem. I'd gotten access to the massive database of what everyone had been searching for, but I couldn't figure out how to sift through it for the combination we needed. Fortunately, I know Lily, who's just about the best in the world when it comes to fooling around with databases. I messaged her and she said she could help, but that she was riding with her boyfriend, Bull, and couldn't be back at her computer for another hour.

I pushed back from my desk, stretched, and looked around for Calahan. And found myself looking right into those clear blue eyes. He was slumped on my couch, staring right at me. *Has he been watching me, that whole time?* A wave of heat rippled down my body and I quickly looked away. I grabbed the tin where I store the granola bars and threw him one while I told him about Lily.

"These are good," he said, unwrapping the granola bar. "Who makes them?"

"My mom. I don't, um... call her much. So she sends me care packages of granola bars. I have a whole freezer full." I looked at my freezer sadly. "I don't want to throw them out."

"You should call her," he muttered.

I nodded. "I know. But we don't get along since...." I glanced down.

"Even so," he said gently.

With anyone else, I would have told them not to lecture me. But I knew where this was coming from: he'd seen Becky lose her mom suddenly and be unable to set things straight. I closed my eyes and held up my hand in defeat. "You're right, you're right. I should. I will. I know how rough it was on Becky."

I opened my eyes and found him staring right at me. "How do you know about Becky's mom?" he asked. He stood up, looming over me. "How do you know about *Becky?*"

My mouth opened, but nothing came out. *Oh shit.*

He turned the full force of those blue eyes on me, his gaze soaking deep into me and reaching right into my soul. *This is how criminals feel, when he interrogates them.* I couldn't lie, when he looked at me like that. All I wanted to do was confess.

And then I didn't have to because my eyes, desperate to escape that gaze, flicked to my computer.

"You hacked me." He said it slowly, as if he was tasting the words to see if they could be true. "You read our messages." His voice turned bitter. "Becky and me."

I started to speak, but he turned away and stalked over to the window. I watched, horrified, as those huge shoulders began to rise and fall: big, shuddering breaths as he tried to control his anger. Oh God, I'd really crossed a line. He massaged his forehead. Rubbed at his stubble. He was breathing faster and faster, the veins in his neck standing out....

I rolled a half inch towards him and extended my hand. "Calahan—"

"*WHAT WERE YOU THINKING?*" He turned and roared it at me, the words a weapon. I shrank back in my chair and instinctively rolled a few feet back. But he was advancing, each stomp of his foot sending shockwaves through the room. "*Hackers!*" he spat. "Don't you have *any sense* of people's privacy?"

I rolled back another foot. "I just wanted to—I only wanted to know what happened!"

"It's none of your business, what happened!" He was almost on me, now, his long legs eating up the distance faster than I could retreat.

"I'm sorry! You're just so... *sad*. All the time. I was just looking for why, I wanted to help!"

Thunk. I'd backed up against a wall. He had me.

He stepped right up to me, his ankles nudging my dangling feet. I had to crane my head right back to look up at him. We stared at each other and the only sound in the room was my tight, shaky panting and his big, shuddering breaths.

"She's dead," he said. It started as an attack, but by the time he reached the second word, his voice was breaking and he didn't look angry, anymore. He just looked lost. And hurt. And disappointed in me. *Why did you have to do this to me?*

I had no words. I was re-running all those messages from Becky in my head. I'd been assuming they broke up. I'd never considered...

oh God. No wonder Calahan was the way he was. And now I'd brought it all back to him—

I'd never felt like such a complete piece of shit. I just wanted to squirm out of his sight. "Calahan," I managed at last. "Sam. I'm sorry."

He turned away. He couldn't even look at me.

"I'll never hack you again," I said.

He still had his back turned, brooding. But I thought I saw him nod his acknowledgment. I had no idea what to do next. I wanted to talk to him about it. I wanted to comfort him. But I couldn't, not when it was so obviously painful for him.

"I think," he said at last, "under the circumstances, I get a free question."

He turned and glared at me, letting me know that the subject of Becky was closed forever.

"Yes," I said immediately. "Whatever you want."

He took a deep breath and let it out, calming down, but a long way from calm. "What's in the dove loft?"

I blinked at him, speechless. I'd been expecting *how did it happen* or *do you miss walking* or even something about sex. "How did you know?" I said at last.

"What you said in the car didn't make sense," he said. "I believe that you want to be high up. But there are taller buildings so that can't be the only reason. You wanted *this* penthouse. I checked and the only thing special about this building is its age. Fancy balconies, gargoyles...and the penthouse has a dove loft on the roof." He stepped closer. "So what's in the dove loft?"

I got it. He wanted to talk about something else, something not Becky. And I more than owed him that.

I swallowed. "Can you keep a secret?"

20

CALAHAN

S HE LED ME to a private elevator that was really only big enough for one person. She backed in first and I had to stand facing her, so close that my legs brushed hers. We ascended, and I closed my eyes and rubbed at them as if I was tired. Really, I was trying to sort through my feelings.

I was hurting. I get through each day by pushing this stuff down inside me. She'd hauled all the memories to the surface, a million glittering, razor-sharp shards, each one slicing deep, the guilt welling up. *Becky. I'm sorry.*

Hacking me had been wrong, but Yolanda had only done it because she was worried about me. And that was my own fault: I'd let her get too close. What the hell was wrong with me? I was normally good at keeping women away. I did it with Hailey, at the FBI, for years. But Yolanda... she'd got under my skin in a matter of days.

The elevator jerked to a stop and I opened my eyes. She was looking right at me, her eyes frightened. *Are we okay?*

I hesitated... and then nodded. I couldn't stay mad at her. Not this woman.

I pushed open the door and stepped out onto the rooftop. All around us were fantastic views of the city. But the rooftop was something all on its own.

I'd been on plenty of rooftops back when Hailey and I were doing surveillance on the Russian mob, and they were just gray jungles of aerials and air conditioning ducts. Yolanda's roof was more like a church: the parapets had little balconies you could step out onto, with gargoyles hunched on the corners, their beady eyes watching the streets below. There were stone benches and even an arch that framed the view of Central Park. And there was a white-painted building the size of a two-car garage with a peaked roof that I guessed must be the dove loft.

Yolanda rolled across to it and opened the door. The only window was a circle of stained glass, high on the opposite wall, so it was dark inside. I blinked as my eyes adjusted and then—

The bottom third of the building must have once been filled with boxes for the birds to roost in: I could still see the marks on the walls where they'd slotted in. But all that had gone. The space was full of something that looked like the inside of a steamship: huge cylinders and pistons and about a million pipes. Suspended above that was a gleaming floor made of metal mesh with some sort of computer workstation. And hanging above *that*—

At first, I thought it was a bird: that was what it looked most like. But it was huge, at least six feet across. I looked at Yolanda.

"It's a drone," she said.

I gazed at it again. "Where did you—"

"I built it." She kept her voice carefully neutral, but I could hear the pride there.

I walked slowly up the ramp and onto the walkway to get a better look. It was nothing like the military drones I'd seen on TV, brutish and bristling with weapons. This was slender, elegant, and gleaming white. Feminine, almost. It was beautiful. But what did she need a drone for?

She pulled a lever and a section of the wall hinged down in front of us. Behind us, another, bigger section hinged down. She could launch the drone from here, I realized, fly it over the city and land it again. But *why?* Why do all this?

She picked up a thing made of white plastic, connected by cables to the computer. It was only when she pulled it onto her head that I recognized what it was: a virtual reality headset. She turned her head and there was a whir as cameras at the front of the drone turned in sync. *She can see through its eyes.*

She groped blindly for me, gripped my arm, and tugged me away from the drone. She hit a button and there was a hiss so loud that it made me clap my hands over my ears, and a thump of metal on metal. And the drone was *gone,* just a speck of white I had to search for against the sky. I knew what the machinery under our feet was, now. A small version of the steam catapult they use to launch fighters off aircraft carriers.

I saw on the computer screen what Yolanda was seeing, a view from the drone as it dived into the canyon formed by two buildings. It banked hard and hooked around a corner, nimble as a bird, windows flashing past almost close enough to touch. Then it rolled and soared high, heading into the blue.

Yolanda laughed. Breathless, delighted, as carefree as a child. She turned her head, looking at the clouds, the tops of the buildings. I'd never seen her grin so wide. I forgot our fight in a heartbeat. You couldn't look at her, when she was like this, and not be happy: it was infectious.

I understood, now. However many thousands of hours she'd sunk into building this, it was worth it. Using the drone, she was free. Who needs to walk, when you can fly?

She soared around the city for close to an hour, showing me how she could ride thermals to stay aloft all day, if she wanted to. Twice, we saw police helicopters and I worried she was going to get caught —God knows how many laws she was breaking, flying an unlicensed drone around downtown New York—but the drone was so silent and quick, she lost them in seconds.

At last, she brought the thing in to land. She pulled off the headset, still grinning.

But then she blinked and looked down at herself, and her face collapsed. She tossed the headset on the desk, spun her wheelchair away from me, and raced out of the dove loft. I caught up to her by the elevator, where she was sitting in brooding silence. As we got in, she muttered, "When I'm in that thing, I forget. But when I come out of it, I remember."

Someone grabbed hold of my heart and crushed it in their fist. All I wanted to do was scoop her into my arms and hold her against me. But I couldn't. If I let her get close to me, she'd get hurt. I couldn't bear to see that happen.

We descended to the penthouse and Yolanda raced back to her desk, her voice determinedly light. "Let's get on with it."

With Lily's help, Yolanda wrote a program that would sift through everyone's search queries, looking for the right combination of math and witchcraft myths. Between them, they got it done in an hour. It was almost frightening, what even just two of the Sisters of Invidia could do.

Yolanda started the program running then leaned back, stretched, and announced she needed coffee. She wheeled over to the kitchen area, the laptop on her knees so she could talk to Lily. Then she put it carefully on the counter while she measured out coffee grounds.

"Hey," said Lily, "turn on your camera. I haven't seen you in weeks. Are you still letting your hair grow?"

Yolanda froze. Her eyes went from the laptop to her desk and back again. "Um—"

And I suddenly realized, *Lily doesn't know.* Yolanda hadn't told even her closest friends about her legs. When she was sitting at her desk, with the camera carefully positioned, Lily wouldn't be able to tell, just as I'd been fooled when I first met her. But out here in the kitchen, the wheelchair was in full view.

"C'mon," said Lily. "I don't mind if you're still in your PJs."

Yolanda stared at the laptop and bit her lip. Her eyes went moist and I could see the guilt on her face. She hated lying. But she wasn't ready to tell the truth, either.

"Yolanda?" called Lily in a singsong voice.

I stalked over, picked up the laptop, and turned the screen to face me. Then I toggled on the camera.

Lily had gone full cowgirl, since the last time I'd seen her. A brown Stetson sat on her head and a red-and-white plaid shirt hugged her curves. There was a wooden wall behind her and for some reason, it was moving up and down. "Calahan?" she squeaked, staring at the screen. "You're there?"

I realized I hadn't spoken the whole time they'd been working on the program. I hadn't talked to Lily since she first sent me to Yolanda, what felt like weeks ago. "Yup."

Lily gawped at the screen. Then she leaned over her shoulder and hollered, "*Bull!*" The sudden movement made the wall behind her rock even more crazily and I realized she was sitting on a porch swing. She leaned close, until the screen was just a pair of big green eyes, and whispered into the microphone. "You're in Yolanda's apartment? How long have you been there? *Is this a thing?!*"

I quickly turned down the volume. Luckily, Yolanda was busy getting back behind her desk, and didn't hear. "Of course not. Just working a case. Yolanda's helping."

I heard heavy footsteps approaching. Then Bull loomed into view, "Calahan?" He took a seat next to Lily and put his arm around her. "What are you doing there?"

Lily gave him a meaningful look. Bull gave me a huge, Texan grin and an approving nod. I felt my neck flush. "It's not like that," I whispered, glancing cautiously across the room at Yolanda. But as soon as I saw her again, I blushed even harder. What was it about this woman? I only had to look at her, hear her voice, smell her damn scent and I was a teenager again.

"Uh-huh," said Lily.

Yolanda nodded to me that she was ready. I quickly said goodbye to Lily and Bull and carried the laptop over to her, only turning it round to face her at the last second. As Yolanda took it from me, her fingers brushed mine and we both froze and just stood there with it held between us. She gave me a solemn nod, her lips pressed tight together, thanking me for stalling Lily, thanking me for understanding. And I nodded back, like, *what are friends for?*

But while she chatted happily with Lily, I brooded. *This is wrong.* Yolanda barely left the apartment. The other two Sisters of Invidia were her only real friends and now it turned out even they didn't know about her injury. She didn't let anyone see the real her, except—

My stomach knotted. *Aw hell.*

I tore my eyes away from her and stared off into the corner. *No.* I couldn't be with her for about a million reasons. Because I didn't deserve love, or happiness. Because no way was I letting another woman pay the price for getting mixed up with my world. Because she needed a genius who understood her, not a dumb jock like me. I shaped my resolve into something iron-hard and unbreakable. We were working the case and that was *it.*

I heard the call end. I glanced at Yolanda and found her staring straight at me. And as soon as I looked into those lush green eyes, as soon as I saw that lock of silky dark hair brushing her cheek, that iron resolve melted like a pat of butter held over a fire.

"Lily says hi," said Yolanda, her voice carefully neutral.

I hadn't heard much of their conversation. I felt my neck heat up again. *What did Lily say?* I nodded carefully.

She stared at me. She *kept* staring at me, as if deciding something. All I could do was stare back into those green eyes and wait.

At last, she said, "Violet."

I blinked. I felt like I'd missed something. Violet *what?* Ultraviolet?

"My *name,*" Yolanda stressed. "Is Violet. Violet Hepler."

I slowly drew in my breath, stunned. "Thank you."

She looked at the floor, flushing. "Yeah, well, now you know why I stick with Yolanda." She frowned warningly and I put up my hands in defense. Fine, I'd call her Yolanda. But I felt honored to know the truth.

At that second, Yolanda's laptop beeped. "We got a hit!" she said.

"There's one person in New York who matches the criteria. Lots of searches for advanced mathematical concepts *and* lots of searches for myths about witches and other people of power. IP address traces back to an apartment on the Lower East Side."

I stood up. "Let's go pay him a visit."

21

CALAHAN

I PARKED UP, switched off the engine, and settled back in my seat.
"So what do we do now?" asked Yolanda.

"We wait."

I'd already knocked on the door of the apartment and gotten no
reply. There were no signs of life, but the sun was setting and he had
to come home at some point. So I'd found a perfect spot across the
street with a good view of the building. And luckily, we'd brought my
battered old Chevy, which was a lot more discreet than Yolanda's
sports car. All we had to do now was—

"Really? We just wait?" asked Yolanda.

I turned to her. "We wait."

She nodded. Seventeen seconds later, "What if he's not back for
hours?"

"Then we wait hours," I said patiently.

She looked at me incredulously. I couldn't help it: I grinned. It
was strange, and sweet, to see her flummoxed. With math and
hacking, everything went as fast as her brain could handle. She'd
never known what it was like to be on someone else's schedule.

I took pity on her and pointed through the windshield. "That
place does fancy coffee, but their pastries aren't great. That one does

old school cup o' joe, but the donuts are amazing. Which do you want?"

"Cup o' joe and donuts," she said instantly.

I brought us big takeout cups of coffee and a box of glazed donuts, still warm from the fryer. Outside, the street was getting dark, the lights coming on one by one. It started to rain in freezing gray sheets that hissed off the sidewalk. People ran past us, hurrying to shelter. But in my Chevy, nursing our cups, we were dry and snug.

"Drinking coffee and eating donuts on a stakeout," said Yolanda. She looked mildly horrified. "Am I a *cop*, now?"

I smirked. "Honorary FBI agent."

She shuddered. Then frowned, realizing something. "Wait, are we *partners?*"

She meant it as a joke. But when we looked at each other, our gazes locked. Something had happened, these last few days. The horrors of the case had bonded us inseparably. We *were* partners.

We switched on the radio and chatted about music and the news and nothing at all. She was easy to talk to, now that I'd gotten past that prickly exterior. And it became comfortable: just the two of us sitting in the darkness, looking out at the outside world.

Like a date.

It's not a date.

But I couldn't stop looking at her. The neon sign of the check-cashing place next to us put blue gleams into Yolanda's black hair and the street lights threw out just enough glow to show me the edge of those soft lips. And then, when a car roared past, its lights would light up her face for a split-second: an instant of a smile, a glimpse of her looking thoughtful. If I missed one, it was gone forever. I didn't want to miss any.

I got it bad for this woman.

I fought to close that feeling down. But, dammit, I couldn't help it.

Two hours went by like two minutes. We finished the coffee and half the donuts, and gave the rest to a couple of homeless guys. After the third hour, the rain stopped and I ran across the street to a Chinese place and brought us back cartons of steaming rice and noodles, sesame chicken and satay beef. We ate, chopsticks clicking in the darkness, people-watching the passers-by. When we'd finished, I told her, "There are napkins in the glove box."

She opened it to get them... and saw the gun lying there.

"It's my spare," I said, patting the one in my holster.

"I've never seen one before." She stared at it as if it might bite her. "Have you ever had to use it?"

"A couple of times."

"Ever have to kill anyone?"

I looked away, then sighed and nodded. "Most people surrender. But just occasionally, you get someone who's really lost it. They won't let you take them in. They come at you and the only way to stop them is to kill them."

Yolanda looked up at the apartment we were watching, its windows still dark. "You think this guy's like that?"

I nodded sadly. "Based on what we've seen so far? Yeah. I got the feeling he might be."

She looked across at me. "Why'd you want to join the FBI?" She said it as if she genuinely couldn't understand why someone would want to. It was a reminder that, to her, the FBI was still the enemy.

I hesitated. I nearly said, "You know, to serve my country," like I say to everyone who asks. But that's not the full story. The full story, I'd never told to anyone except Becky.

"Back in high school," I said, "I played football. Only thing I was any good at. My life was practice, practice, practice, and trying to buy a keg for a team party. You know, jock stuff. But..." I sighed. "I had a thing for comic books. I liked them, even though they were for nerds, back then. I used to pay one of the geeky kids to slip them to me, so I didn't have to go to the comic book store." I shook my head. "I don't even know *why* I liked them. They were dumb. In the real world, there weren't any guys in capes, or billionaires cleaning up the streets."

"Anyway, my final year in high school... a couple of guys on the team, Frankie and Ralph, they come into the locker room crowing about how they'd got one of the cheerleaders drunk and taken turns

with her behind the bleachers, even though she'd *pretended* she
hadn't wanted it."

I heard Yolanda suck in a breath.

"The next day, the girl goes to the cops. She has a split lip and a
black eye. And the team just closes ranks. Even the coach, who's
worried about losing two kids who are heading for football
scholarships. He started talking about how we all had to stick
together and how none of us had heard Frankie and Ralph boasting
about anything." I grimaced, remembering. "He said the little slut
must have wanted it. He said she must have gotten drunk afterwards
and fallen over."

"And I looked at these two guys, who I knew were going to get
away with it, who were going to go off to college and do the same
thing there, and I realized the comic books were lying. There were no
heroes. Just guys like me."

"I didn't want to do the right thing. I knew what would happen if I
did. But if I didn't, no one else would. So I went to the cops and
testified to what Frankie and Ralph had said in the locker room."

"What happened?" asked Yolanda quietly.

"Frankie and Ralph were charged, but one of their dads had a
fancy lawyer who talked their sentences down to a slap on the wrist.
None of the other guys would even talk to me. I got frozen off the
team, which meant I didn't get the football scholarship I'd been
hoping for. And the cheerleader dropped out of school. Doing the
right thing had done basically nothing."

Yolanda grabbed my hand and squeezed hard.

"But... I couldn't stop doing it," I said. "I'd figured out that if idiots
like me don't take some sort of a stand, things will get even worse. I
managed to get into a second-rate college and get a degree, then I
joined the NYPD and got on the detective track. After five years of
that, I joined the FBI."

I looked across at Yolanda. It was almost completely black in the
car, now, and I couldn't see her expression. But when she spoke, I
could hear the emotion in her voice. "You are *not* an idiot," she said.

"I'm no genius. Most of the time, I don't even know what you're talking about."

"But you understand people. I wish I could."

We sat in silence for a while. The car rocked as a truck thundered past.

She glanced down at her legs, and then at me.

"I already used up my stupid question for the day," I said.

She swallowed. "I'm giving you a bonus one on account of you being a decent freakin' human being."

"You don't like talking about it," I countered.

"No," she agreed. "Not unless the person asking actually cares."

I stared at her in the darkness. The traffic had died away and the only sound was our breathing.

"Yolanda?" I asked. "What happened to your legs?"

22

CALAHAN

"I was running," she said.

I wasn't ready for how hard that hit me. I'd only ever known her like this, I'd never thought of her running or walking or even standing. *Oh God....*

"I didn't even *like* running." I saw her head tilt in the darkness and she stared down at her legs. Her voice was hollow. "But my brother, Josh, loved it and he was always trying to get me to go outside more, so once a week we'd go for a run. We normally ran a loop around the Riverbank State Park but we'd done it so many times, I wanted to switch it up a little. So we decided to go across the JS instead."

I froze. "You were there?!"

She nodded in the darkness.

My stomach twisted and I felt the nausea rise inside me. The JS is burned into the psyche of every New Yorker. *That's* what happened to her?

The Jonas Salk Bridge, or "The JS," as New Yorkers dubbed it, had been an epic, multi-billion dollar construction project. Connecting New Jersey and Manhattan, it was designed to take some of the load off the George Washington Bridge. The mayor had been elected on a platform of getting it built and when it was finished, everyone, even the naysayers, had to admit it was something special.

Named after the New York-born inventor of the polio vaccine, it was a colossal structure made of smooth white stone, its span hanging from gleaming steel cables, its towers rising high above the Hudson River. By day, it was shining and bright, but as the sun went down and the stone turned gold and orange, it became truly beautiful. Everyone loved it. Tourists flocked to take pictures of it. Traffic improved. They printed special commemorative postage stamps.

Three weeks after it opened, America turned on the morning news to see the bridge, loaded with traffic, trains, and pedestrians, collapsing into the Hudson River.

I'd rushed over there along with every FBI agent in the city, on or off duty. I closed my eyes and instantly, I could see what had greeted me when I arrived. The bridge had broken into pieces and most of it was already under the water. In places, the debris had piled up and chunks of concrete and steel broke the surface like islands. The water was filled with cars and debris and screaming, terrified people. If there's a hell, that sight is the closest I ever want to get to it.

We'd presumed it was a terrorist bomb, at first. But it wasn't.

"You know why it fell?" asked Yolanda in the darkness. "I mean, exactly why?"

I shook my head. I wasn't capable of speech, thinking of Yolanda in the middle of that.

"One number," she said tightly. "Just one. One tiny error in the architect's calculations that nobody spotted. I went over the blueprints, afterwards, trying to understand. One little error, but it meant that every car that drove over the bridge was creating a shearing force across the central tower. Way down inside, where no one could see it, the whole thing was cracking."

She swallowed. "My brother and I were running on the pedestrian walkway, under the road. We were..."—her voice went tight—"*buried.*" She was staring at the stoplight down the street, the reflection in her eyes turning red, amber, green. "The first thing I remember was how black it was," she said. "I mean *black*. I opened my eyes and I couldn't tell I'd opened them. I was lying on my back on a concrete slab, and there was another slab on my legs, pinning me. I called out for Josh, but he didn't call back. I was all alone."

She kept staring at the traffic light. I realized she was reassuring herself that she wasn't still down there.

"An hour went by," she said. "And then I heard Josh call my name. I've never been so glad to hear anything in my life. He was trapped too, maybe twenty feet below me, and he'd just woken up. I couldn't see and I couldn't move, but I wasn't alone."

She drew in a slow breath, fighting to stay calm. "Hours went by. No light, no sound except the sound of each other's voices. I don't want to think about what it would have been like, if he hadn't been there. I would have gone insane. We talked to each other, told each other it was going to be okay. We did math problems in our heads, calling out the numbers to each other." She turned and looked sharply at me. "I know that sounds stupid, but—"

"No," I said gently. "It doesn't."

"And then, after about six hours, I felt something hit my cheek. A drip of water. And once it started, it didn't stop. Drip, drip, drip, coming from somewhere above. A *long way* above because it's going really fast by the time it hits me. And I realized it was much worse than we thought—"

She broke off and looked away, her lungs filling as she sucked in air. I saw the panic that was coming and groped for her hand in the darkness. Found it and grabbed it with both of mine. Her whole body had gone tense. "Yolanda," I said quietly. "You don't have to—"

She shook her head fiercely, mad at herself. "Yes I do." She took a moment, gathering her strength, then forced the words out. "We realized we were below the surface of the river, in an air pocket in a pile of debris. The water was leaking in. We were going to drown."

"We had to move, so I started trying to figure out some way of lifting the slab that was on my legs. I reached down and felt around, trying to find out exactly how I was pinned...." She paused. "And that's when I realized I *wasn't* pinned. The slab I'd thought was pinning me was just lightly resting against my legs. I wasn't trapped, I just couldn't make my legs move. I made the effort in my head and they didn't respond. Sometime during the collapse, something had hit me hard enough to shatter the bones and damage the nerves."

"Josh knew something was wrong," she said. "I don't know how. He heard it in my breathing. He asked me what was wrong. And..." The headlights of a passing car lit up her face just as she turned to the side and stared out of the window, her lips pressed tight together. "I told him I was fine. I figured we were going to die anyway. I didn't want him to worry about me." She looked down at her legs. "And maybe, if I didn't tell him, it wouldn't be real."

That was how it started, I realized. Not telling Lily, living alone, so she didn't have to see people react to the wheelchair.... It had all started in that awful darkness. *If no one knows, it's not real.*

"We lay there for hours, listening to the water slowly filling up. And then... I heard something above me. They were digging through to us. We were going to be o—okay!"

I didn't miss the hitch in her voice, the little gulp. Tears were seconds away.

"The noise got closer. Drills, heavy machinery..., and a light. Blinding, because it was the first light I'd seen since that morning. Someone was shining a flashlight down at me. I yelled to Josh that we were going to be okay. But then...."

She stopped. Her hand squeezed mine and I squeezed back. When she spoke again, the raw emotion in her voice made my heart break. "The debris pile was like a house of cards. Every time the rescue workers moved something, the pile shifted and settled lower and more water flooded in. They knew it was risky, but they could see where I was and they figured they could get to me before it all collapsed." Her voice grew tortured. "They didn't realize Josh was there as well, further down."

She twisted around and stared at me, eyes wild, and cheeks glistening with tears. "*I tried to tell them!* I was yelling, *stop! My brother's down there!* But they were using drills, and banging, and yelling to each other, they couldn't hear. And I felt everything shifting and moving below me, and I could hear him screaming—" She swallowed. "And then the screaming sto—stopped."

I silently cursed. I was in pieces, listening. I just wanted to—

"They got a rope around me," she croaked. "I was yelling at them, I can't leave Josh. But they were in a panic, the whole debris pile was caving in. They hauled me out. About a minute later, it all collapsed. They were happy, they were celebrating that they'd saved me, but Josh was—"

I leaned forward and grabbed her. Pulled her into my arms and wrapped her tight and the hell with keeping my distance.

23

YOLANDA

H IS ARMS hooked under mine and I was lifted effortlessly out of my seat. Suddenly, my face was between those huge, hard pecs, my tears soaking his shirt.

He held me in the dark as the pain came out of me in hot, angry, tearful bursts. "It should have—He was—"

His arms had wrapped around my back and he squeezed me tight. "I know."

That made it worse because clearly, he didn't understand. "You *don't!* He was—He was smarter, and funnier, and he had friends, he was *normal*, he was—he was *better!* It should have—"

My voice shredded and I descended into wordless sobs. But he just held on tight. And at last, when my crying had slowed enough to hear it, he put his lips to my ear and he said, "I know."

And this time, I heard what I'd missed before. It wasn't just a platitude. I could hear the raw pain in his voice. He *did* know. He knew what it was to think: *it should have been me.*

Oh God. Becky.

I wrapped my arms tighter around him. I was a wreck and I knew I couldn't help him now, but my God, somehow, I was going to.

He held me until I'd cried myself out, my eyes burning and all my defenses lying open. All I could do was state facts. "They only got eight people out," I said. "Eight, out of over three hundred that had been on the bridge."

"I remember," he whispered. "I remember the stretchers."

I thought of being carried to the ambulance, blue and red flashing lights and camera flashes as we'd moved through a crowd of workers and volunteers, police and paramedics and FBI agents. Calahan and I must have passed within six feet of each other.

I told him about the hospital and the moment the doctor told me I'd never walk again. When I told him about my boyfriend dumping me, Calahan's face turned murderous. I told him about being pushed out of my job and spending more and more time in my apartment. And I told him how it felt to lose my twin. "There aren't many people like us," I said. "No one else understood me like he did. Not even my folks." I shook my head. "I don't see them much, now. I want to, but whenever I see them, they want me to move back to Oregon. But I can't give up on New York, and Josh wouldn't have wanted me to. They mean well, they're just still grieving for him. We all are. We never even got to bury him."

We weren't alone. Over a year later, hundreds of families were still looking for closure. There was just no practical way to recover bodies buried under thousands of tons of rubble at the bottom of the river. The disaster still haunted the city: there were charities for the affected families, grief counseling and countless investigations and inquiries. The architect who'd designed the bridge had taken his own life just days after it happened, when he found his mistake.

"Everyone said I was lucky," I said. The darkness made it easy to talk, to admit things I'd never told anyone. "I mean, I survived. But...." I looked down at my legs.

"You don't *feel* lucky," Calahan said gently.

I nodded. Then I shook my head. "And then I feel guilty. I know I'm privileged. Most disabled people can't convert their apartments, or work from home, or—"

"Listen," he said, his voice like iron. "You've got nothing to feel guilty about. You came through hell. You're br—"

"Don't say that! Don't say I'm brave. I'm not brave, I didn't have a choice."

"You dealt with it."

I said nothing. That was one part I couldn't tell him.

But he picked up on my silence. "Yolanda?"

I looked away. And saw someone going into the apartment building across the street. I drew in my breath and Calahan followed my gaze and snapped to attention. A moment later, the lights in the third floor apartment came on. It was him.

"Okay," said Calahan. "Wait here."

Before I could say anything, he'd opened his door and was hurrying off across the street. *Wait! Should he be doing this alone?*

I watched him slip inside the building. Moments later, up at the third floor window, I saw a man walk into view, his back to me. He opened the apartment's door and I saw Calahan in the doorway, his mouth moving as he talked to the guy. The guy suddenly bolted and I gave a moan of concern as Calahan chased after him. He slammed the guy against a wall, but the guy punched Calahan in the stomach, doubling him over. Calahan reached for his gun—

There was a flash, and the lights in the apartment went off.

I sat bolt upright in my seat. *Shit!* I couldn't see a thing. *What do I do now?!*

I pulled out my phone and stared at the screen in a panic. Should I call 911? Call the FBI? Calahan hadn't left any instructions for if things went wrong.

I stared up at the window, straining my eyes, but I couldn't see a thing. That guy could be killing Calahan. Or he could have already shot or stabbed him and run, and Calahan could be lying there bleeding out—

I looked at my phone again, then stuffed it in my purse. I opened the glove box and grabbed Calahan's spare gun. Then I wrestled my chair out of the car and got my ass into it. My heart was racing. I felt sick. *What the hell am I doing?*

I wheeled myself across the street.

24

YOLANDA

THE RAIN had left everything so wet and slick that my hand slipped off the door handle twice before I finally managed to haul the door open. Or it might have been that my hands were shaking. The gun felt incredibly heavy in my lap.

I wheeled myself into the deserted hallway, my breath coming in big, panicky gulps. *I can't do this! I should just turn around and go back to the car. Call for backup.*

But what if there wasn't time? What if by the time backup arrived... it was too late?

I wrestled the panic back down. I'd take it one step at a time. First step: get upstairs. The elevator. I could do that. I rolled forward and reached for the button marked "3."

But before I could press it, the elevator hummed into life and started to ascend. One, two, three—

It stopped on the third floor. Someone had called it there.

And then it started to descend.

Shit! The killer. The killer was on his way down, maybe alone, maybe with Calahan as a hostage. I grabbed the gun and slid my finger over the trigger. I'd never even held one, before. *Is this right?!*

The elevator reached the second floor. I pointed the gun with both hands, aiming at the slit between the sliding doors. The muzzle jerked up and down with each shaky breath I took.

The elevator reached my floor. I held my breath. The doors opened—

Calahan. Standing beside a guy in his sixties. Both of them saw me at the same time. The old guy flattened himself against the rear of the elevator. Calahan's eyes bugged out. "*Whoah!*" he said. "Whoah, whoah! Put it down!" He motioned for me to lower it. But I couldn't, I was still in shock, my heart racing.

Calahan skirted sideways, stepped around the gun and gently took it from my hands. Both of us slumped in relief. Then the anger arrived. "What the *fuck* are you doing?" he demanded.

"I thought you were in trouble! I saw the fight!"

Calahan jerked his head at the man in the elevator. "Mr. Avakian got spooked when I said I was a fed. His immigration status is a little... unclear." Mr. Avakian looked at the floor. "He made a run for it, we tussled." Calahan rubbed his stomach, then muttered half-admiringly, "He's got a mean jab, for an old guy."

"But the lights went out!" I said.

"A lamp got knocked over and the breakers tripped." Calahan's tone hardened. "What were you *thinking?* What if I *had* been in trouble? You could have been killed!"

He glared down at me, but behind the anger there was something else. He'd unconsciously stepped closer, looming over me protectively. I wasn't used to that. I'd never had anyone worry about me like that.

"I just didn't want you to get hurt," I mumbled.

Calahan scowled but then looked away and cursed under his breath. I bit my lip. *He's not used to having someone worry about him, either.*

He finally looked at me, pinning me with those clear blue eyes. "Don't ever do that again!" Then he paused, considering. "But if you ever do..." He held the gun in front of me and showed me. "You had the safety catch on. Slide that like *that:* then you're ready to shoot."

I nodded. Then I looked questioningly at Mr. Avakian.

"He's the landlord," said Calahan. "Rents the apartment to a guy I think is our man, going by what I saw up there. Mr. Avakian was checking the place because the guy hasn't been here in a few weeks and the rent is due. There's math stuff all over the place. Maybe you can get something from it."

We rode the elevator up and Mr. Avakian got the lights back on. As soon as I saw the place, I knew Calahan was right. There were shelves of books on advanced mathematics. There were books on witches, several different versions of the Bible and other religious books, even some stuff on the occult. And there were four notebooks filled cover-to-cover with equations.

Calahan checked the other rooms, then came back. "No clothes in the closet, refrigerator's empty. He used this place to plan but he left before the first killing and he hasn't been back since. And he won't." He kicked a cupboard. "We missed him."

"The landlord must have a name, details...."

"He paid in cash. I already ran the name, it's fake. Got a description: tall, lean, long hair. Not a lot to go on." He squatted down in front of me, his eyes pleading. "Anything you can tell us would help."

I started reading through the notebooks. It was getting late and Mr. Avakian made us thick, dark coffee to keep us going. After a few hours, I rubbed my eyes and called Calahan over. "I recognize some of the equations in two of these books from the two killings," I told him. "They're like rough drafts."

"Four notebooks. Four killings?" Calahan's voice grew bitter. "He's planning two more?"

I nodded. "That'd be my guess."

Calahan leaned over my shoulder to peer at the page of equations. I tried not to think about how good it felt, to have his body so close to mine. "Can you use these to get ahead of him? Solve the equations in advance?"

I shook my head. "They're just rough notes, not the full thing." I closed the notebook with a sigh of frustration. Then I noticed something and held it up to the desk lamp. There was a word scrawled on the front in pencil, almost invisible against the dark cover. But when I angled the light just right..."*Merytou*," I read. "Any idea what that means?"

Calahan shook his head. I pulled out my phone and did a quick search. There was only one hit: a book, written almost twenty years ago, on French folklore. One of the chapters was called *The Merytou*. The author was a guy called Warrington Hobbs.

A few minutes of searching and I had a phone number for him, with an international area code I didn't recognize. It rang eight times before finally going to answerphone. I left a message saying I was working with the FBI and needed his help.

"I'll have this place searched," said Calahan, and sighed. "But I don't think we'll find much."

We had nothing to go on unless I could solve the equations for the next murder to find out either *where* or *who*. We already knew the *when* and we only had a day and a half. "I better get back to my chalkboards," I told Calahan.

He drove me back to my apartment. By the time we arrived, the sky had clouded over again and this time, it looked as if it would be a full-on storm. I hesitated just inside my door. After all the time we'd spent together, separating was hard. "You want to come in?" I asked.

He shook his head. And when I looked up at him, my stomach knotted because those gorgeous blue eyes were clouded with pain. He was looking at me but he was somewhere else. "There's something I've got to do," he said.

And he was gone.

25

CALAHAN

FTER IT HAPPENED, the counselor had said it was important
to have a plan for dealing with anniversaries. He said
anniversaries could be "crisis points."

Yes, I saw a counselor. You think Carrie would have let me keep
working, if I'd refused?

So I had a plan for each anniversary of Becky's death. Work, to
keep me busy, friends, to get me through it. Light a candle and don't
go anywhere near a bar.

But with each year, it got harder. First my friend and colleague
Kate ran off to Alaska. Then, last year, my best friend, Hailey, had left
the FBI to be with her Russian boyfriend. This year, there was no one
I could hang out with to fill the silence. What made it even harder
was that I'd spent all day with a woman who made me feel things I
hadn't felt in years. By the time I dropped Yolanda back at her
apartment, the guilt was threatening to rise up and swamp me. I
wanted her so bad and I didn't deserve her. I didn't deserve anyone,
after Becky.

I'd done all the work I could. I didn't have any friends I could turn
to. But there was one part of the plan I could stick to and I clung to it

like a drowning man clings to a lifebelt. I drove through the streets looking for a church.

Becky....

Becky was a musician. She had a day job in an office to help pay the bills but she was a musician in the same way I'm an FBI agent. She had long, copper hair and played electric fiddle in a folk band. She wore long skirts and low-cut blouses and she had a tattoo of roses winding up her back that I liked to kiss.

She was my antidote. I'd come home from seeing all kinds of horrible shit and I'd wrap her up in my arms and bury my face in her hair and just inhale her and everything would be okay.

She balanced me. She was an air person, like Yolanda, and she made me try stuff that wasn't physical, that took me out of myself. Like singing. I thought it was dumb, at first, but she persuaded me to try it and I found I actually kind of liked it. A few times, after a gig, when most of the crowd had stumbled home and the bar owner had locked the doors, I'd joined Becky's band in some Irish folk song. And when the drums were thumping and the feet were stamping, I felt...I don't know, some sort of Irish kinship resonating down through the two hundred years since my ancestors came to America. It felt *right*.

I hadn't sung since she died. I figured I never would again.

I pulled up outside a church and scowled at it through the windshield. *What the hell am I doing here?* I hadn't been inside one since last year.

Stick to the plan.

There was a flash of lightning and thunder rumbled overhead. The rain was going to start again any minute. I hurried over to the church door and then tentatively pushed it open. It was a really old place, all stone and silence. I seemed to be the only person there. I saw the rack of candles over in the corner and turned that way but then I stopped and frowned.

I felt something and it wasn't to do with Becky, or grief, or guilt. It was like the feeling you get when you pull back the drapes and open the windows in a dark, stinking room. Walking into the church, I felt like I'd been cleansed.

I shook my head and marched over to the candles. Put five dollars in the tin, knelt down and lit one. And as soon as the flame flared into life, the pain and guilt hit me, a black hole sucking me in from the inside. I hadn't realized how much I'd been bottling it up all day. "I'm sorry, Becky," I whispered. My breath vibrated the candle flame, as if she was answering, and that made me draw in a huge, shaky breath. I'd underestimated. *Really* underestimated. I felt like there was a whole reservoir full of black water behind a dam and I only had a tiny tap to release the pressure. I had to let it out or the whole thing was going to crack, but I didn't know how. When I left here, all I had to go back to was an empty apartment.

There were people I could call. Hailey was in St. Petersburg, but she'd pick up the phone in a heartbeat, day or night. I could call Alison and ask to spar with her. Getting my ass kicked by her would be a relief compared to this. Hell, I could call *Carrie,* she might be my boss, but we look after each other.

Or I could call Yolanda. That was the option that was hardest to resist.

But I didn't deserve comfort or relief. I knew what I deserved. And if I let the pressure build and build, maybe the dam would blow wide open and that would give me the guts to do it.

I closed my eyes and remembered. I thought of Becky's laugh, her grin, the way I used to twirl her round in Central Park. I began to shake, my eyes going hot. *Becky....*

A noise, behind me. I spun and stood, blinking through tears, one hand going to my gun—

A priest, carrying a set of keys. I dropped my hand away from my gun, shamefaced, and quickly wiped my eyes. "I'm sorry, Father," I muttered. "Didn't mean to keep you."

He had wispy white hair and one of those placid, kindly faces you only see on the deeply devout. "Take as long as you need."

I shook my head and headed for the door.

"We open again at seven," he said, following me. "You're always welcome, if you want to talk."

I was already out the door but I stopped and looked back at him. I wasn't going to church, tomorrow. The way I was feeling, I was pretty sure I wasn't going to see another sunrise. But my mom didn't raise me to be rude to priests. "Thanks," I mumbled.

And then suddenly, the priest's face changed. There was a second of shock and then it contorted, not just angry, but *hurt* and when he spoke, he had to grate the words out through gritted teeth. "But before you come back, you wash that filth off your hand!"

I was gaping. *What the hell?* I followed his gaze to my hand, which was still wrapped around the edge of the door. I pulled it back and stepped back in shock.

He slammed the door and locked it.

The first heavy drop of rain hit my head, but I barely even registered it. I stared down at my hand in confusion, then walked over to a street light to examine it.

The priest had been looking at the pairs of letters I'd scrawled on my hand in the spider house.

26

YOLANDA

I T HAD STARTED to rain, but I couldn't say when: when you're deep, time becomes as runny as caramel and an hour can seem like a minute. I was vaguely aware of a drumming against the windows and I knew there must be lightning because there were flashes through my closed eyelids. But I hadn't opened my eyes once.

I was close. I could feel it. I'd figured out about ninety percent of the equations that would tell us where the next killing would be, but the last ten percent...the numbers just didn't make sense. What was I not seeing?

There was a very familiar bang on my door. I worked my way back up, like going backwards up a long, spiral staircase, until I finally surfaced and sat there blinking at my chalkboards. It felt like it had taken longer to surface than usual. The killer's equations had a hypnotic weight to them, dragging me down....

I shook it off and rolled over to the door. The apartment was almost dark. I hadn't bothered to turn the main lights on when I came in because I'd known I'd just be sitting there, *deep*. Now, with the thunder and lightning outside, it was eerie. I opened the door and standing there, backlit by the light from the hallway, was Calahan.

God, he looked amazing. Windswept and determined. His hair

was soaked and drops of water were rolling over those high cheekbones and down his stubbled jaw. He was wearing a long gray raincoat over his suit and it was so wet with rain, it shone like steel. And his eyes... that look I'd seen earlier was still there, he was in pain... but he looked *sure,* too, certain of something for the first time in this whole crazy case. He looked like some knight arriving at a princess's tower with a declaration of war... or love.

"What?" I croaked.

"We were wrong."

"About what?"

"About everything."

I rolled backwards so he could come in. He stalked across the room: he was so fired up, he couldn't stand still. I recognized the mood because it's the same way I get, when I've solved an equation. "Those letters on the spiders? They weren't initials, they form a sentence. We just didn't recognize it because it's in Latin. *Ave Satanas. Welcome, Satan.* It's from a Black Mass."

"*What?!*" I don't normally mind the dark, but suddenly it gave me the chills. I switched on a side light, but the little pool of warm light didn't reach very far.

Calahan kept pacing. "I had this wrong from the very beginning. I'm FBI: I see bodies, I think *murder.* And I assumed the writing on the walls was a message for us. But the killer doesn't hate these... witches, people of power, whatever you want to call them. That's why there's so little violence. He just needs their blood."

"*Why?*"

"Because they're special and so, in his mind, their blood is special. He thinks it has power, that's why he uses it."

"So the killings aren't the point. Writing the message is the point. *Why?* What's so important about the message?"

Calahan went silent. A flash of lightning lit up the room and I saw how pale he'd gone. He stared into my eyes and I could see he didn't want to say the words that were coming. But he had to because they were the truth.

"It isn't a message," he said. "It's a spell."

We stared at each other for a few seconds. "I don't believe in magic," I said at last.

"Neither do I. But I think the killer does."

I could feel my heart starting to race, sick fear winding up from my ankles like someone was wrapping my bones in freezing, wet silk. "This is *math,*" I snapped, waving my hand at the chalkboard. "It's as far from magic as you can get!"

"The world runs on math," he said. "You said so yourself. It's a universal language. Spells used to be written in old English because that's what they used back then. But if you were creating a spell *now,* wouldn't math be the perfect language?"

I was shaking my head, nauseous at the thought of something I loved being twisted into— "No. No! Math isn't—It's about hard science, it's *nothing like* magic!"

"You said that some of the equations were to do with astrophysics. Wormholes. That's like a rip in space, right? A door that connects two different places? Sounds a lot like magic to me."

A flash of lightning lit up the chalkboards. Even written out in white chalk, the equations suddenly looked unsettling. I remembered how they'd looked at the crime scenes, written in glossy, dark blood. How the killer had formed them into disturbing patterns. Tentacled monsters. Spiders.

Calahan was right. I looked up at him, and I could feel that I'd gone pale, too.

"I'm not saying I believe in it," he said gently. "Only that the killer does."

I thought about what this meant. It explained a lot. "This is why the time and place and who he's going to kill next are written at the scene," I said. "He's not bragging to the police, he's *working it out.* Each... *sacrifice* is a spell and part of the spell tells him what to do next. That's why the locations are so random: he's not choosing them willingly, he's going where the numbers tell him."

"So the spell's in four parts," said Calahan. "He wrote rough drafts of all four in that rented apartment. Now he's doing each part in turn. Two so far, two to go. What's it *for?*"

"What do you mean?"

"I mean: spells do something, right? They put a curse on someone or they make someone fall in love or whatever, so what does this one do?"

I shook my head. "I haven't been able to figure out the main body of it. I don't know if I'm not smart enough, or not crazy enough. But..."

"What?"

Maybe it was the darkness or the rain rushing down the windows outside, but it suddenly felt very cold. I wrapped my arms around myself. "Those letters that turned out to be Latin, *Welcome, Satan...* they tie in early on. If the spell is a machine, that part's like the power source."

"And what does it do? I mean, what *would* it do, if it was real?"

I thought about all the parts I hadn't solved yet, the stuff to do with wormholes and string theory. The more advanced you get in physics, the weirder it gets. Particles called *charm* and *strangeness.* Black holes. The God particle. And the killer had taken all that and created a spell with it, supposedly powered by the devil, penned in the blood of people said to be witches.

"What does it do?" I echoed. "I don't know. But it scares the shit out of me."

Calahan closed the distance between us in two quick strides. He dropped to his knees, wrapped his arms around my back and pulled me into him so that my chin was on his shoulder and his stubble rasped against my cheek. My whole upper body pressed against the warm, hard wall of his chest and abs. "Me too," he admitted.

I squeezed him tight and he squeezed me tight and we stayed like that while the lightning flashed and the rain pounded down. This case was taking its toll on both of us. It didn't matter that this stuff wasn't real. There was something about it that was unsettling on a deep, primal level. We needed each other: we were the only two people in the world who understood.

Gradually, we calmed... and the mood shifted. Neither of us

moved, but I became aware of his lips, almost brushing my earlobe, and how my breasts were pressed tight against his pecs.

We'd hugged because we needed to. Now we were holding each other because we wanted to.

A tension started to build. My fingertips were throbbing with the feel of his body. The temptation to just go exploring, to roam over the hard muscles of his back, was almost too much to resist. And I could feel him toying with my hair, rubbing a lock of it between his fingers. I started to breathe faster, and with every breath I inhaled the intoxicating scent of him—

He suddenly pushed me back, just enough that he could stare into my eyes. I swallowed, my chest tight. His lips parted. Was he about to—

He jumped to his feet and turned away from me. His hands bunched into fists: he was teetering on the edge of control. Then he shook his head savagely and pulled out his phone. "I'm going to need to bring Carrie up to speed on all this," he said. He started to type out a message.

I just stared at him, my heart breaking. Something was wrong. It wasn't the first time he'd pulled away, just as I thought something was going to happen. But it was different, tonight. *He* was different. I'd seen it in his eyes earlier and I could see it again now. I was worried about him.

I swallowed and looked away. "I'll come. You'll need me to explain the math."

He looked up, surprised. Remembering how much I'd hated visiting the FBI last time.

I set my jaw and stared back at him, determined. I wasn't going to desert him when he needed me most.

"Thanks," he said with feeling. More typing. "OK, we're meeting her first thing tomorrow morning."

I nodded. This time, I'd dig out a suit and blouse so that at least I didn't feel so underdressed.

Calahan shoved his phone in his pocket and moved towards the door. "I gotta get going."

I rolled after him. "Calahan?" He didn't turn around. "Sam?"

He was already halfway out the door. He stopped, but he didn't turn around.

"You okay?" I asked.

He turned just long enough to look me in the eye and I saw that I was right. That pain he always carried inside had bubbled right up to the surface. He'd been able to fight it back down when he was telling me about the spell, but now it was back.

"I'm fine." His voice was ragged.

I opened my mouth to say something... but the door slammed shut and he was gone.

I tried to convince myself that everything was okay. I told myself it was just my imagination. I was upset because I'd thought he was about to kiss me and then he didn't, and so I was assuming something must be wrong....

But it wasn't that. I'd gotten to know him pretty well, over the last few days. I'd never seen him like this.

I managed to work for two hours before I couldn't bear it any more. I had to know that he was okay. I messaged him, letting him know how I was doing with the equations. No reply. I tried again, ten minutes later. Still no reply. And he *always* answered messages, he was never not working.

I'd promised I'd never hack him again. But this was different, I was worried.

Within minutes, I'd tracked his phone's location. He was in a bar across town. From the photos I found online, it was a real dive. *See? He's fine. He's just having a drink. You're not his mother.* I leaned back in the chair.

But that look I'd seen in his eyes. I knew what it was like to lose someone you loved. Every day was hard. But tonight, he'd seemed—

Tonight.

I lurched forward and grabbed for the mouse. Brought up the messages between Becky and him and scrolled right to the very end.

The last message was sent four years ago today. It was the anniversary of...*oh, God, Calahan!*

There was a roll of thunder. The storm was right on top of us and through the window, I could see the rain hammering my stone balcony, pouring in torrents out of the mouths of the gargoyles. Driving was going to be hell and when I got there, there was no way I'd get parked right outside. I'd have to wheel myself down dark streets surrounded by drunks in a bad area of town.

But he needed me.

I grabbed my purse and headed for the door.

27

CALAHAN

I SAT AT THE BAR, hunched low, hand gripping the whiskey glass. The bartender knew by now to refill it when it emptied. I'd stopped counting after eight.

I drank and I thought. I thought about meeting Becky for the first time and how I'd followed her band like some crazed stalker, going to every gig, in the hope of talking to her again. I thought about our first date and the first time I'd kissed her. I thought about the first time we'd had sex, in the backseat of my car, way out of town on a dirt road, after we'd broken down.

And when I'd thought about all of that, I just relived the day she died. Everything I'd said. Everything I hadn't said. Every wrong decision I'd made. All building up to that moment, that one second, when I tried to wake her up—

And then I relived it again. And again and again and again.

Any man would have been lucky to have her. Any other man, *any other man* and she'd still be here, alive and singing and telling bad jokes and never being able to find her butterfly hair clip. Why did she have to fall for *me?*

If I could change it, if I could go back in time and change it so we never met, but she was alive, I'd do it in a heartbeat. She'd deserved better. She'd cut through all my jadedness, made me see the city in a new way, through her eyes. And now that unique perspective was gone forever. No one else would ever know her.

Thanks to me.

I knew what needed to happen. It had been coming ever since that day, creeping towards me each time I dreamed of her and woke up alone. It had gained ground when friends at the FBI, like Kate and Hailey, moved away. I just hadn't had the guts...until now.

My plan was simple. Lock the door from the inside, sit on a chair, put the gun against my head.... I was determined to make it as easy as possible for whichever cop ended up investigating. I'd never been much good with words, but I'd force myself to write some kind of note, just to remove any doubt. Each drink made the self-hate burn hotter. Each reliving of that day made the guilt mount, black waves of it hammering against the dam, cracking it open—

I drained my glass, slammed it down, and tossed some bills on the counter. I got up from my stool, turned around and—

For a second, I thought I was seeing things. She couldn't be *here*, in this place. She didn't belong in a place like this.

Yolanda looked me up and down. "I'm taking you home," she said firmly.

I gawped at her. Then I shook my head, which sent the room spinning. "Fuck off," I slurred, and turned back to the bar. I felt a stab of shame as soon as I'd said it. But why couldn't she just leave me alone?

The hiss of tires behind me. Other drinkers muttering as they moved aside to let her past. She stopped right behind me and I could feel her eyes boring into my head.

I finally turned to look at her. Her hair was tangled and windswept. Her clothes were soaked and the wheels of her chair were glistening with dirty water: she looked like she'd gone through every puddle in New York. And God, she must have come through the backstreets to get here. At night, in *this* neighborhood.

For me.

The thought terrified me and the fear came out as anger. "What the hell are you doing here?"

"I told you," she said. "I'm taking you home."

"I'm *going* home!"

She cocked her head to one side and glared at me. But when she spoke, I could hear the concern in her voice. "Not alone, you're not."

I froze. Did she know what I was planning? *Stupid.* Of course she didn't. How could she? But the look in her eyes....

Enough of this. I headed for the door again, stepping around her. But she was faster than me. She shot forward and got in front of me and suddenly there wasn't enough room for my feet. I staggered and fell forward, catching myself on the arms of the wheelchair. Our faces were a foot apart.

I scowled at her. I can be intimidating, when I want to be. I've stared down mobsters and junkies, guys with guns. I was twice her size—

She didn't shrink back. She looked me right in the eye. "You can stay here and argue or you can come with me. But I'm not letting you out of my sight. Not tonight."

Goddammit, she's as stubborn as me. My scowl faded and I just stared at her. She wouldn't give up on me. No matter how many times I pushed her away.

Without warning, all the feelings I had for her slammed into me, so powerful I could barely breathe. Things I hadn't admitted even to myself. Things I never thought I'd feel again.

But feeling those things made the pain and guilt rise up like a tidal wave and sluice through me. I actually staggered and would have hit the floor if I wasn't holding Yolanda's chair.

I had to fight my feelings for Yolanda. I had to fight the guilt and loss. That left me nothing to fight *her.* When Yolanda put her hand on my arm, her cool skin soothing and calm, I couldn't find the strength to push it away. I muttered a curse...and nodded.

She led me out of the bar and through the rain-slick streets. I was stumbling-drunk, the world hazy and muffled with just occasional flashes of sharp memory. I remember being horrified at how far she'd had to wheel herself and how scary it must have been. I remember reaching her car and her helping me in. I must have dozed off as she drove because the next thing I remember is struggling to get my key in my lock and then stumbling into the elevator in my apartment block. And then I was slumping forward and my bed was coming up to meet me.

28

YOLANDA

"Calahan?"

No response. He'd hit the bed like a sack of potatoes and now he was out. God, how much had he drunk? He was going to have one hell of a hangover when he woke up.

I leaned back in the chair and watched him, relieved but worried at the same time. For now, he couldn't hurt himself but what about tomorrow, and the next day, and the next?

One step at a time. One thing was for sure: I wasn't leaving him alone tonight.

For the first time, I looked around at his place. It was a small apartment, just big enough for one person. It could have been cozy but he hadn't decorated it that way. He hadn't decorated it *at all*.

There was a sun-bleached and heavily patched punch bag swinging from a hook in the corner: that must be how he stayed fit. There was a picture of him shaking hands with—wait, was that the *President?* I lifted it down and looked more closely. No doubt about it, that was him. When had that happened?

The tables and other surfaces were covered with paperwork. Old FBI case files, cold cases dating back twenty years. *This is how he spends his time. He works his ass off all day and then he comes home and tries to catch the bad guys who got away.*

I silently wheeled myself over to the bed and watched him sleep. I remembered what he'd told me about his school days and why he'd joined the FBI. He might be a reluctant hero but he was a crusader. Once he took a case, he wouldn't back down, wouldn't quit. I understood that sort of merciless focus but I knew the price it extracted from you, too. We all need someone to decompress with, to offload to. I'd had my brother and when I'd lost him, I'd retreated from the outside world. Calahan had had Becky and when he'd lost her, he'd buried himself in bars, one night stands and cold cases. Spiraling down and down until, tonight—

I reached out and put a hand on his cheek, his stubble rough against my palm, and all the feelings I'd been having for him swelled up, filling me until it felt like I'd burst. *Calahan!*

I stayed that way until morning.

29

CALAHAN

"Calahan?"

I vaguely remembered that that was me, but being awake was much too painful so I burrowed further into sleep.

"Calahan?"

That voice, though. That almost made the pain worth it. So soft and calming, like the wind gently sighing through a forest. A voice I recognized....

"Calahan!"

I remembered where I'd heard it before. I jerked awake, blinking and rolling over on my side and—

ARGH! Opening my eyes was like staring into the sun. And as soon as I moved, someone started pounding my head with a sledgehammer and everything in my stomach tried to leave. I screwed my eyes shut and kept very, very still.

"Here." That beautiful voice again. "Drink this."

A cool glass was pushed into my hand. I drank deeply, tasting Alka-Seltzer, and started to take stock. The pillow, the bed...that all felt familiar. This was my place. But then how was I hearing her voice?

I cracked my eyes open, just a narrow slit, and—

"Hi," said Yolanda shyly.

I just stared at her in complete incomprehension.

"I would have let you sleep," she said. "But we've got that meeting with Carrie. You need to get in the shower."

Slowly, horrifyingly, it started to come back to me. The bar. The drinking. Deciding to end it all. And then her arriving, and—

Telling her to fuck off.

It was a blank, after that. But she must have gotten me home and then....*she stayed here all night?*

I wanted to speak but I couldn't. I was sweating and nauseous and my mouth felt like sandpaper. So I just let my expression say it. *Why?*

She gave me a nervous smile. "Partners, right?"

I stared at her and—*dammit,* I couldn't stop it. I was too exhausted and hungover to hide it and I knew it was shining through like a goddamn searchlight. I was helplessly, hopelessly, besotted with this woman.

I nodded and looked at the floor, and she looked away into the corner. "Partners," I agreed. Then, with only a little help from the bedpost, I levered myself up and staggered off to the shower.

I turned it on ice cold. The world snapped into focus and my brain came awake. *What if she suspects? What if she guessed I was planning to end it all?* The idea was horrifying. No one suspected how close to the edge I was, not even Carrie. I couldn't let anyone find out. I was ashamed enough already.

As the water hammered down on me, I tried to reassure myself. If she knew, she would have said something, right? I'd just brazen it out. I've always been good at hiding my feelings.

Except...I rubbed at my stubble and muttered a curse. Except when those soft green eyes were watching me.

30

YOLANDA

I HEARD the water turn off. A few seconds of toweling off and then—

If I'd been thinking straight, I would have expected him to emerge with just a towel around his waist: he hadn't taken any clothes in with him. I could have prepared. Braced for impact. But I was too busy worrying about how the hell I was going to talk to him about last night, so the first I knew of it was when he swung open the door and I was staring right at his glistening pecs.

Since the first moment I saw him, I'd always thought that Calahan looked great in a suit. Even with his rebellious, disheveled look, he still fooled you into thinking he was...well, maybe not respectable, but civilized. But take the suit off him and he was resolutely blue collar. He looked like he'd been shaped in a foundry with hammers, surrounded by sparks and fire. His shoulders were too big, too solid, to work in an office: I could see why he'd played football in high school.

His chest, with its curving pecs the size of my head and dusky pink nipples...that hadn't been built at some upscale Manhattan gym, surrounded by stockbrokers. He was just *big,* full *of unapologetic* brute force. And those abs, with their hard, tan ridges and deep valleys I wanted to run my fingers along...they didn't look like they'd been carefully toned with planks and crunches, they looked like they'd gotten that way from Calahan tightening them to protect himself in fight after fight. His body was so gloriously raw and physical, so real.... I had an overwhelming urge to throw my arms around his neck, squash my breasts against his chest, and let his damp body soak through my top. I wanted to revel in how solidly rooted he was in this world, instead of my floaty, insubstantial world of ideas. And then I wanted him to take all that solid hardness and use it to pin me and spread me and—

I flushed. "We should get going."

He nodded. Grabbed a fresh suit and shirt from the closet and pulled out a pair of soft gray jockey shorts. He stuck his thumbs into the top of the towel...and hesitated, looking at me.

Oh! I flushed all over again, and quickly spun the chair so my back was to him. I heard him unwind the towel from his waist and finish drying himself off. Then the heavy *whump* of the damp towel hitting the floor—

I was staring at the refrigerator in the kitchenette. It was polished stainless steel and the reflection of the tan, naked giant behind me was surprisingly clear. I felt the flush travel all the way down my neck and I wasn't sure if it was from staring at those hard, muscled thighs and what was swinging between them, or the fact that he seemed to be staring at a point down and directly in front of him. Staring right at *me.*

I watched his body disappear piece by piece beneath his suit. Only when he was tying his tie did I dare to spin around. But looking at him started me blushing all over again. Now that I knew what was under his clothes, I couldn't get it out of my mind.

"My car's downstairs," I told him. "But I need to stop off at my place on the way."

~

A half hour later, now wearing a charcoal gray suit jacket and skirt, I opened the door of my car, swung myself into the driver's seat, and stowed my chair behind it. I slammed my door, turned to Calahan and—

He was just staring. Downwards.

"What?" I demanded.

His mouth moved but nothing came out.

I followed his gaze to my skirt, then rolled my eyes. "They're legs, Calahan. I do have them."

He looked out of his window, embarrassed, and passed me a huge takeout cup of coffee. "I got these across the street while you were, um...changing."

I took it and gulped gratefully. I'd spent the night sitting next to his bed and I'd barely dozed. But I wasn't so sleepy that I missed the way he stumbled on *changing.* Like he'd been thinking about me getting changed, while he was waiting down here.

I stowed the coffee and hit the gas. We drove to the FBI building in silence: I had no idea of how to broach the subject of last night. But at some point, we needed to talk.

When we arrived and I swung myself back into the chair, Calahan did a double-take. Not at my legs, this time: at what I was wearing on my feet. Glossy black leather pumps with a three inch heel. I smirked at him. "I don't actually have to walk in them," I said. "Might as well take advantage."

Inside, we met up with Carrie and the rest of the FBI team who were assigned to the case. Carrie took us all into a meeting room and, this time, I didn't feel like someone's nerdy kid sister. *The suit was a good idea.*

Together, Calahan and I told them how the messages were actually spells. "Just to be clear," I said, "We're not saying this stuff is real. But the killer believes it is."

Everyone started talking at once. And while they were debating possible strategies, my phone rang. "Hello?"

The voice was straight out of one of those lavish period dramas set in Britain, the ones with butlers and scandals. "Miss Hepler!

Warrington Hobbs. I'm sorry I took so long to return your call, I was at the library until really quite late." His voice was incredible. It was like he'd been frozen in the 1920s and just recently thawed out. "Now, as to your enquiry. I do recall writing the book you mentioned. It was some years ago, while I was traveling in Europe. I wanted to preserve the traditional French folklore before it was lost forever."

"There was a whole chapter about the Merytou," I said. "What is it?"

"A wise woman," said Hobbs. "A sort of seer, or soothsayer. Very few were ever born but when they were, they were treated with great reverence because it was believed they could see the future."

I leaned into the phone and closed my eyes, blocking out the rest of the room. "And how did the French recognize this...wise woman? Was there something physical about her, a sign?"

"Oh yes," said Hobbs. "According to legend, a Merytou always had six fingers."

I thanked him profusely and ended the call. Then I brought everyone up to speed on the word we'd found at the killer's rented apartment. "That's his next victim. A woman with six fingers." I was already typing in search queries into my laptop. "Polydactyly," I read aloud. "It's not all that rare. There are hundreds of cases each year."

"Okay," said Carrie. "We have to find her before he does. "Something like that would be on a person's medical records. We'll have to get a judge to grant an order to search the central medical database. Then maybe we can...."

She trailed off. Everyone else was listening attentively but I was typing furiously.

"Yolanda?" Carrie asked nervously. "What are you doing?"

I said nothing and just kept grimly typing.

Carrie frowned at Calahan. "What's she—" She glanced at me and then back at him. "Wait, is she—"

Calahan sighed and gave an apologetic smile. *Probably.*

Carrie jumped to her feet and raced around the table. I heard the intake of breath behind me when she saw the National Medical

Database logo on my screen. "*Stop that!* Are you *crazy?!*—That's a *federal crime!*"

I felt her reaching for me. *Quick!* I made one last flurry of keystrokes. Carrie grabbed my forearms and—"*Done!*" I said triumphantly. My screen started to fill with medical files.

"Oh Jesus," said Carrie quietly, letting go of my arms. I twisted around and, when I saw how pale she'd gone, my triumphant smile faded.

Calahan got to his feet and came around the table. "Okay, now I know Yolanda's methods might be unconventional—"

Carrie lost it. "*Unconventional?!* She just hacked a federal database. That's *ten years* in federal prison!"

"We didn't have time to wait around for a judge," I mumbled.

"She's right, Carrie," said Calahan.

Carrie's face had gone from white to red. She snapped her arm out like a weapon, her finger pointing at Calahan. "She's a civilian, Calahan, but you know better! Don't you start defending her just because—" Her eyes went to me, then back to him. Calahan and I both reddened. Carrie shook her head, incredulous. "Do you have any idea how much trouble you could be in?" she asked me. Then she waved her hand at the rest of the table. "How much trouble *this office* could be in?"

I swallowed and looked at the floor. I'd never had to worry about other people. I'd always worked on my own. "I can just throw it away," I said. *Please don't make me throw it away.* My finger hovered over the *Escape* key—

Carrie sucked in a long breath and let it out. "No," she said. "Let's catch this son of a bitch." She pinned me with a look. "But we're a team here, Yolanda. No more lone gunman stuff."

A team? An unexpected warmth blossomed, deep in my chest. I hadn't been a part of something since the accident. Not in person, face-to-face.

"And any more hacking and I'll slap the cuffs on you myself," Carrie added.

I nodded meekly. "Yes ma'am."

She nodded for me to show them what I'd found. I was gaining more and more respect for this woman. A lot of people would have thrown away the hacked information and risked the killer going free, just to cover their asses.

I connected to the big screen at the end of the room and it filled with medical files. "Even eliminating all the men, there are over a hundred cases of polydactyly in New York," I said. "Not many babies are born with it each year, but the victim could be any age so I've gone back eighty years. We have to narrow it down."

Calahan started pacing. "He's not going to want someone who's had surgery to remove the extra finger. He wants to *see* she's this special person of power. So remove any surgical cases."

Over half the files disappeared. "That leaves forty-six."

Calahan thought some more. "Put up the photos of their hands." Images filled the screen. In most cases, the extra finger was more like a stump, branching off another finger. "Our guy's going to want the classic case. The perfect example," said Calahan. He went right up to the screen, looking closely at each photo. "This one!"

It was a photo of a hand with a fully jointed extra finger coming off the hand. It looked so natural, you had to blink and count carefully to see that, yes, there really were five fingers and a thumb. I brought up the details. "Clara McConnell. She's twenty-four. Lives in Queens." There was another photo, a headshot, and I brought it up. Clara was pretty, with long red hair and pale skin and a cute little smile that made me want to smile, too—

My stomach suddenly lurched. Seeing the photo made me realize how far I'd slipped into...*cop mode,* I guess. I'd become so wrapped up in the case, I'd been thinking of these people as *possible victims* but.... I reached out and touched Clara's picture on my laptop screen. She was real. She was alive, somewhere out there, with friends and family and a life, and she had *no idea* what was going to happen to her tomorrow. I drew in my breath in horror...and instinctively, I looked at the one person who could help me protect her.

Calahan nodded to me, his jaw set. "It's okay." He grabbed the phone. "I'm calling the NYPD. They can have a black-and-white at her house in three minutes."

"Have them bring her here," said Carrie. "We'll keep her safe until we've caught this fucker."

I warmed to her even more.

While we waited for Clara to arrive, everyone took a moment to stretch their legs and get coffee. Calahan poured us both a cup from a steaming jug. "Careful," he warned. "It's cop coffee."

I didn't know what he meant until I tasted it. If coffee was music, this was someone banging steel bars together an inch from your ear. I recoiled, grimacing, but I could feel my body being bludgeoned into wakefulness. Cop coffee, it turned out, was *functional*.

The elevator pinged and Alison swept in, wearing a leather biker jacket over her suit and carrying a crash helmet. "Hey," she said. "I just came from the apartment our killer rented. Search is done, nothing new."

"You ride a bike?" I asked, shocked and a little awed.

She put the crash helmet down on her desk. "It's faster, in traffic."

I watched her as Calahan brought her up to speed on the spell theory. Like me, she couldn't keep still. Except, where I fidget awkwardly, she flowed effortlessly, shifting her weight sexily from foot to foot.

And while she listened to Calahan, she gave me a long, suspicious glance.

I was right. She has a thing for Calahan! We were in competition: a beautiful, confident, half-ninja FBI agent who roared around New York on a motorcycle and...me.

At that second, Carrie stuck her head out of the door of the meeting room and hollered. "*Calahan!*"

All three of us rushed over there.

Carrie's face was grim. "NYPD got to Clara McConnell's apartment. She's not there. Signs of a struggle."

My stomach went into a tight, hard knot. "He already took her. Oh God, he's keeping her somewhere and tomorrow—"

Carrie looked me in the eye. "*When* tomorrow?"

"Eight thirty-four am," I said immediately. Then I swallowed. "But we don't know where."

Carrie looked at her watch. "Then you have less than twenty-four hours to find out."

I looked around me in horror. Carrie, Calahan, Alison...they were all looking at me.

I was Clara's only chance. And I had no clue how I was going to figure it out.

31

CALAHAN

I KNEW something was up as soon as I arrived at her apartment. I'd been there enough times that I was learning her ways: normally, I'd knock and there'd be a delay while she woke herself up from being *deep*. But today, the sharp little buzz of the door unlocking came instantly, like she'd stabbed the button in frustration.

My second warning was that she was still in her suit. Hell, I wasn't complaining: it meant I got to see those luscious thighs and the way her white blouse clung to the full curves of her breasts. But wearing a suit wasn't Yolanda's way. She was more comfortable in jeans and a hoodie. It was past ten at night: she'd come home from the FBI office over twelve hours ago. Why hadn't she changed into something more...*her?*

Then I saw the chalkboards. Every square inch was packed tight with equations. Chalk dust was thick as mist in the air and more was smudged on her clothes. She must have filled the boards and wiped them clean again a dozen times. My chest tightened. She hadn't gotten changed because she hadn't stopped working since she got home.

She glanced up at me, then scowled at the chalkboards. "I can't get it," she snapped. "I have *no idea* how to figure out the location part." She ran her fingers through her hair, leaving white chalk smudges. "And without that, we can't stop Clara's mu—"

Her throat clamped down as she tried to say *murder*. I crossed the room in three big strides, the protective need welling up inside me. Now that she'd seen Clara's face, the case was even more personal. And she was burning herself out trying to solve it. I could see the exhaustion in her eyes: she'd been doing complex math for twelve hours straight, most likely without even stopping to eat. "You need to take a break," I told her.

"What I *need* is to solve this!" she snapped, and hurled a piece of chalk at the chalkboards. It shattered, leaving a white starburst. "But I'm not smart enough," she said bitterly.

I squatted down in front of her. "The hell you're not," I growled. "You're working too hard. You need some downtime."

"We can't afford downtime," She turned the chair and started to move past me, towards the chalkboards.

I grabbed the chair and held it fast, my temper flaring. I wasn't mad at her, I was mad at myself. I'd involved her in this thing and now it was destroying her. What if she pushed herself too hard and her mind snapped? I'd never forgive myself if something happened to her. "You need a break!" I told her.

And just for a second...she saw. I was so worried about her, so frustrated with myself, that I couldn't hide it. She looked into my eyes and she must have seen just how much I cared. Her own gaze softened.

I looked away, my face going hot. *Dammit!*

"Coffee?" she mumbled hopefully.

"No. Enough coffee. You drink more coffee than anyone I've ever met! What you need is to get out of your head. Turn that big brain of yours off for a few minutes."

She blinked at me. "I...I don't know how to do that," she said slowly.

And I realized she really didn't. I could see it in her eyes: her brain had been spinning all day, gaining momentum like a flywheel. Without the satisfying pleasure of solving the problem, she didn't know how to spin it down and in the meantime, it wouldn't let her sleep, or rest. *She's never had this, before. She's never come across a problem she can't solve.*

I squatted there staring into those beautiful, lush green eyes, helpless. I'd always known I wasn't right for her. I'd always known that she was a genius and I was a big, dumb lunk. But I'd never felt more out of my depth. I didn't know what it was like to have a brain like hers: how the hell could I help her shut it down?

Unless...unless a big dumb lunk was just what she needed, right now.

I knelt in front of her and lifted my hand, palm facing her. "Hit me," I said.

"What?!"

"Hit me," I said again. "Hit my palm with your fist. It's what I do, when I need to wind down, I pound a punch bag."

She shook her head, "I'm not really...." She trailed off. *I'm not really the hitting things type.*

"Maybe you need to be, now and again," I told her stubbornly. "Now hit me."

She sighed in frustration and then gave my palm a half-hearted tap.

"Like you mean it."

She punched my palm, this time putting some of her frustration behind it. The wheelchair rolled back a little way. That frustrated her even more: she slapped the brakes on and then hit me again, even harder.

"Good." I held up my other palm alongside the first. "Keep going."

She still looked reluctant but that last hit had given her just a taste of the release that was possible. She punched the other palm. Then the first again. And then she started alternating: left, right, left, slowly at first but getting steadily faster as the excess energy began to pour out of her. Her pummeling became savage, bitter, her fists stinging my palms, and I knelt there and soaked it up, urging her on with my eyes, drawing the frustration out of her. At last she whacked my palm and let out a long yell of anger that made my heart ache—

She stopped and rocked forward in the chair, panting, her fists still touching my palms. "Better," she admitted.

I nodded, relieved, and gazed at her, taking in her hair, all mussed and dotted with chalk dust, her cheeks flushed from the workout. She chose that moment to lift her head and suddenly, I was looking straight into those amazing green eyes....

And it hit me, full force. Everything I'd been holding back.

For days, I'd been grimly restraining myself, using all my strength to resist. But for one brief moment, I was so relieved that she was okay that all my defenses were down. The need picked me up like a wave and carried me, unstoppable. The blood was singing in my ears.

Without consciously willing it, my hands closed, capturing her fists. She swallowed. The room went silent.

I mustn't do this. I knew that.

But letting go of her hands was impossible. And every second I stayed in contact with her, the desire built and built—

We stared at each other, neither of us daring to breathe.

And then, simultaneously, we lunged at each other.

32

YOLANDA

OUR LIPS MET and the white-hot shock of it flashed through me. Then the pleasure rumbled through me like thunder, vibrating right down to my fingertips in pink waves.

I'd spent way too much time, since I'd met him, watching those lips. I'd focused on the way that full lower lip pressed against the hard upper one on the *p* of *suspect* and, especially, on the *B* of *FBI*. And now that softness was working at *my* lower lip, stroking over it in a way that made my whole body go weak. Meanwhile, that hard upper lip was attacking firm and fast, demanding I open up. And I did.

One, two, three beats of my racing heart. Then he broke the kiss and we were staring at each other from just a few inches away, both silently asking the same question. *Did we really just do that?* I'd gone heady. It couldn't be real. But my throbbing lips said it was.

Then we were kissing for the second time. He was so big, so out of control, that he would have knocked me back against the back of the chair if I'd let him. But as soon as his lips touched mine again, it was as if a current had been switched on inside me. My spine went rigid and I was bolt upright against him, pressing back, drinking in the feel of him. My hands groped and found his shoulders and a tremor went through me as my fingers slid out, out, *out,* marveling at the size of him. My lips flowered open under him and then the tip of his tongue was teasing mine. My hands came alive, tracing the glorious, solid swells of his biceps over and over.

We broke and stared at each other again. This time: *yes, this is real, this is definitely happening.* I was panting, half-drunk on the feel of him, and my lips were so super-sensitive I couldn't speak. But we didn't need to speak.

Both of us glanced at the big leather couch at the same time.

He kissed me again, full-on and animal. Then his arms hooked under mine and suddenly I was being lifted up out of the chair, my ass skimming the thick leather arm of the couch before I gently touched down in the center seat. He moved closer, his kiss pressing me back until my head pushed against the top of the couch and he was kissing down into me. I was pinned, sandwiched between him and the couch and there was no better feeling in the world. The pleasure was rolling down my body, making me twist and thrash against him. And then I heard the creak and felt the cushion dip as he climbed onto the couch. His knee speared down between my thighs: so thickly muscled, so big and solid. My breathing went shaky.

His hands found my hips and then slid under my jacket and all the way up my sides, the warmth of him throbbing into me through my blouse. They skimmed the sides of my breasts and the pleasure leapt and danced, slamming around inside me. I slid my fingers deep into his thick black hair, tangling them in it, then drew in a shuddering breath as his pecs pressed against my breasts.

My hands slowly slid from his head down to the back of his neck and then to his back. When I felt how he'd gone hard, how every muscle was like *rock* in his excitement, I melted: I wanted to just cling to that hardness forever and mold myself to him. He hunkered over me like a beast, huge and unstoppable: after all that time restraining himself, he was finally loose. His kisses came faster and faster, both of us breathless—

He suddenly hooked his hands under my arms and pulled me

along the couch, twisting me around so that I was on my back. I got my hands behind me and helped, lifting and scooching, as impatient as him. He lifted my legs up onto the seat and then—God, I was lying full-length and he was climbing atop me, knees straddling me.

He was big anyway but from this angle he looked massive, looming over me, those wide shoulders and broad chest filling my view. He gazed down at me and there was no battle in his eyes anymore, no conflict. His course was decided. There was only one way this would end.

I saw his eyes go to my blouse, then my skirt. I swallowed. *Which one first?* I could hear my heart pounding.

He seemed to make up his mind and slid a hand up my leg, under my skirt. He gave a shocked, little intake of breath when his fingers brushed the bare skin of my upper thigh and he realized I was wearing hold-ups, not pantyhose. His eyes gleamed, delighted.

Then he reached down with his other hand, stretched my blouse away from my body and popped the first button one-handed. He wasn't going to choose, he wanted both, *now*.

He slid his hand up between my legs. My skirt rose higher. There was a sudden stab of cold fear as I realized he was about to see the scars on my legs. He glanced down at them, then up. Our eyes met—

And all I saw there was lust. He'd seen them. He didn't care at all.

His fingers stroked me through the front of my panties and I drew in a strangled groan. He growled in response, torn between just taking me and savoring the moment. He started to rub me, tracing the shape of my lips through the thin material of my panties, and I ground my ass in response. He stared down into my eyes and slowly smiled. He was enjoying seeing me get more and more turned on and the thought of that turned me on even more. The pleasure was taking over, aching currents of it whirlpooling out from where his fingers stroked, and I bit my lip and closed my eyes.

Seeing me bite my lip seemed to do something to him. His other hand came to life again, popping button after button on my blouse. The instant it was unfastened, he spread it wide, baring me. I opened my eyes and saw him gazing down at my breasts and then, with a growl of victory, he shoved the bra cups up and out of the way and just...*feasted.* There was no other word for it, his eyes just ate me up and it made a depth charge of hot pride sink all the way down and detonate between my thighs. And then he was lunging forward again, his head dipping towards my chest and—

I sucked in my breath and grabbed his head with both hands as his mouth enveloped a nipple. God, he knew just how to do it, too, just how to swirl with his tongue and bite using the softness of his lips and the hard edges of his teeth. He used both his hands, cupping my breasts, squeezing them, and my world descended into licks and sweeps of his tongue, kisses and sucks and hot pants across my spit-wet skin. Then it got even better because he slid his knee up between my thighs and suddenly I was rocking against him, grinding myself towards the brink. He crushed my breasts together with his hands and alternated between them with his mouth, faster and faster, and I could feel the hot hardness of his cock through his pants—

He broke off and looked down into my eyes and something passed between us. *Yes.*

His hands dove under my skirt and then my panties were sliding down my legs and off. He reared up onto his knees and before he could work his belt, I had hold of it, jerking the leather through the loops, my eyes locked on the bulge just beneath it. His pants came free. He shoved them down and—

Oh. I swallowed and a hot throb went right down my body, ending between my thighs. I actually felt myself *twitch.* I tried to look up at his face but my gaze kept being drawn down. It matched the rest of him, big and solid and determined, ready to plunge into me and—

"Go slow," I said. But even that came out breathy and urgent. I flushed. *Go slow. But hurry.*

He pushed my skirt up a little higher. Nudged my legs apart and lowered his body between them and *oh God* that feeling of his weight pressing down on me, of being spread—I grabbed at his shoulders, then started frantically unbuttoning his shirt, needing him skin on skin. I heard a condom being rolled on, then the first hot touch of him against me, hot hardness slipping on wet flesh—

My head rolled back against the couch arm as he began to move into me. He *did* go slow. He had to, because he was big. But I was soaking and every tight millimeter sent silver pleasure right up my spine, lashing and twisting and feeding a deep, molten core. He dipped his head, his lips close to my ear, and growled, "Been dreaming about doing this since I met you."

I blinked and panted. He'd been dreaming about me, too? "How was I?"

He pressed forward with his hips and we both gasped. "Fantastic." Another push. "Awesome." He groaned. "Not as good as this."

He lifted himself a little and planted his hands on my shoulders, pinning me in place. I looked up into his eyes and gulped. The lust on his face took my breath away: he needed all of me, *now*—

I quickly nodded. I did, too.

I saw his muscled ass rise as he drew back a little and then—

Both of us cried out in pleasure as he thrust *hard, deep.* I grabbed for his shoulders and clung on, my body flexing against him as he filled me, inch after glorious inch. I moaned as I felt him reach my very limits, the coarse hair at his base grazing my lips. We lay there gazing into each other's eyes. I could feel every breath he took, every throb of his pulse.

He laid kisses on my forehead, waiting until I was used to him...and then slowly, he began to move. Each time his hips drew back, it was a loss that made me groan. Each time that muscled ass drove him into me, I went wild, my hands slipping under his shirt to rove across his back. He lowered himself, taking his weight on his forearms, and it got even better: now his pubis ground against my clit each time he moved, and his chest stroked my breasts.

As he started to go faster, it felt like each out stroke was sucking silvery pleasure into my core and each in stroke was compressing it into a ball as dense and hot as the core of a star. I pulled on his shoulders, drawing him down to me, and we kissed long and deep, panting against each other's lips as his hips rose and fell.

It built until I moaned. Until my hands grabbed and clutched at him, fingers digging deep into the tan muscle of his shoulders, his back and finally his ass. The pleasure was scrunching down tighter and tighter, becoming so intense I couldn't keep still: I stretched up and matched him kiss for kiss, laying them on his lips and cheeks and neck as he did the same to me. The leather couch was firmer than a bed and as he sped up even more, I bit my lip in ecstasy. Every bit of force he used was going into *me,* instead of being lost in the mattress, and it was incredible. There was a glorious, dark pleasure in being...hammered. Slammed.

Pounded.

I could feel the orgasm thundering towards me and I knew he was close, too: every muscle in his body had gone hard. I kissed his lips, open-mouthed and desperate—

He took his weight on his elbows and cupped my face in his hands, holding me still for a second as he thrust. I was so close to coming, I had to blink a few times before I could focus on those clear blue eyes.

When I did, I saw something. An openness I'd never seen in him before. We were *together,* in a way I knew I wouldn't be able to explain to anyone else. More than boyfriend/girlfriend. More than lovers. More than partners.

We trusted each other. And to both of us, that was worth more than anything else in the world.

He gave a low growl and buried himself inside me a final time and then we were wrapping each other in our arms, binding ourselves together as we came. We were so close, I could feel every shudder and jerk, every gasp and groan, and I wasn't sure which were him and which were me.

When it was finished, we lay there, neither of us willing to loosen our grip.

Inseparable.

33

CALAHAN

AFTERWARDS, we went up to the roof and sat side by side on one of the stone benches. It was a clear night and, even with New York's light pollution, there were still plenty of stars to see. But I couldn't stop looking at her.

It was more than just her beauty and her spirit. I felt...*awed* by her. When you boil it right down, what I do—stopping people from hurting each other—is about the simplest, most earthly thing you can do: hell, people have been enforcing the law since people first started living in towns. I glanced down at the city. My job took place down there, in dirty alleys and dirtier boardrooms, wrestling with people, be it in a fist fight or a courtroom. But Yolanda...she was *up there,* doing things in her mind that I couldn't hope to understand. I had to tell her.

The wind blew her hair and I reached across and tucked a stray lock behind her ear. "What you do," I said, struggling to put it into words, "is amazing. You know that, right?"

She shook her head. "What you do *matters.* Catching killers *matters.* Math...most of the time, it's just obscure papers being read by other academics. It doesn't make any difference to ninety-nine percent of people. And then when I see what the killer twisted it into...." She shuddered and I put my arm around her and pulled her tight into me. "I think we need more people like you, less like me."

"Bullshit," I said calmly. She turned to look at me in shock and I gently lifted her chin so that she was looking up at the stars. "Without math, there'd be no space travel."

I kept my fingers under her chin. When she spoke, her soft skin rubbed against me and it was difficult not to just grab her and pull her down to the floor for another round. "I never figured you for someone with one eye on the stars," she said.

I shrugged. "With some of the stuff I've seen people do to each other, down here...I kinda like the idea of someone making a fresh start, up there."

The wind was getting up and she shivered. I went downstairs, grabbed my raincoat, and wrapped it around her like a blanket. Then I pulled her sideways so she was cuddled up against my side.

I stroked her hair and kissed the top of her head and she smiled, but her gaze was focused on an apartment building a few blocks away, its windows almost all dark. "They don't know," she whispered sadly.

I knew what she was thinking because I'd thought the exact same thing, hundreds of times. I hugged her even tighter and put my head next to hers so she could feel my nod.

There's a weight that comes from being a cop. You see a city at night and it's like watching a child sleep, unaware of all the danger that exists. They don't know and that's good, because they'd go crazy if they did. It's not their job to know, it's ours. But it can be lonely.

I hated that Yolanda had crossed over to my side. The urge to protect her had gotten even stronger, after what we'd just done. It was like a physical ache. But for the first time, I had someone to share things with. Becky had always calmed me and comforted me but she'd still been a civilian. After everything that had happened, Yolanda was effectively a cop.

The wind whipped across the roof and Yolanda shivered again and stuck her hands deep into the pockets of my coat to warm them. Then she frowned and pulled something out. "What's this?"

It was the torn-off corner of a wrapper, in a plastic evidence bag. "I forgot about that," I said. "Picked it up at the first crime scene. I'll put it into evidence tomorrow."

She cuddled into me and it was a while before she spoke again. "Sam," she said. "This—I mean, what we just did...it's not just...?" Before I could answer, she took a shuddering breath and continued, "Because if it is, just tell me. It's okay, I'm just saying I want to know—"

I grabbed her hand, knitted my fingers with hers and squeezed. "No," I said. "It's not just that." I kissed her knuckles and she relaxed against me. But inside, guilt was eating away at me. I was telling the truth. I didn't want this to be a one-night stand or a fling or a friends-with-benefits. I wanted to be with her. But....

But she didn't know what I'd done. If I didn't tell her, the secret would gradually poison us. Secrets always do. And if I did tell her, she might hate me.

She deserved a proper relationship and that's what I wanted to give her. I just wasn't sure I could. And before I could even wrap my head around that—

"We need to talk about last night," she said quietly. "In the bar."

I nodded. "I'm sorry I yelled at you. I was just, uh...I'd had a bad day. I was drunk. Thanks for getting me home."

Silence for a few seconds. Just long enough for the hairs on the back of my neck to start to stand up, for the cold horror to rise in my belly.

"That wasn't what I meant," she said.

I turned to her and she turned to look at me. I could see it in her eyes. *She knows.*

It felt as if my stomach fell the whole forty stories to the ground. I finally knew how a suspect must feel, when I tossed the evidence in his face in an interrogation room. I was exposed, every layer stripped back right to my core. But I still tried to brazen it out. "I was feeling low, that's all it was—"

"You were planning to kill yourself."

And there it was, simple and unvarnished. My face went hot. I wanted to throw up. I jumped up off the bench and took a staggering step away from her. "No! No, I wouldn't—"

"Sam, I could see it in your eyes."

Oh God, it was over. *We* were over, almost before we'd begun, because how could she like me now, now she knew I was so weak? I turned my back on her and started to stalk away towards the elevator.

She raised her voice. "I know that look. *I've seen it in the mirror!*"

I stopped and spun around. So many emotions flooded my brain in just a few seconds. Shock, first. Then anger, that she'd say something like that when it wasn't true. And then the slow, sickening realization that it was. In two running steps, I closed the distance between us and fell to my knees in front of her, my hands gripping her shoulders. "*What?!*" I rasped.

"Usually," she said, "It's when I finish using the drone. But sometimes it's as soon as I wake up. When I *remember.* I came up here and—" She looked down at her legs. "When the contractors were renovating the dove loft, I had them remove a section of parapet from the roof." She nodded to the west. "Over there. There's a gap where there's nothing to stop me. I could just go the edge, tip myself out of the chair and—"—her voice cracked—"It would be like flying, for a few seconds."

I gave a groan of horror and pulled her to me, locking my arms around her back like I was never going to let her go. My humiliation was forgotten. All I cared about was—"*No!*" I growled into her neck. "*No,* you hear me? *No,* not ever. You got that straight?"

I felt wetness where her face was pressed against my cheek. And then *her* arms locked tight around *my* back. I drew back just enough to look into her eyes. The raw determination there hit me like a punch in the chest. This was an ultimatum. A promise that had to go both ways.

It was the hardest thing in the world to give up and I did it in a heartbeat. Because it was *her.* "Okay," I managed, my own eyes going hot. "Okay."

We clung to each other like that for a long, long time.

34

YOLANDA

H E LEFT as dawn broke. We both agreed, in that self-consciously sensible way people have the morning after sex, that he had to get back to the FBI and I had to get to work. But that didn't make it any easier to let go of him, as he hunkered down to kiss me goodbye in my doorway.

I was still reeling from how much things had changed in one night. It felt like I'd stepped through a door to a parallel universe, one in which I had a boyfriend. One in which I *could* have a boyfriend. And it wasn't just about the sex, however mind-blowing that had been. For the first time since my brother died, I didn't feel alone. When I was with Calahan—I still couldn't think of him as *Sam*—I felt...grounded. I knew he'd keep me anchored and I trusted him more than I've ever trusted anyone.

Maybe that's why I admitted to him about sometimes feeling suicidal. I've never told anyone that before. I always thought they'd think I was weak, or ungrateful. I mean, I survived the bridge, I lived when my brother died. Suicide would be the ultimate act of selfishness. But Calahan had understood. He'd been that low, too. And now we'd made a promise. Both of us had something more to live for, this morning.

The difference was, he knew *why* I'd sometimes been that low. My broken, useless body, being cut off from society, the guilt of having survived. But I didn't know why he had. It wasn't as simple as losing Becky. It was more than loss and survivor guilt. It was something darker, something that was growing inside him instead of fading, dragging him into a downward spiral. I couldn't help him unless I knew what it was. But I wasn't going to make the mistake of prying again. I'd just have to hope he could open up to me.

I took a shower, threw on some jeans and a hoodie...and stopped. There was something on the kitchen counter, a plastic bag. *Crap!* It was that scrap of evidence I'd pulled out of Calahan's coat pocket. I'd had it in my hand when we'd come down from the roof and I must have put it down and then forgotten to give it to him. Now that I could see it properly in the light, I could see it was the corner of a wrapper, only about an inch across. It was red, but not a bright, fiery red. More like the purple-red of a cherry, with a tiny curl of creamy white at the edge.

I put it down and went to work on the chalkboards. It had been good to get out of my head: Calahan's punching trick had worked...in fact, just being with him was the perfect antidote to all the time I was spending *deep*. With him around, maybe I'd be able to worry a little less about my mind snapping.

But for now, it was back to work. I was still trying to figure out the location of the next murder using the equations from the previous one. But whatever I tried, the numbers came out way, way too big to make sense. And—

I looked over my shoulder at the evidence bag. Something was scratching at the very back of my mind. That color combination, cherry-red and cream. A memory....

I shook my head and went *deep*, fitting the equations together in my head like jigsaw pieces. But an hour later, I emerged no closer to figuring it out. And we were running out of time: Clara would be killed in less than three hours.

I needed coffee. I shot over to the kitchen and started to make it, venting my frustration on anything and everything: slamming down my mug, stabbing the button on the coffee machine, grinding the coffee beans like they were personally responsible for my failure. *What if I can't solve this? What if Clara dies because I can't find the answer?*

As soon as the coffee was brewed, I took a big gulp. Then I grabbed the bag of beans to put them back. Only I was in so much of a hurry that they slipped through my fingers and landed on the floor. *Crap.* At least they hadn't spilled. I picked them up and stuffed them back in the freezer.

I was halfway back to the chalkboards when that memory itched at the back of my mind again. The cherry-red and cream wrapper....

I spun around, went back to the freezer, and pulled out the bag of coffee beans. Then I dropped them on the floor again.

That was it. That sound. I closed my eyes and did it again. Not right, but close. I sat back in my chair, sipped more coffee and groped for the memory, like trying to grab a fish that's the same color as the water around it. Little...*things.* The sound of hard little things, rattling in a packet—

And suddenly it was there, bright and clear at the front of my mind. My eyes snapped open. There was a crash as my coffee mug hit the floor but I just stared fixedly ahead, unseeing.

Oh *no.*

The realization was like being slowly dunked in freezing black oil, the sickening, slick touch of it crawling up my body until it drowned me. *No....*

I erupted into life. I grabbed the evidence bag, threw open the door and raced down the hall. The elevator ride down seemed to take hours, with me staring at my reflection in the mirrored wall, white-faced and staring, *come on, come on....*

I shot across the parking lot and swung myself into my car. A few seconds later, I was tearing through the streets, asking the GPS to take me to the nearest grocery store that would be open this early in the morning...

When I got there, I screeched to a stop right outside the doors, flung out my chair and lifted myself into it. I was inside the store before I realized I'd left my car's door wide open, but I wasn't going back now.

I needed to know.

I shot along the aisles, searching for the right one. *Where the hell is everything?* I hadn't been in a grocery store since the accident, I got everything delivered. I cursed and searched the signs and eventually found the candy aisle, tipping up on two wheels as I swerved around the corner. I was dimly aware that everyone was looking at me, and that this was some sort of milestone: I was *out,* on my own, surrounded by people, and I'd barely even noticed. I couldn't have done this, a week ago. But I didn't care about any of that, right now. I just needed—

There. Cherry-red wrappers, swirled with creamy white. And... they were out of reach. I muttered a long string of curses but it did no good. I was going to have to—

I took a deep breath. Felt the stab of helplessness but did it anyway. "Um...Sir?"

An old man turned around to look at me.

"Could you please pass me a packet of those?" I asked, pointing. "I can't reach."

He gave me a kindly smile and passed one down. I thanked him and stared at the packet. *Toffee Cores.* Spheres like little planets with a glossy, hard coating that melted on your tongue to reveal a mantle of milk chocolate and finally a core of hard, chewy toffee. The packet had a cherry-red background and curly cream lettering. I compared it with the fragment in the evidence bag.

Identical.

I ripped open the packet and hard brown spheres rained across the floor, bouncing and rolling. The smell hit me, sugary sweet and chocolatey with a hint of buttery toffee—

Noises around me. A crowd of people had gathered and a shop assistant was nervously approaching, looking at the candy scattered around me. "Miss? Miss, are you okay?"

I didn't answer. I just sat there, stock-still, the memory exploding in my mind.

I was kneeling on his bed, my arms wrapped around him. "It's okay," I told him. "It's all okay, now." And as I held him in the dark, I offered him the bag of Toffee Cores to comfort him. He took one and sucked it, glad of the distraction. His chest was still heaving with fear, his cheeks shining with tears.

When he was six, my brother Josh went through a stage of night terrors. Toffee Cores were what I'd give him to comfort him, when he woke up sobbing at two in the morning. The stage passed. We grew up. I hadn't thought about them in years.

But for a while, Toffee Cores used to be Josh's best defense against the monsters in his head. What if they still were?

What if now, as an adult, he'd started eating them again, subconsciously craving their comfort, because he'd repeatedly been exposed to something far more terrifying than any childhood monster? What if that was why the fragment of packet was at the crime scene?

What if my brother was alive...and what if he was the killer?

35

YOLANDA

I PACED. One long, hard shove on the wheels to send me down to the end of my apartment. A light pressure from my hands to slow myself, as I approached the wall. A quick turn. And repeat.

I'd been having the same circular argument with myself for over an hour.

It's just a coincidence. A scrap of candy wrapper found at a crime scene, the same candy my brother used to eat, twenty years ago, when he was a scared kid. I'd been to the manufacturer's website: they sold over two hundred thousand bags of Toffee Cores in the US every day.

It doesn't even make sense, I reasoned. *Josh is dead.*

But a little voice inside me whispered: *they never recovered the body.*

If he had survived the bridge, he would have come home, I told myself sternly. *He wouldn't have disappeared for an entire year.*

But he was smart enough to have written these equations, the little voice said. *He was always smarter than you.*

I'd never known a problem like this. Math is all hard, solid numbers and beautiful, intricate mechanisms that connect them. It might be complex, but it's always *certain.* This was anything but. I just kept going round and round—

I clamped my hands down hard on the wheels, jerked to a stop, and yelled in frustration. "*Stop!* Just stop!" I sat there panting, staring at my useless legs. *Be rational.* Yes, Josh was smart enough to have written the equations but he wasn't crazy. He was the most level-headed person I'd ever known. And like me, he didn't believe in superstitions. He wouldn't chase after witches or write spells. And Josh would never, ever, hurt anyone.

I took a deep, shaky breath and forced myself to be calm. And when I did, the whole thing seemed stupid. *Of course it's not Josh!* For one thing, I would have recognized his handwriting.

I was exhausted and stressed out of my mind, scared I wasn't going to be able to save Clara. So when I'd come across this one coincidence with the candy wrapper, I'd latched onto it and concocted this whole crazy theory as a solution to all my problems. If it was Josh, we could catch the killer *and* I'd get my brother back. It was laughably childish, in the cold light of day. *I'm really losing it.* The thought sent a chill through me. Losing my mind has always been my greatest fear.

A familiar thump at my door. I opened it and tiredly waved Calahan in. "You okay?" he asked immediately. "Thought I heard you yell, on my way up the hall."

"I'm fine," I lied.

He squatted down and looked at me. God, those blue eyes, the way they demanded the truth. He knew I was lying. But there was no way I was going to tell him I was cracking up. I looked away. "I'm just frustrated," I told him. I nodded at the chalkboards. "I still can't solve it. And we've got less than an hour before Clara—" I closed my eyes, tears pricking at the corners of them. All that time I'd wasted, chasing ghosts! What was wrong with me?

"Talk me through it," said Calahan. "Even if I can't understand, It might help."

I sighed. "To determine a location, you need a couple of reference points. Like, you'd tell someone a coffee shop is one block west of *here* and two blocks north of *there*. But I don't know what the reference points are. And the math doesn't add up...not unless the reference points are stupidly distant."

He screwed up his face, confused. "You mean they must be outside New York?" I shook my head. "Outside the US?"

"No, way further than that. They'd be way out in space. So my math must be wrong."

He started to pace, just like I had. He finally stopped in front of the window, arms stubbornly crossed, and my heart melted. He was so far out of his comfort zone, with this stuff, but he still wanted to help.

He saw something and frowned. Tilted his head to one side as he considered. He glanced over his shoulder at me but then looked away.

"What?" I asked.

"No. Nothing." He looked at his feet, embarrassed. "It's dumb."

I rolled over there. He was so much smarter than he gave himself credit for: I wished he could see that. "Tell me," I said gently.

He sighed. Scowled. "What if your math is right and the numbers are meant to be that big? This guy thinks he's doing magic, right?" He nodded at what he'd been looking at: the moon, just visible in the morning sky. "Didn't people used to do rituals when the stars or the moon or whatever were in the right place?"

I was already running the numbers in my head. "The moon's too close, " I said despondently. "And the stars are too far away." Then it hit me. "But...wait, the *planets....*"

I did a one-eighty and raced over to my computer, bringing up a list of the planets and their distances from the Sun. Then I shot across to the chalkboards. "Read them out to me!" I yelled. "Start with Mercury and work outwards!"

He read them out and I started scribbling them down, cursing as it all finally began to make sense. How had I not seen this before?! "It's to do with the orbits," I said, writing furiously. "It's as if the orbital paths are visible, and the light reflected by the planets is casting shadows of them onto New York, and where the lines appear to cross...."

I closed my eyes and went *deep*. Time melted away as I hurtled through the solar system, planets spinning around me. I imagined their paths as thin strands of silver wire, casting a spider web of shadows down onto Manhattan. I just had to figure out exactly where everything would be at the precise instant Clara would die—

I heard my name from somewhere very far away. Then again. "What?" I grated without opening my eyes.

"Thirty minutes left," said Calahan, his voice tight.

I was staring at Neptune as it spun in front of my face. "I know," I managed. "But right now, I'm trying to calculate the orbits of nine planets, all moving at thousands of miles an hour."

"What can I do?" asked Calahan.

"Shut the hell up." Then I reached out, found his hand in the blackness, and squeezed it, and he squeezed back.

I lost myself in space. At first, I moved, turning my head to watch the planets spin by, sweeping my hands around me to trace their orbits. But as it all folded down—as everything does—into beautiful, simple math, I grew very still. I knew time was slipping away but I almost had it, *almost had it*....I wound my hair into a bun, then let it out very, very slowly—

My eyes flew open and I exploded into life, plugging the orbits I'd calculated into the killer's equations. My chalk went *tak tak tak* on the chalkboard. "How long?" I asked without turning around.

"Not long," said Calahan tightly.

Tak tak taktaktak—*Yes!* "Plug these coordinates into a map," I yelled, and read them out. By the time I'd raced over to the computer, Calahan had entered the numbers and we watched together as the map scrolled and zoomed.

"It's downtown," he said. He scribbled down the address and we both hurried towards the door. As he jogged along the hallway, he pulled out his phone. "I'm calling in backup. We only have thirteen minutes."

I shot past him. "We'll take my car. I can get us there in eight."

36

YOLANDA

W E GOT THERE FAST but the NYPD were faster. An army of officers were already swarming into the building, asking each other *what the hell?* And I understood because it made no sense.

The building was a shopping mall.

A big black SUV roared up and Carrie and Alison jumped out. Carrie stared at me incredulously. "You're telling me he's going to sacrifice Clara in a goddamn mall? There must be a thousand witnesses in that place. Security cameras everywhere. Why would he come here?"

I shook my head. "He's not like any normal killer. He's going where the math tells him to go and it says to go here. I'm sure of it."

"My guess is, he'll find some quiet storeroom, or a closed-up store," said Calahan. "We've got to tear this place apart. He's got her here, somewhere, and we only have four minutes!"

Carrie looked at him, looked at me...and nodded.

I let out a long sigh of relief. She believed us!

"I'll make sure the NYPD have all the exits locked down," said Alison. "Even if we can't find him in time, we can sure as hell stop him leaving. Wish we knew what he looked like." She ran off.

My stomach lurched. Just for a second, I considered...what if it *was* my brother? I could give them a description....

Calahan saw my expression and grabbed my arm. "What is it?"

I shook my head and looked away. "Nothing." *God, what's the matter with me?* My brother was dead. I knew it couldn't be him. But the crazy theory was still haunting me and I'd been a half second away from blurting it out. At which point Calahan would realize I'd completely lost it. Or even worse, he might believe me and send the cops looking for a guy who'd been dead for a year, while the real killer slipped the net.

I risked a glance at Calahan. He was giving me that look: he knew I was hiding something. But to my relief, someone called him away.

I took a deep breath. We'd got here in time: just. That was all that mattered. We could stop the killer. We could save her.

But as the time ticked away, I started to panic. Reports were coming in every few seconds from the close to one hundred officers and FBI agents searching the mall...and none of them could find anything suspicious. Just as the deadline arrived, the last officer reported in: nothing. *What are we missing?*

Carrie lowered her phone from her ear. "The security office has been through every camera. No killer." She gave me a worried look. "Is it possible you were wrong?"

"No!" I snapped. "No, the math is solid. *This* is the location, *This* is the time, it's happening right now! She's—" I spun around on my wheels, trying to look in every direction at once. "She's *here,* somewhere! We have to find her! He's killing her *right now!*"

Carrie nodded. She got it. She was as worried as I was. But there was nothing she could do. The killer just wasn't there. Carrie ordered the mall searched again. And then a third time.

We searched for two hours and found nothing.

"Maybe we scared him off," offered Carrie. "He got here, saw all the cops—"

"No," said Callahan. "Not this guy. He plans each killing, he knows exactly where and when, he'll have had some plan...." He looked at me helplessly. *All* of us looked helpless, even super-agent Alison.

An FBI agent ran up to Carrie. "There are a lot of press outside. They want to know why the mall's closed off." Carrie cursed.

"We missed it," I mumbled. "He was right here and we missed it."

"Not possible," said Alison firmly. "We've checked the entire mall. Are you *sure* about the location?"

I felt my face heat. What if I was wrong? What if the murder had happened a block away, what if Clara was lying dead somewhere and it was all my fault? But I was so sure of my math. The two coordinates had put the location exactly here.

And then a chill crept across my mind. *Two* coordinates. Two dimensions. We hadn't thought about—

I looked down at my feet. "What's underneath the mall?" I asked in a strangled voice.

Calahan got it immediately and cursed. He grabbed a janitor, almost pulling the poor guy off his feet. "What's below us?" he yelled.

"Nothing," the man shrugged. "I mean, there's an old subway tunnel, but they closed that back in the sixties."

"How do I get there?"

"You can't! Not from here, there's no connection to the mall. You'd have to go to the station on Broadway and then follow the tunnel back until it branches."

Calahan was running almost before the man had finished speaking. Carrie whipped out her phone and called the New York Transit Authority and told them to shut down the trains.

I raced over to the window and looked down the street. I could see Calahan running at a dead sprint, shoving people out of the way. At the end of the street, he disappeared into a subway station.

Minutes passed. Carrie, Alison and I all looked at each other, our faces white. Carrie was sending him backup, but what if the killer was still there?

My phone rang. My hands were shaking so much, I could barely hit the button to answer. "Hello?"

Calahan was panting. "I'm here,"

He must be right below us. I looked down at my feet, as if I had x-ray vision. "And?"

More panting. Then he whispered a curse. "And we're too late."

37

YOLANDA

I T TOOK ME fifteen minutes to get down there. I had to navigate the crowds on the street, then find an elevator and a ramp down to the tracks, and finally pick my way through fallen debris in the old, abandoned tunnel. Twice, I had to double back to avoid piles of bricks that someone with working legs could have just climbed over. But I wasn't giving up. I owed Clara more than that.

As I got closer, I started to feel that familiar *wrongness*. I slowly lifted my phone, pointing its flashlight at the curving walls of the tunnel. The surface was alive with equations, all glistening wetly in the beam. Fresh blood. With all the competing flashlights sweeping back and forth, it almost looked like the writing was alive. I shuddered and pushed myself another few feet.

And then I saw what was ahead of me and my hands locked up on the wheels. My body just refused to go any further.

There's a feeling you get when you're standing on the edge of a cliff. Even when there's no wind, you feel like the drop could just grab you and pull you in. This was like that, but a thousand times worse.

Ahead of me, there was...*nothing*.

The tunnel didn't end in a wall or a barrier. It ended in void: a featureless, matte black nothingness that filled it floor to ceiling, darker than the deepest, darkest hole. When I swept my flashlight beam across it, the light was swallowed up.

I shifted in my seat, panic clawing at me. It felt as if I was going to fall forwards into it...and once inside, I'd never stop falling.

The equations changed as they got closer to it. They stretched out as if being pulled, twisting and spiraling towards the blackness and then vanishing as they reached it.

It looked like...it looked like a black hole.

And right at its mouth, stretched out on the floor as if being sucked in, was Clara.

Fighting every instinct, I forced myself forward. In my head, I knew it was an optical illusion, just like the tentacled things and the spiders at the other crime scenes. But knowing that didn't take away the panic. *The floor's level,* I told myself, *it must be.* But it didn't feel that way. It felt as if I was inching the wheelchair down a steep slope towards the void, and at any second I was going to start sliding and be unable to stop.

By the time I reached Clara, I was a sweating, nauseous mess. I looked down at her face and wanted to weep. Except for the paleness of her skin, she looked just like she had in the photos. The woman we'd sworn to protect. *My fault. If I'd been a little smarter, if I'd thought in three dimensions instead of two....* I couldn't take it any longer. I had to look away.

Calahan was kneeling over her. He looked up at me and, from the look on his face, the guilt was eating him up, too. "You shouldn't be down here," he muttered.

"I can manage," I said, and moved back a little. One wheel went into an unseen dip and I lurched sideways, almost spilling out of the chair.

Calahan jumped up and grabbed my shoulders, steadying me. Then he glared. *See? I told you!*

I glared back, then looked away, my face going hot. I was defensive, as usual, I wanted to prove I didn't need his help, or anybody's. But I could feel the tender strength of him as he loomed over me, ready to shield me from anything, and that made me melt.

"Thanks," I muttered.

He grunted. Something had changed. He'd always been protective but now that we were together, it felt like it was dialed up to eleven. *He's worried something bad will happen to me...oh God, is that what happened to Becky?*

I wanted to ask him but I couldn't. I'd seen the pain talking about it unleashed. I had to wait for him to tell me. *What if he never can?* What if this thing just kept eating him up from the inside and there was nothing I could do about it?

I tried to focus. We had a job to do. But when I started to look at the equations, I found I couldn't concentrate. The black void was almost close enough to touch and I kept feeling like I was going to fall sideways into it. It was the psychological equivalent of standing next to the speakers at a thrash metal gig, impossible to ignore.

I thought that if I proved to myself it wasn't real, it might help. I wheeled myself slowly forward towards the blackness.

"Careful," warned Calahan.

I kept going, getting closer and closer. It was impossible to see where the end of the tunnel was. I knew there must be something solid there but the blackness made it impossible to get any sense of depth or distance. I held one hand out in front of me, rolling forward inch by inch—

"Don't!" said Calahan in sudden panic.

Too late. My fingertips brushed something soft. Powdery and yet greasy....

I looked down at my hand in revulsion. My fingers were coated up to the first knuckle in—*filth.*

All subways are dirty. The soot from all the traffic on the streets finds its way underground and it mixes with the rat droppings and the human debris, the skin cells we slough off every day, the bacteria and viruses we leave behind. All of that mixes together and blows through the air as tiny particles, too small to see. Blow your nose, after a day riding the subway, and the tissue will be black.

The tunnels...they're the dirtiest of all. A thick, sticky layer of muck builds up over everything. *This* tunnel was a dead end and every time a train passed by it, the dirty air was rammed into it with no way to escape. It had built up on the end wall, where I was now standing. And after fifty years of the dirt drifting into the corners, undisturbed, there *were* no more corners: the end wall had become a perfect bowl shape. A smooth blackness made of concentrated filth. *That's* what the killer had used to create his black hole illusion. And I'd just put my hand in it. I wanted to throw up.

I returned to Calahan, wiping my hand over and over on my hoodie. I was going to have to throw it out. I wanted to burn everything I was wearing and take a very long shower. The stuff must be in my hair, in my lungs. Worst of all, the stuff coated the floor. Clara was lying in it, just discarded like a toy, like she was *nothing*. That thought brought me close to losing it. *This is our fault! We should have stopped him!*

More cops arrived. "No one touch anything!" Calahan yelled. "We haven't got photos yet! Where's the photographer?"

"On her way," said Alison, walking over. "We didn't plan on needing her. We thought—"

She broke off guiltily but I knew what she'd been going to say. *We thought we were here to catch the guy.*

I didn't want to look at Clara's body but I forced myself. I could feel tears burning at the corners of my eyes. It was just so *wrong*. She'd been young and alive, with friends and dreams and—I felt my throat close up. I wanted to scream and rage: who could do something like this?

The doubt crept into my mind again. *My brother?*

No. No way. My brother would never hurt anyone.

Clara's hand was resting palm-up in the dirt, her five fingers curled slightly as if reaching for something. The tears finally came, rolling down my cheeks. I stretched down to her. "I'm sorry," I whispered. "I'm so, so sorry." And brushed her palm with my fingertips.

Her hand closed on mine.

38

YOLANDA

I SCREAMED. Calahan was at my side in two big strides. He saw what was happening and hollered down the tunnel: *"PARAMEDIC! Get the paramedics in here!"*

He squatted down beside Clara, shaking his head in disbelief. "I checked her pulse when I found her," he said. "I couldn't find one...."

He'd gone sickly pale. *Oh God, if she dies, because he missed it....*

The paramedics ran up. Calahan frantically gave them the story and then we backed off to let them work. They rigged up bags of blood and saline, filled needles and pushed them into her veins. I grabbed Calahan's hand and squeezed it tight.

It seemed like an eternity before one of the paramedics turned to us. "She's stabilizing," he said. "She barely had a pulse, the blood loss had slowed it right down. Not surprised you missed it."

"Will she make it?" demanded Calahan.

The paramedic hesitated, reluctant to promise, but he relented when he saw the look in our eyes. "Her chances are good."

We both let out a long sigh of relief. It was the first good news we'd had in a long time. And with the guilt lifted, I could think clearly for the first time. We knew how to solve the location equations, now. I could work out the one at this crime scene and that would tell us where the final killing would happen. This time, we could stake out the place well beforehand. We could finally catch this guy.

Alison hurried over. "We found something," she said, and held up an evidence bag. In it was a tiny square of thick paper, smaller than my fingernail, with a smiley face on it. Calahan and Alison exchanged knowing looks. "That explains a lot," said Calahan.

"Does it?" I looked between them, feeling stupid. "What is it?"

"LSD," said Alison.

I drew in my breath. Partially because it *did* explain a lot. I hadn't been able to understand how anyone with such a precise, mathematical mind as the killer could also draw stuff that was so disturbing. But a mathematician who was tripping on LSD...that would make sense.

Mainly, though, I was relieved because that proved once and for all that the killer wasn't my brother. We'd both known kids at college who took acid, claiming it "opened their minds," but we'd been drilled too heavily as kids on how fragile our minds were. No way would he ever do drugs.

"Okay," called one of the paramedics. "We're ready to move her."

They began to lift the stretcher. Alison, who'd been searching the scene beside them, jumped up and stepped back out of the way—

It seemed to happen in slow motion. Her foot came down on a loose piece of debris, she stumbled, fell backwards—

I saw what was going to happen. "*No!*" I screamed.

Alison hit the tunnel wall, slid down it and landed heavily on her ass. She sat there stunned for a second. Then she looked behind her at the wall and her face fell as she realized what she'd done.

She panicked and her hands went back towards the wall to try to push herself up. "No!" yelled Calahan. "Don't move!"

She froze, her face pale. Meanwhile, the paramedics lifted the stretcher and hurried Clara off to the hospital.

Calahan ran over to Alison and I arrived a few seconds later. Calahan held out his hand. "We'll do it in one move," he told her. He was trying to keep his voice level but I could hear the fear and so could Alison. She nodded, eyes huge, and took his hand. With one big heave, he pulled her to her feet....

I stared at the wall. Where she'd fallen, a patch of equations a few feet square had been reduced to a smeared mess. Alison clapped her hand to her mouth as if she was going to be sick. I knew how she felt.

"Yolanda," said Calahan shakily, "which equations were those?"

"The location for the final killing," I said in a small voice. "There's no way to work out where it's going to be."

39

YOLANDA

T HE OTHER FBI agents gathered around Alison, reassuring her that it was an accident, that it wasn't her fault. But she just shook her head, inconsolable.

Calahan turned to me. "If we can't figure out where," he said, "can we at least figure out when?"

I nodded. The time equations were still intact and I had a good handle on them, now, after having figured them out twice before. But the tunnel wasn't the easiest place to concentrate, filthy and claustrophobic and the equations were only lit by my shaking flashlight beam. The walls made every tiny sound echo and everyone was talking at once.

"Everybody shut up!" yelled Calahan. "Let her think!"

They all went silent. I flushed at suddenly being the center of attention. But to my surprise, there were no sneering faces and no one rolled their eyes. They were looking at me with respect. I was one of the team, now.

I read through the equations and then went deep...and soon, I had the answer. "Tomorrow morning. Ten thirty-one a.m."

We all looked at each other, worried. We had less than a day to stop the last killing.

"What about the *who?*" asked Calahan. "If we can figure that out, we can protect them."

I began to search the equations. I was getting a feel for how the killer's mind worked, now, so I could go faster than before. And I was focused: I knew how important this was.

But the longer I worked at it, following the twisting, spiraling paths of equations, the more I felt myself being drawn in. The rest of the tunnel, Alison, even Calahan, all faded away until it was just me and the numbers. Normally, that's heaven. But this was unsettling, like the difference between swimming in warm, blue water where you can look down and see the bottom, and suddenly realizing you're out of your depth, far from shore, and you're not sure you have the strength to swim back.

Someone touched my arm and it felt...*distant*. Like my mind had slipped right out of my body. I focused on the sensation and groped my way back to the surface, which took a frighteningly long time. Then, with a sudden lurch, I was back in my chair, blinking at Calahan.

He was kneeling in front of me, face taut with worry. "Are you okay?"

My mouth didn't seem to work, yet. Almost as if I was getting used to having one, again. "Wha?"

He leaned closer. "You went quiet. You didn't move. *For over two hours.*"

That was the longest I'd been deep in a long time. What was more worrying was that I hadn't had any sense of time. If he hadn't pulled me out, how long would I have been in there?

Would I have come back at all?

I shook it off. Compared to what Clara had been through, this was nothing. We had to catch this guy: the risk to me was acceptable. And I'd found something, while I was in there. "The equations give a phrase," I told Calahan. "*Veiled one.*"

"A bride," he said immediately. "He's going to kidnap some woman getting married."

"That doesn't narrow it down much," said Carrie. She must have arrived while I was deep. "You know how many weddings there are every day in New York?"

I frowned. "It doesn't feel right. Brides aren't *special,* not in the way this guy wants."

"Lots of tradition and folklore to do with weddings," countered Calahan. "Not seeing the groom before the day, all that stuff. Might be to do with her being a virgin, being pure."

"Or it could be a woman in mourning, at a funeral," said Alison.

Carrie cursed under her breath. "We're talking about hundreds of women. We can't protect all of them."

I nodded, thinking. Neither answer felt right, to me. The other killings had all been people of power, born special.

Born special.

"Shit," I said aloud. Everyone looked at me.

"You got something?" asked Calahan.

"Maybe," I said uncertainly. I pulled out my phone and hesitated. I knew exactly who I had to call, to see if I was right. I just didn't want to do it.

Carrie, Alison and Calahan all looked at me, waiting.

I sighed...and dialed.

She answered on the third ring and the way she said my name, joyful and hopeful, made me screw my eyes shut and hang my head. I felt like the worst daughter in the world. "Hi, mom."

"You sound different," my mom said immediately. "Better."

Right then, down in the dark, surrounded by blood and too close to the killer's warped mind, I didn't feel good. I felt awful. But then I looked up and saw Calahan. He took my hand in his big, warm one and—I *did* feel better. Hell with Calahan was better than sitting in my apartment without him. "Yeah," I said to my mom. "I'm...doing okay."

We talked and it was so much easier than I'd been expecting. She didn't try to convince me to go back to Oregon. We even sketched out plans for her to come to New York. Whatever change she sensed in me, it was making her less worried about me, in a good way.

I squeezed Calahan's hand.

"Look," I said. "I need to ask you something. It's kind of weird.

Back when you were a midwife...didn't you tell me you'd once delivered a baby with, like, something over its face?"

"A caul," she said immediately. "Mr. and Mrs. Penning's son." I swear, my mom remembers every birth. "It's like a film. It's part of the amniotic sac."

"And didn't there used to be a superstition," I asked, "that babies born like that were special?"

"Oh goodness, yes. There are all sorts of legends."

I had to ask carefully: I didn't want to lead her, or put ideas in her head. "And wasn't there some other name for it, aside from *caul?*"

I prayed that I was wrong.

"A veil," said my mom. "They used to call it a veil."

I managed to thank her and end the call. But then my chest closed up so tight in fear that I could barely speak.

"Yolanda?" asked Calahan. "Tell us."

"A kid," I choked out. "He's going after a kid."

40

YOLANDA

IT WAS TOO MUCH. Everything I'd seen, Clara and the void and being deep for so long and now...my mind rebelled and locked up. Not a *kid*. Not a little kid, taken and *bled* and—

Calahan bent and cupped my cheeks in his hands. "Hey," he said. But I just stared through him, seconds from going into full-on panic. "*Hey!* Look at me. *Look at me!*"

I focused on him.

"Nothing," he said, "is going to happen to that kid." There was an iron in his voice I'd never heard before, a will that went way beyond his usual stubborn need for justice. He wasn't fucking around. That child was under his protection. I nodded.

"Let's think," he said. "How would he find a baby born with a caul?"

"Midwives," I said. "Midwives would remember something like that. He'd ask them."

Calahan rubbed at his stubble. "So he'd go to the hospitals. Starting with the biggest one. Let's go!"

We hurried back down the tunnel, up onto the platform and through the subway station. We rode the elevator up to street level, emerged onto the street and—

I cried out as a million camera flashes hit me at once, blinding me. Before I could stop, I'd rolled into a sea of reporters, all shoving mics under my nose and yelling questions at me.

"Are you working with the FBI?"

"How many bodies are down there?"

"We have reports of symbols on the walls. Is this a satanic cult?"

They pushed in on all sides, towering over me, blocking out the daylight. I tried to find a way through but it was a solid mass of people and, from low down, I couldn't see the edge. I backed up but my wheels hit a curb hidden by the crowd and I nearly flipped over. I clutched at the chair's arms, my breathing going tight.

And then someone came crashing through the crowd from behind me, knocking reporters aside like skittles. "*Get back! Get away from her!*" He broke through the final few and I saw Calahan's furious face. "*FBI!*" he yelled. "Clear a *goddamn* path and let her through!" He glanced down at me as he passed: *you okay?*

I nodded mutely.

He stepped around me and then walked ahead, opening up a path for me with glares and shoves. We were almost through when a reporter pushed in front of me, filming me with a handheld camera. "Is it true the FBI was searching the shopping mall while the murder was happening here? *Did you get it wrong?*"

The guilt washed over me like ice water. I just sat there gawping at the camera, unable to escape.

Suddenly, the reporter rose into the air. He panicked, looking down at his feet in disbelief as they left the ground. Then he was tossed aside and landed sprawling on the sidewalk. The whole crowd went silent.

"I *said,* get away from her!" said Calahan in a dangerously quiet voice.

There was a silent explosion of warmth in my chest. I'd never felt so protected.

Calahan marched ahead of me, clearing a path, and a few seconds later we were free of them. The reporter he'd thrown got to his feet. "That's assault! I'll sue the FBI! *I'll see you fired, asshole!*"

"Get in line," muttered Calahan, and led me towards my car.

41

CALAHAN

I SPENT the first few minutes of the journey silently raging. How *dare* they? How dare they scare her like that? Every time we stopped at a stop light, I looked across at her and had to resist the urge to pull her into my lap, wrap her in my arms, and just keep her safe from everything. Between the crowd and that prick's accusation, they'd really shaken her up. She was still breathing too fast and her eyes were too wide, staring determinedly at the street ahead, one step from tears.

"Hey," I said the next time we stopped. I waited until she looked at me. "You didn't get it wrong," I said firmly. "You figured it out in time to save Clara's life. No one else could do what you're doing. You're the smartest person I've ever met."

She flushed and looked back at the stop light. She still wasn't good with compliments but her breathing slowed a little.

"Now let's stop this son-of-a-bitch," I said. "Okay?" I covered her hand on the steering wheel and squeezed.

She nodded.

A few minutes later, we were at New York Presbyterian, the biggest hospital in the city. Someone showed us to the right department and I marched in—

And stopped.

I'd been so focused on getting there, I hadn't really stopped to think about what an obstetrics department would be like. There were babies *everywhere*: moms in bathrobes carrying them carefully, premature babies wriggling weakly as they were transported in their little heated greenhouses, and, on the other side of a big pane of glass, rows and rows of babies in the nursery in babygros and little hats.

And Yolanda was staring at them, transfixed, as silent tears shone in her eyes.

I suddenly remembered Central Park. *Aw hell.* I had to make this fast and get her out of there.

I grabbed the nearest midwife, flashed my badge and asked her to round up all her colleagues. Then I addressed the group. "I'm Special Agent Calahan with the FBI. We need to know if anyone's been in here asking questions about babies born with cauls."

The midwives all looked at each other and then hustled a short woman in her sixties to the front. "There *was* a man," she said nervously. "I spoke to him last week. A reporter from the New York Times." She looked worried. "I mean, he *said* he was a reporter—"

"Can you describe him?" asked Yolanda sharply.

The midwife gave a description that sounded a lot like the previous glimpses people had gotten of the killer: a lean man in his twenties with long dark hair.

"His eyes," said Yolanda urgently. "What color were his eyes?"

The woman shook her head. "I'm sorry, I don't remember."

I frowned. Why was Yolanda so focused on what the killer looked like? "What did you tell him?" I asked.

The woman was twisting her hands together guiltily. "We get caul births occasionally but I told him I only knew of one case where I still remembered the name. The boy's five, now, and he goes to the same school as my grandson, that's why I know it." Her face crumpled. "Oh God, did I—Is he in danger?" She looked between Yolanda and me, devastated. I got it. Her whole job was to bring children into the world. The thought that she might have put one in harm's way....

Yolanda wheeled herself forward and took the woman's hands. "It's going to be okay. We'll make sure he stays safe. We just need the name and the name of the school."

I looked on, amazed. I couldn't believe how much Yolanda had grown from the isolated, prickly woman I'd first met.

"Harry Brammer," stammered the midwife. "And the school is Central Park West One, Manhattan Avenue."

Yolanda patted the woman on the arm in thanks. Then she spun around and shot towards the parking lot with me close behind her.

42

YOLANDA

W E SPED through the streets. I could push it up to sixty when we hit a clear stretch but this was daytime in Manhattan and clear stretches were hard to find. Most of the time, we were crawling through traffic and both of us could feel the tension. We'd got to Clara too late to prevent her being kidnapped. We couldn't let that happen again, not to a five year-old kid. "I want a light," I muttered.

"What?"

"I want a red flashing light and a siren," I said. "Can't we get me one of those?" Then I leaned on the horn as someone pulled out ahead of me. "Get out of the way!"

"Why'd you ask about his eyes?" asked Calahan.

Shit. I kept my eyes straight ahead. "Just thought it might help. Every detail's important, right?"

"And at the shopping mall, when Alison said she wished we knew what he looked like, you looked worried. What's going on?"

Damn him. He didn't miss a thing. I stayed quiet.

"Yolanda, do you know something? Do you have a suspicion? Some mathematician you went to college with? A professor?"

I sat there turning it over and over in my head. It *couldn't* be him.

Even if he'd somehow survived the bridge, my brother was no killer. He'd never been into superstitions and magic and he'd never take LSD. Yes, he could have grown his hair long and that would make him fit the description but there were millions of dark-haired men in their twenties. The only real piece of evidence I had was the candy wrapper and that was laughably flimsy.

I could feel Calahan's eyes burning into me. I didn't dare look at him because I know I'd wilt under that gaze.

I couldn't tell him. It was crazy, it probably meant *I* was crazy. He'd lose all faith in me. And saying it out loud: *what if my brother is alive...*that would make the idea real. I was just starting to heal from his death: this would rip the wound wide open again. When it turned out I was wrong, it would be like losing him all over again. And I *had* to be wrong because Josh would never do something like this.

"No," I said. "I don't know anything."

It was a long time before I felt his eyes leave me. And when I finally dared to glance across at him, he was scowling out of the window. My stomach knotted. He knew I was lying and it was driving a wedge between us.

A few moments later, I pulled up outside the school. Calahan waited for me to get the chair out of the back but I waved him on. "Go, go!" He nodded and ran. Both of us remembered the NYPD getting to Clara too late. For all we knew, the killer was in there now, spiriting the kid away.

When I caught up to Calahan, he was leaning against the visitor's window, trying to stay calm while he talked to the woman inside. "Harry *Brammer,*" he told her, for what sounded like the third time.

"And what class is he in?" asked the woman.

"I don't *know* what class he's in!"

The woman peered at her screen. "Blake, Bosco...*Brammer.* Got him. Let me just check where he is...."

I reached up and curled my fingers around Calahan's, feeling ill. We were too late again. *You just missed him. A man who said he was his father took him for a dentist appointment—*

"Classroom 16A," the woman announced. "Geography."

Both of us stared at her in disbelief. "He's *here?*" asked Calahan. "For sure?"

The woman looked between us, bemused. "I can have him brought out to you, if it's important."

Calahan just *slumped,* his head dropping as he gave an amazed, exhausted chuckle. I grabbed his jacket and turned him to me, then threw my arms around him. He leaned down, pulling me to him and almost lifting me out of the chair. The relief was like a drug. I felt shaky and lightheaded. We'd done it. Finally, *finally,* we were ahead of the killer. We'd be able to keep the kid safe.

Ten minutes later, Calahan was embroiled in a full-on shouting match with Harry's teacher, the principal, and the vice principal. They wanted to keep Harry in school until his parents got there. Calahan wanted to take him to the FBI building now, to make sure he was safe. Neither side was giving an inch.

And me? I was somewhere I never thought I'd be.

I was babysitting the kid.

The two of us were sitting outside the principal's office like we'd been caught cutting class. Harry had a mop of sandy hair that no comb could tame, too many freckles to count and big, solemn gray eyes. I hadn't spent much time around kids but he seemed small, for five. He swung his legs like pendulums, his feet not touching the floor.

"Am I in trouble?" he asked at last.

"No." I said firmly. "Not at all. We're just here to make sure nothing happens to you."

"Why would something happen to me?"

Crap. Hurry up, Calahan. I was no good with kids. "There's a man, a bad man, who might try to hurt you. But *we're not going to let that happen.* I promise."

He nodded. Then, "Because I'm small?"

I stared at him, completely thrown. "What?"

He shrugged. "Is that why he wants to hurt me? Kids pick on me because I'm small."

"Yeah, well...people can be assholes." Then I winced. "Forget I said that last word."

He looked at my wheelchair. "What happened to you?"

"That's—" I bit back my instinctive response. "Some really heavy stuff fell on my legs and now they don't work anymore."

"Oh. That sucks."

I liked this kid.

Calahan marched out of the principal's office. "Let's go," he said. 'Harry, we're going to take you somewhere safe."

The principal was shaking her head. "Agent Calahan, I'd really rather wait for Harry's parents—"

Harry's face fell. "You're taking me somewhere? No! I want to wait for my mom!"

I pulled Calahan aside. "Maybe we *should* wait."

He glared at me, exasperated. "You, too? What's the matter with you? This place isn't secure! What if the killer comes in here with a gun and starts shooting? What if he pulls the fire alarm and grabs the kid from the yard while they're evacuating? We're taking him to the FBI. It's the only place we can guarantee he'll be safe."

I could hear that iron in his voice again, like I had in the tunnel. *It's the kid,* I realized. Kids in danger put Calahan into full-on daddy bear mode. I bit my lip, going a little melty inside. *He'd make a wonderful dad...*and then my stomach lurched as that thought reached its conclusion. *He just needs to find someone who can give him that.*

I blinked furiously and glared at the ceiling. I'd been a mess ever since I saw all those babies. *Focus, Yolanda!* One thing was for sure: arguing with Calahan, when he was in this mood, wouldn't do any good. He was going to protect this kid no matter what.

I took a deep breath. "Okay, fine." I went back to Harry, whose lip was starting to wobble. "Harry, this is Agent Calahan," I said, pointing. "FBI."

Harry looked at him, then whispered to me. "Is he really an FBI agent? He looks kind of a mess."

Calahan scowled and rubbed at his stubble.

"I promise you he's real. He has a badge and a gun and

everything," I said. "He's with me and he's really okay when you get to know him. We're going to take you to the FBI building. Trust me, it's pretty cool."

Harry looked uncertainly between us. "Okay," he mumbled at last.

With the principal still muttering that she wasn't sure about this, we got Harry strapped into the back seat of my car. Calahan let out a long sigh of relief as we pulled away. A moment later, he muttered, "Thanks."

I nodded.

Calahan glanced at Harry in the rear-view mirror. "You're good with him."

I looked at him in shock. I could see in his eyes that it wasn't a throwaway comment. He was telling me he'd noticed there was something going on with me. He could see I'd been freaked out at the hospital. I looked away, embarrassed, focusing on the road ahead.

Calahan gently slid his hand over mine on the steering wheel and squeezed.

"Are you two in love?" asked Harry from the back seat.

That made me flush. Calahan and I looked at each other.

There was a deafening bang as a truck rammed into our car.

43

YOLANDA

I MUST HAVE blacked out for a second. When I came to, everything was wrong. I was leaning on Calahan so hard that my seatbelt was cutting into me painfully, but when I tried to straighten up, it felt like I weighed a thousand tons. There was a huge white balloon pressing against my head and neck and my face was wet, even though it wasn't raining.

It took me a while to figure out that the car was on its side, and I was slumped in my seat, hanging down towards Calahan, who seemed to be unconscious. The side airbag had gone off, probably saving my life.

I twisted around and looked right into Harry's tearful, terrified face. "Are you okay?"

He nodded. *Thank God.* Then, "You're all...." Harry pointed to his face. "Blood."

Now I knew what the wetness was. "It looks worse than it is," I told him, and hoped that was true. "Just hold on, it'll be okay."

I turned back to the front and checked on Calahan. He was stirring and mumbling but he wasn't making much sense. There was blood on his head: he could be concussed. I tried to remember what happened. *This is all my fault,* I realized with a sickening lurch. We'd been distracted, Calahan had touched my hand, I looked at him.... I must have not seen the truck.

Movement in the wing mirror caught my eye. Someone was approaching from behind, maybe a cop or a passer-by. I struggled to see—

Not a cop. The mirror was cracked but I could make out a man in jeans and a leather jacket with long, dark hair, walking purposefully towards our car.

It hadn't been an accident.

Oh God. Oh no. "Calahan!" I shouted. "Wake up!"

Mumblings and groans. He was out of action. And even if he could help, I was on top of him. He couldn't get out until I moved. It was up to me.

The man had almost reached the car. I frantically unfastened my seatbelt and almost went slithering down into Calahan's lap. I had to cling onto the steering wheel just to stay in place.

My door swung open. The sun was right overhead and it blasted down into my face: all I could see was a silhouette as the man reached behind me, over my wheelchair, to Harry in the rear seat. "No!" I yelled. "No! Don't you touch him! Harry! Don't go with him!"

Harry was screaming and kicking, terrified. I heard his seatbelt come free. Then the man was hauling him out of the car. "No!" I yelled. "No!"

I got one hand, then the other up onto the door sill and heaved myself up onto the side of the car, like lifting myself out of a swimming pool. The car rocked unsteadily as I dragged myself up and made a grab for the man. But he was already out of reach, walking away with the struggling Harry in his arms.

"Yo—YOLANDA!" screamed Harry.

I dragged myself along the car, reaching uselessly after them. I was sobbing, tears stinging where they ran into the cuts on my face. *Just make my legs work this once,* I thought desperately. *Just let me walk for thirty seconds. That's all I ask. Please!* But my legs stayed useless, dead weights. And the man was getting farther and farther away, heading for a parked car. "Calahan!" I yelled in desperation.

There was a groan and a lot of cursing from inside the car.

My vision was blurring with tears but I could see the man struggling to open the car door while keeping hold of the wriggling child. "Calahan, *he's here! He's got Harry!*"

There was a *thump* and the sound of cracking glass. Another *thump*. Then the whole windshield broke free of the car and went skidding along the street. Calahan climbed out through the hole, cursing up a storm. He got to his feet and started stumbling towards the man, taking two steps right for every one forward, clearly concussed. He pulled his gun and aimed it, the barrel swaying drunkenly.

"*No!*" I yelled in panic. "No! You might hit Harry!"

Calahan grimaced but didn't fire. He started running towards the man, still staggering. But by now they were in the car—

When he was still six feet away, the car started up and roared away. Calahan chased it for a few more steps and then fell to his knees.

We'd lost them.

44

YOLANDA

I SAT in my wheelchair with a gauze pad held to my forehead, watching the chaos around me. FBI agents were going over the truck the killer had used to ram us, hoping to find a clue. The school principal was giving a statement to another pair of FBI agents. A tow truck was in the process of righting my car. And right in front of me, Carrie was listening as Calahan gave his side of things.

"I'll take the heat," he said as he finished. "You can make it clear that I was acting on my own. Hell, tell them I ran it past you and you told me not to do it, if it helps."

Carrie sighed and looked around at the scene. The principal was giving all of us an evil glare. "No," she said. "That wouldn't be right. It was the wrong call but it wasn't a dumb one. I'll support you. But I'm not sure I can save you. I'm not sure I can even save myself."

I listened, stunned that she was willing to put her neck on the line for Calahan. My boss at the security firm would never have done that for me.

Carrie went off to try to smooth things over with the principal. Calahan sat down on the step of an ambulance, next to me. "I should have listened to you," he said.

"You were just trying to protect Harry."

But Calahan just sighed. I understood how he felt. We'd delivered Harry right into the killer's hands. Whatever happened to him now, it was on us.

There was a crash from down the street. The tow truck had just succeeded in pulling my car back onto its wheels. It was a write-off, one side caved in as if punched by a giant. It was a miracle we'd all survived.

"How's your head?" I asked.

He touched the lump on his scalp and winced. "I've had worse. How's the face?" He reached for my gauze pad.

I flinched away. "I'm fine."

"You're *not* fine. Let me see."

This time, I let him remove the gauze from my forehead. He kept his face carefully neutral.

"Bad?" I asked.

"You'll have a scar," he said breezily. "But just a little one. Under your hair." He climbed up into the ambulance, talked with a paramedic, and came back with cotton wool and water. "We need to clean you up."

I explored my cheek with my fingers and realized the gash on my head had bled a lot: that whole side of my face was caked in dried blood. "I look that bad, huh?"

It was just meant to be a quip, but Calahan caught my eye and gave me a look. *No. Never.* I flushed and sat there obediently while he slowly cleaned my face. I knew it wasn't about getting the blood off me. It was about being quietly together, just for a few minutes, before he got called away again.

Carrie returned. "We found the car a few streets away. It was stolen, as was the truck. We have an APB out for a man and a boy but I'm not hopeful. They could be anywhere in the city by now."

She looked at me. "You're our best hope, now. Go do what you do."

My heart sank. With the location equations wiped away, I had nothing to go on. If I was their best hope, we were screwed. But I nodded. "Yes ma'am." I hadn't planned on calling her that. It just slipped out. But it felt right. I looked at Calahan. "What are you going to do?"

He pushed himself up to standing. "I'm going to see Harry's parents," he said. "And tell them how I lost their kid."

He walked off. I went to call after him but then stopped: there was nothing I could say. All I could do was try to catch the killer before he hurt Harry.

An FBI agent dropped me at my apartment. I wheeled myself over to my chalkboards and took stock. *What now?*

We knew the *who* and the *when* of the next killing: Harry, 10:31 tomorrow morning. But I couldn't solve the equations for *where* because Alison had accidentally destroyed them. There was no math for me to work with.

I sat there despondent for a few minutes. Then I caught sight of my reflection in the window and scowled at myself, just like Calahan would. *Get a fucking grip,* I told myself. So what if things had gone wrong? There was a five year-old out there, scared out of his mind, and his only chance was me. I wasn't just a mathematician, I was a hacker. How would the hacker part of me approach this? If it was a tech problem, if there was a missing piece I didn't have...I'd reverse engineer it.

I sat bolt upright. That was it. I had to recreate the equations we'd lost. Instead of just solving them, I had to write them.

I had to put myself in the killer's mind. I had to think like he thought.

The idea made my insides turn cold. Just working with this stuff was scary enough. Creating it myself would mean going even deeper into that bottomless black. What if I couldn't get back?

I checked the time. It was almost four in the afternoon. Harry would die tomorrow morning. I was the only chance he had.

I went to work.

45

CALAHAN

I KNOCKED, but she didn't answer the door.

I was exhausted, emotionally and physically beat. I'd spent almost an hour with Harry's parents, explaining what had happened. The worst part was, they hadn't gotten mad. I'd been ready for anger. I actually would have welcomed it. God knows I deserved it. But instead, when I told them how I'd lost their son, they just...collapsed. Their faces crumpled, their shoulders dropped and they fell into each other's arms. I'd done that to them. Me.

I told them the FBI was using every resource to find their son. And then I went back to the office and worked with the other agents for the rest of the day and into the night, chasing every scrap of a lead we had. But the killer and Harry had disappeared. I'd tried to check in with Yolanda, but she wasn't answering her phone. Now, it was past eleven at night and I'd come to her apartment to check in with her. But she wasn't answering her door, either.

I knocked again. And again, really hammering, this time. Then I cursed and stepped back from the door, preparing to kick it—

The door swung open. But the Yolanda who answered wasn't the one I knew.

Her silky black hair had turned flat and greasy, as if she'd been running her fingers through it for hours. Her normally pale skin looked gray and there were dark circles under her eyes. But the worst part was her eyes. They were normally so lush and green, so calming. Now, the color seemed to have drained away and they stared right through me. *What the hell happened to her?* I'd seen her less than eight hours ago, but she looked like she'd been gone for weeks.

She mumbled something unintelligible and wheeled herself deeper into the apartment. The wheels crunched over sheets of paper, all of them filled with scribbled equations. And the paper got deeper as we went, drifting like snow: in the main room, it was over my ankles. More hung from the ceiling and walls, the sheets taped together in long lengths. And twisting across them were the black tentacles I remembered from the first crime scene, hundreds of tiny equations making up the shape.

By the time I'd finished looking, she was back to working. She bent low over her lap, scribbling equations on a piece of paper, her hand moving eerily, unnaturally fast.

"Yolanda?"

She didn't look up, didn't say hello.

"Yolanda?" Nothing. She'd only answered the door because my knocking had gotten too distracting. Now I'd stopped, I was irrelevant.

"*Yolanda?*" I reached out and touched her shoulder. She jerked so violently, the wheelchair almost tipped over and I had to grab the armrests to steady it. Her eyes snapped wide in panic and she flattened herself against the backrest like a cat in a thunderstorm.

"It's okay! It's okay, it's *me!*" By the last word, my voice was raw with desperation. The lack of recognition in her eyes was terrifying. We stayed there staring at each other for two seconds, three—

And then the color seemed to come back to her eyes. She blinked, nodded, and mumbled something I couldn't hear, then turned away from me and wheeled herself over to the kitchen counter.

I followed. "What's going on? Are you okay?"

She began making coffee. But it felt...wrong. Normally, she was so quick and deft that I had trouble following her. Now, she stared at each item for a second before she picked it up, as if she couldn't quite remember how this world worked. And when she tried to scoop the grounds, her hands were clumsy and shaky. As if she was still getting used to having a body again.

I'd never seen anything so disturbing. "What have you been *doing*? What is all this?"

She started to speak but had to stop and work her lips before she could form syllables. "We don't have the equations. So I have to recreate them. I have to do what he did, think like he does."

I looked around in horror. She'd taken her mind to that place where the killer lived, where black magic, theoretical physics and complex math all combined. "When I came in, you were *gone*."

She shrugged. "I was deep. You've seen that before."

"No. No, this was different, *you* were different. You answered the door, but it wasn't you. You didn't recognize me. It was like you were sleepwalking."

She rubbed her eyes. "How long since the car crash?"

"Eight hours."

That got her attention. For the first time, she took a proper look around the apartment. I don't think she believed me until she looked out of the window and realized it was night. "Jesus," she muttered.

I knelt down next to her. "I'm worried about you," I said, looking her in the eye.

"I'm fine." She lifted the end of one of the dangling paper streamers and looked at it. Then she cursed and ripped it down. "I need to get back to work." She turned away.

"What? No!" I grabbed her shoulder and turned her back to me. "I don't think you should go deep again. Not into this stuff. This isn't good for you." I was thinking back to what she'd told me about how fragile minds like hers were. I was no psychologist but the way she'd been a few minutes ago: absent, disassociated, whatever you want to call it...that couldn't be good, for someone like her.

"Calahan," she said. "We have less than *twelve hours!* I need to go deep. I need to go *deeper!*" She grabbed another streamer of paper and ripped it down. "It isn't working! I can recreate the parts of his equations but not the whole thing. I can't see how it all links together, I can't see the...the—"

She pointed helplessly at the ceiling. Where all the equation tentacles she'd drawn would join, a *body,* the heart of it all. There was just a blank space.

"You need a break," I said firmly. And I took the pen from between her fingers. She made a grab for it but I was too fast. "Just sit there," I told her.

She sighed. "Like I have a choice," she said darkly.

That made me smile in relief. There was a little of the old Yolanda still in there. I raided her kitchen cupboards and found noodles, vegetables and enough ingredients to make a sauce. I started chopping.

She wheeled herself closer. "You can cook?" she asked in amazement.

"I have hidden depths." I poured her a big glass of water. "Drink that."

She glugged it down and then stared at the empty glass. "Didn't even realize I was thirsty."

"I bet you haven't drunk anything in eight hours." I threw everything into her wok and started pushing it around. The scent of sesame seeds and five spice filled the room.

She winced, remembering something "Crap. I'm sorry. How did it go with Harry's parents?"

"They're in pieces," I said.

"And you?"

"The FBI's launching an investigation into my handling of things." I tried to shrug it off. "Not my first time." I tipped the noodles and vegetables into a bowl and pushed it towards her. "Eat. No arguments."

She reluctantly picked up some chopsticks. But once she'd started eating, she didn't stop until the bowl was empty. "Thank you," she said. "Okay, I *do* feel better, I admit it."

I smiled at her and she smiled back. But then she held out her hand for her pen. "Now I need to get back to it."

I looked at her, worried. Some color had returned to her face and her eyes were a little brighter. I turned her pen over and over in my fingers.

Her smile disappeared. "Come on, this was the deal." She reminded me, just a little, of a junkie. She *wanted* to be working. Needed it.

"I don't want you going in there again," I said.

She huffed in frustration. "'*In there?*'" She tried to brazen it out. "Ultimately, however weird it is, it's just math. It can't hurt me."

"It's *not* just math and you know it!" I was getting angry, now.

She crossed her arms. "You said you didn't believe in magic."

"I don't. But thinking like the killer thinks, going to that place in your head...I think it's dangerous." I sighed. I took hold of her shoulders and when I felt that gorgeous, smooth skin against my fingers, all the anger went out of me. My voice softened but my grip on her shoulders tightened protectively. "And I don't want anything to happen to you."

We looked into each other's eyes and both of us relaxed a little, climbing down. She leaned forward and touched her forehead to mine. God...this was still our *first day* together. It seemed like weeks ago that we'd finally kissed, finally had sex, but that was only last night. Today should have been all about getting to know her better, spending time together. Instead, we'd been through hell.

I gently pushed back and laid a soft kiss on her lips. She gave a little groan of need and slipped her arms around my neck. I teased her lips with my tongue, exploring her, and she relaxed into it, her body molding to mine. It wasn't urgent and primal, like the night before. It was tender and caring. *This* is what we'd both been needing all day: each other.

A voice in my head screamed that I didn't deserve this, that she'd hate me if she knew the truth.

I wrestled it down and managed to silence it. For now.

When she broke the kiss, her anger was gone but her eyes were big with worry. "Sam, we don't have a choice. Harry's going to die tomorrow morning." Her eyes went to the sea of paper on the floor. "Even if it isn't good for me, I have to do this."

I sighed and rubbed at my stubble. But however hard I thought, I couldn't come up with another plan. She was the only chance we had. And even though every cell in my body was screaming at me to protect her, I knew she'd never forgive herself if Harry died. "Okay," I said at last. "But I'll stay here with you. I'll make sure you take breaks. Water. Food. Coffee. Make sure you don't go *too* deep."

She nodded, relieved, and held out her hand. "Deal." We shook on it. And then kissed again.

I gave her her pen back. She found a fresh pad of paper. And my phone rang.

It was the hospital. I'd asked them to call me if there was any change in Clara's condition. She'd just woken up.

"Go," said Yolanda as soon as I told her.

I hesitated, uncertain. I really didn't want to leave her alone again. But if Clara could give us a lead on the killer, we might not even need the math anymore. We might be able to pick up the killer right now, save Harry, and end this whole thing.

"Go," she said again. Was it me or...was there a part of her that seemed almost eager? As if she was desperate to submerge herself in the equations again...and not because of Harry?

"You promise you'll take breaks?" I said. "And not go as deep as you did before?"

She nodded.

I debated for another few seconds...then I kissed her one last time and ran.

46

YOLANDA

WHEN HE'D GONE, I just sat there staring at the door for a moment. I could still feel the touch of his lips on mine, the rasp of his stubble on my cheek. I thought about what he'd done, how he'd come to check on me, got me out of whatever weird, super-deep state I'd slipped into, *cooked* for me. He'd ignored my anger and rudeness, even put my safety ahead of the case. All while he was dealing with his own problems, like the FBI investigation into his conduct. If he was found at fault, it could be the end of his career and the FBI was Calahan's whole life. But he'd put all that aside to look after me. And that made me examine my own feelings.

I'd felt things for him since we first met. But I hadn't fully acknowledged how much things had changed...*deepened.* It wasn't just lust, anymore. It went beyond friends, beyond partners. When he wasn't around, it was like an ache, a need. When he smiled, it was like fireworks going off in my chest. When something was bothering him, I'd move mountains to fix it.

I was in—

My heart gave a big, bass-drum boom.

I swallowed. *That.*

And what troubled me was, *despite* that, there was part of me that was relieved he was gone because it meant I could get back to the equations.

That scared me. Really scared me. The killer's math was *wrong,* on a soul-deep level, but it called to me even more strongly now than when I'd first seen it. It was addictive.

I didn't want to go back in there. I was shaken by what it had already done to me. Calahan had been right, the only way to do this safely was with regular breaks. But he was gone. There'd be nobody to pull me out.

I debated. But really there was no argument at all. Harry was out there, somewhere.

I put my head down and started work. But less than an hour later, I surfaced with a yell of frustration. It was just like before: I could recreate the killer's strings of equations but I didn't understand what I was trying to do. It was like being fluent in a language but not knowing *what to write.*

I checked the time. It was almost one in the morning. In less than ten hours, Harry would be killed. I closed my eyes and I could see him wriggling in the killer's arms, screaming over his shoulder for me to help him.

I couldn't let him die. But I'd run out of ideas. How could I take the final step? How could I think more like the killer? How could I open my mind enough to see the big picture?

And then it hit me. There was one more thing I could try.

As soon as I thought of it, a chill crept up my arms and down my spine. I was already risking my mind, doing what I was doing now. If I did this, I'd stand a real chance of losing my sanity.

Harry's terrified wail echoed in my ears.

I called a cab.

47

YOLANDA

LESS THAN fifteen minutes later, I was wheeling myself through the doors of the FBI building. By now, people knew who I was and they knew how urgent the investigation was. It wasn't hard to convince them that I needed to check a piece of evidence that had been booked in earlier that day. Or, once I was down in the evidence lock-up with the box from the crime scene, to slip what I needed into my pocket.

As I thanked them and wheeled myself out of the room, my shoulders tensed, waiting for someone to yell, to grab me, to throw me in jail. But nothing happened. One thing about being in a wheelchair: no one ever suspects you.

I was heading for the elevator when a voice behind me called, "Yolanda?"

I spun around. *Alison.* The thing I'd slipped into my pocket felt like it was red hot and glowing through my clothes. *She's going to know....* "Hey," I said weakly.

She looked exhausted but determined. "We've been chasing up leads all day. No sign of Harry or the killer. Have you and Calahan got anything?"

Me and Calahan. If Calahan knew what I was about to do, he'd go ballistic. "Working on it," I muttered. She still intimidated the hell out of me. "I better get back to it."

I hurried on and was almost at the elevator when she called out to me again. "Yolanda!"

I stopped and turned around again. Alison caught up to me, opened her mouth...and then stopped, as if she didn't know what to say. I frowned. This wasn't like her at all.

"I'm sorry," said Alison, looking at the floor. "I know I screwed up."

She lifted her eyes to me and suddenly, I wasn't seeing the perfect, intimidating super-agent. I was seeing *her,* the woman behind the mask. And she was terrified. "If Harry dies..." she whispered.

I nodded quickly. I had no idea how to handle this. I'm not good with people: it had taken this long just for me to be halfway normal with Calahan. "It was an accident," I told her. "It could have happened to anyone." I reached out and hesitantly squeezed her arm.

She gave me a weak smile. God, this whole thing had really shaken her. I understood that she wasn't used to failing, but it was more than that....

For the first time, I wondered what it must be like to be a female agent. There were vastly more men than women, from what I'd seen. Maybe it meant working harder, being better. *Never* screwing up. And never showing weakness.

I stopped being intimidated and started feeling sorry for her.

"It's going to be okay," I heard myself say. "What I'm—What Calahan and I are doing, it'll work. We'll find Harry."

She nodded gratefully. Then, just as I was about to go, she grabbed my hand. "Calahan," she blurted.

I frowned and waited for more. But her lips had pressed together into a tight line: she couldn't find the words. Then I looked into her eyes and saw it: a deep, protective love.

Oh. *Oh!*

I flushed. I'd thought the suspicion I'd seen in her was from jealousy. I'd thought she held a candle for him. But no.

"He's like a big brother to me," managed Alison. "He believed in me, when I was coming up. One of the only people who did."

I nodded quickly, ashamed I'd got it so wrong.

"A lot of women have tried to get to know him, since Becky," said Alison. "But he hasn't gotten close to any of them. Not like he has with you. So I hope it works."

I swallowed and nodded, my cheeks going scarlet.

"But break his heart and I'll break your face, wheelchair or not. Okay?"

I nodded hard and we went our separate ways.

A cab ride later, I was back in my apartment. Only then did I finally dig in my pocket and bring out the little evidence bag. I held it up to the light, staring at the little LSD-soaked squares of blotting paper.

They scared the hell out of me. I knew how fragile my mind was. And mixing hallucinogens with the killer's disturbing blend of magic and math, plus very little sleep...it seemed like the perfect recipe to break me. But it was the only way I could think of to get in his head, to see things like he did. If I didn't do this, Harry was dead. Calahan and Alison would blame themselves and I knew I'd never forgive myself for not trying.

I stared at the blotting paper for three more breaths. And then, before I could change my mind, I grabbed one, put it on my tongue and swallowed it.

48

CALAHAN

THE HOSPITAL was a washout. It was a relief to see Clara awake and talking and the doctors said she was expected to make a full recovery. And Clara was eager to help, even though she was still weak. I questioned her for hours and it helped confirm a lot of things we'd only been able to guess at. Yes, the killer had jabbed a needle into her neck to dose her with something when he kidnapped her. Yes, she'd been kept semi-conscious while he drained her blood and yes, it had been almost painless, though terrifying. But she couldn't tell us anything useful about where she'd been kept and her description of his face was frustratingly vague. Blue or maybe green eyes, long dark hair, good looking. I thanked her and headed for the exit.

Alison called as I was stalking angrily down the hallway. She didn't have good news either, and was hoping I did. "Yolanda's working on the math," I told her. "That's our best lead." *Our only lead,* I added silently. Alison went quiet, which wasn't like her. "What?" I asked at last.

"She's nice," said Alison.

"Didn't think the two of you got on."

"Well, she's a freakin' genius. That's pretty intimidating. But I've got to know her a little, now." She hesitated. "She'd be good for you, Sam."

I didn't know what to say. "Uh-huh."

"I don't mean just sex, or short term. I mean she'd make you happy."

"Mmph."

"If you let her."

"Mm," I muttered.

"Sam," said Alison quietly. "You deserve to be happy."

I stopped, at that. I felt my arm tense up, ready to throw the phone. *No. No I don't.* That was what made it so hard. I'd never been drawn to anyone in the same way I was to Yolanda. But I couldn't be with her, not really *be* with her, as long as I kept my secret from her. And if I told her, I had no idea how she'd react. I imagined her face crumpling in disgust, in disappointment that I wasn't the hero she thought I was, and my chest closed up tight. I couldn't take that. Not from the woman I was falling—

I screwed my eyes shut. *Don't think that way.* I tried to change the subject. ""When did you suddenly become best friends, anyway?" I asked Alison.

"We had a talk, tonight."

I frowned. "*Tonight?*"

"She was here, at the office...maybe an hour ago?"

I froze. When I'd left Yolanda in her apartment, nothing had been more important to her than getting back to the equations. "What was she doing there?"

"Taking a look at some evidence, I think. She was coming out of the evidence lock-up when I saw her. Wait, you didn't send her?"

I didn't answer. My mind was racing. What the hell could she want in the evidence lock-up?

Then I got it. *Oh God. Oh no.*

I ended the call and ran for my car. Slapped the red light on the dashboard and roared off, siren wailing. And prayed I got there in time.

49

YOLANDA

A T FIRST, there was nothing. *Maybe it's defective. Maybe I'm immune.*

I closed my eyes, sat back in the chair and tried to go deep. It felt just how it always feels, like sinking into sun-warmed, glutinous mud, a comforting heaviness around my mind that blocks out the outside world. I sank down and down....

I waited impatiently for something to happen, for my mind to open and have some mystical revelation. *What if it doesn't work?* Harry would die. None of us would ever forgive ourselves. *Come on!*

And then I felt something. A coldness, spreading along the base of my spine, as if I was lying in bed and had knocked over a glass. I'd sunk all the way through the warm, comforting mud. And below me was a layer of icy water.

I let out a shuddering cry as I fell clear of the mud and the water closed around me. It was much thinner than the mud and I could feel myself falling faster and faster. The water didn't hug me the way the mud had: it felt distant and uncaring: I tried to grab onto it but it slipped between my fingers. And there was too much of it, I was at the center of a huge ocean with nothing for thousands of miles in any direction.

I plunged, the surface suddenly miles away.

Down and down, picking up speed. And then I burst through the bottom of the water and I was in a void. Not air, just *nothing,* a blackness, chillingly cold. It felt as if I was outside the world, outside time. I was behind the scenes of the universe, away from all the people and sunlight and laughter and children, all those *distractions* that stop people like me thinking. I could focus and when I did—

I could see. I could see how it *all worked.* I drew in a slow breath, exhilarated. Planets sweeping round in their orbits, quantum physics, exotic matter. Language, belief, religion, magic, all so *simple.* It was as if the cogs of my mind had been clogged with sand, all these years, and the perfect blackness had blown it all free. I could see the killer's plan, now, the spell I needed to reconstruct. I didn't know what it *did,* but I understood the mechanics and I started writing it down, my pen flying. *Why didn't I try this sooner?* It felt amazing, as if my IQ had just doubled. I loved it. I didn't want to stop.

And then the blackness moved.

It was so quick, it was gone before I fully saw it. Just a hint of something like a bat's wing. There was nothing for long moments. Then the floor shifted, becoming alive. It wasn't a floor, it was a million scurrying somethings with too many legs.

I wasn't surrounded by blackness. I was surrounded by things *made of* blackness. And they wanted me, wanted to touch me and own me, and crawl inside my brain. They told me how what happened in the world up there didn't matter. Only they mattered.

*Oh God...*my stomach knotted as I realized. This place allowed me to think because it removed me from the distractions. But the distractions were things I wanted, things I needed. Calahan, my friends, sunlight....

Children.

Down here, it was just me and the...*things.*

They were black against black so I could only glimpse them when they moved. A river of spiders scurrying up my ankles, up my legs, under my jeans. I opened my mouth to scream but my voice was choked off, twisting black tentacles cutting off my air, covering my eyes and ears, dragging me deeper into the black. *No! I want out! I want to go back!*

My mind strained for the surface, a part of it lunging upward while the rest was carried down, down, down. My mind stretched out thinner than a pencil line, thinner than a hair, thinner than an atom. It went *tight.*

No! I screamed against the darkness.

My mind snapped.

50

CALAHAN

I HAMMERED on the door of her apartment. "Yolanda? *Yolanda!*"
No answer. I put my ear to the door and listened, holding my breath.

A cry. A sob that got inside me and tightened like a fist around my heart. Back when I was starting out in the NYPD, we were called to a domestic dispute. We got there to find a drunk husband beating the hell out of his wife: there were literally dents in the drywall where he'd been slamming her against it. On the floor in the corner, their six year-old had been watching, hands clamped over her ears, unable to process the horror of watching daddy beat mummy. She'd made that exact same keening, *let me out of here* cry.

I cursed, took one pace back, and kicked the door down.

The apartment was in a mess, half of the lights off and even more paper strewn on the floor than before. *Where is she?* "Yolanda! Yolanda!" She'd gone quiet, as if she was hiding. Hiding from *me?* "Yolanda!"

Then my heart stopped. The wheelchair was on its side in the hallway. She must be so far gone, she'd tipped herself out of it and then crawled...*somewhere.* I searched frantically, checking the kitchen, the bedroom, behind her desk. Scared, hallucinating, she must have crawled somewhere, looking for safety, but where....?

Then my eyes fell on the elevator that went to the roof. I wanted to throw up. *Oh Jesus no, please. Not the roof.* It was dark and she was seeing things, what if she crawled right over the edge?

I'd taken one running step towards the elevator when I thought I heard something: a terrified little sob. I spun on the spot. I didn't hear it again but I've gotten good at homing in on sounds. It came from...*there,* down the hallway and—

I burst into her bedroom for the second time. Not behind the bed. Not under the bed. What if I was wrong? What if I was wasting time and she *was* on the roof? But I was sure I'd heard something.

I put my hand on the closet door. *Please, please, be in here—*

I pulled the door wide. Big green eyes blinked up at me. I drew in a shuddering gasp of relief.

She was sitting on the floor, hugging herself. I dropped to my knees. "It's okay," I told her. "It's okay, I'm here now."

I reached for her but she recoiled, her eyes going even wider and a throaty moan of horror rising from her chest. She flattened herself against the back wall of the closet, looking around for a way to slip past me and escape. I drew back, but in the second I'd managed to touch her, I'd felt her trembling. Not the momentary shudder of fear but a *shaking,* constant and uncontrollable, raw animal fear. "It's okay," I told her again. But she just shrank back even more.

I knelt there staring at her, desperate to help but with no idea how. It would have been scary to see anyone in that state, but when it was *Yolanda,* with her awe-inspiring brain, it was heartbreaking. "Please," I choked out. But there was no reaction except fear. The Yolanda I knew wasn't in there, or if she was, she was too far gone for me to reach. I was too late.

I remembered another night. Another woman. Kneeling over Becky's body, willing it not to be true. *This is my fault. It's my fault, again. I brought her onto this case. I got her involved, because I liked her.* "Yolanda, I'm sorry," I whispered. "Oh, God, I'm so sorry." *Her mind. Her most precious thing.* I'd destroyed it, just like I destroy everything.

I tried to take her hand but as soon as my fingers brushed hers, she jerked away. My stomach lurched: she felt waxy and cold, as if she wasn't in there, anymore. "Yolanda!" I said, my voice cracking. But she just shrank back: wherever she was, words were too much, too frightening. Of course: her head was full of those fucking equations. Letters, numbers, words: they all must seem like part of the same evil.

"Shh," I tried, forcing my voice to be gentle. "*Shhh!*"

I kept repeating it, calming her the way I would a terrified animal. I eventually managed to slip an arm around her and pull her gently to my chest but she still didn't surface. She just lay there trembling, staring at things I couldn't see.

I felt my eyes go hot. What if she was *gone?* What if I—what if *no one* could ever reach her again? What if thanks to me, the woman I loved was trapped in there forever? My heart felt like someone was slowly ripping it down the center. The tears started to roll down my cheeks. *Oh God, Yolanda....*

The thought of losing her made me realize how wrong I'd been. I'd been so convinced that I didn't deserve her, so scared that she'd hate me if she ever found out the truth, that I'd held back. I'd thought I couldn't be with her. I should have taken the chance and opened up because now it was too late...and the truth was, I couldn't be without her.

There was only one thing I could think of to comfort her: the folk song Becky had taught me, an ancient lullaby. The words were in Gaelic and I had no idea what they meant, but the tune made me think of a safe place with a crackling fire in the grate. *Home.*

Tears running down my cheeks, I sang.

51

YOLANDA

I'D STOPPED SCREAMING. I didn't dare open my mouth because the things that crawled and slithered and scuttled in the darkness might get into me. I could sense a huge creature beside me and it kept muttering dark incantations, making me shrink away. I prayed for death.

But then...there was a sound I recognized as coming from another world. One that I'd lived in, once, many years ago, a world with color and light. *Music.* And with it, a voice I recognized. It reached past all the monsters and plugged straight into my soul. I couldn't remember names or faces but I remembered feeling safe, around that voice. I clung onto it with both hands and all my heart and I felt it begin, very slowly, to lift me.

The monsters grabbed and pulled. The ones that had managed to get inside my head told me how I wasn't good enough, how he wouldn't want me, how *no one* would want me, anymore. But I clung even tighter to that slender thread of song and felt myself being hauled *up, up, up....*

The first thing I saw was a shirt, a little mussed and creased. *He's always rumpled.* And I sobbed because it was the most welcome sight I'd ever seen.

Gradually, my trembling stopped and the shapes around me solidified into walls and floors. I lifted my cheek from his tear-damp shirt and looked up at him.

His voice cracked and broke. "*Hey you,*" he managed.

I put both arms around him and hugged him very, very tight.

"Are you...okay?" I could hear the fear in his voice but I couldn't speak, yet. I nodded, firmly enough that he could feel it. "*You're okay,*" he exhaled. He crushed me to his chest. Then he pushed me back, hands gripping my forearms so hard it almost hurt. I had to blink a bunch of times before I could focus on him, but when I did, when I saw the look in his eyes, my heart lifted and swelled like a balloon. He was so overcome, he couldn't speak: his hands just squeezed at my arms. "*Don't ever do that again!*" he croaked.

I nodded weakly. I realized I could see, even though the lights were off in the bedroom. It was daylight outside!

He saw me looking at the window. "It's a quarter to ten," he said gently. "You were...wherever you were, for eight hours."

And from the look on his face, he'd been with me, trying to coax me home, for almost all of it. "Sorry," I rasped, shocked at how rough my voice sounded. I needed about eighteen gallons of water. My head was pounding and I felt like I might throw up if I so much as moved. "Eight hours," I echoed, then shuddered, remembering. "Felt like longer."

And then it hit home: I looked down at my empty hands: no pen, no pad of paper. "It didn't even work," I mumbled. I'd spent eight hours shaking in a closet like a coward. In less than an hour, Harry would be dead. We had nothing and it was all my fault. I wanted to weep, but I had no tears left.

Calahan pulled me back into his arms and hugged me tight. "You did everything you could," he said. His arms locked tight around my shoulders. "More than you should. More than was safe."

He retrieved my wheelchair and helped me into it. I headed for the bathroom, trying not to cry. My head felt like it was cracking open and my stomach was churning. I'd never even really had a hangover before, let alone an acid comedown.

I turned into the bathroom...and froze.

"Calahan?" I croaked. Then, louder, "Calahan?"

He burst in behind me, looking for the threat. Then he stopped, just as I had.

The white-tiled walls were covered in black marker pen. At some point during my trip, before Calahan had arrived, I'd crawled in here and written. I'd written *the whole thing.*

"It worked," I said in awe.

52

YOLANDA

I YELLED for Calahan to get me paper and pen while I started working through the equations in my head. Somehow, in the depths of my bad trip, I'd managed to recreate the killer's work: now I had to solve it. And I only had forty-five minutes.

Calahan pushed paper and pen into my hands. His fingers kept contact with mine for just a second longer than needed and when our eyes locked.... Something was different. The pain and guilt in his eyes was still there but he looked...*determined*. Freed. His expression said, *we need to talk*.

I nodded. But we'd have to think about that later. I didn't have time for my hangover, either. I pushed the nausea and headache and everything else away and just *focused*. Planets spun in my head, moons rising and falling. I frantically scribbled numbers, sketched orbits, and finally drew lines that converged on the Earth...*there!*

I spun on the spot and shot off towards my desk, fallen papers lifting like leaves in my wake. My stomach knotted when I saw the clock at the bottom of the screen: 10:19. Harry would be dead at 10:31. Calahan leaned over my shoulder as I typed the coordinates into a map program. The map re-centered and then zoomed to show a particular building.

"I know that place," said Calahan, stabbing the screen with his finger. "Used to be a chemical factory. They started to demolish it to build apartments, but the EPA shut the project down because the place is a toxic nightmare." He pulled out his phone. "I'll call Carrie."

"Call her on the way," I told him, already heading for the door. "We've only got twelve minutes!"

~

The factory was only a few blocks away and with the siren wailing on Calahan's car and a little use of the sidewalk, we made it in three minutes flat. We screeched to a stop outside a huge red-brick building close to a hundred years old. There were still signs of the aborted plan to demolish it: dumpsters filled with waste and a garbage tube that snaked down from the top floor. The EPA had fenced the whole place off and warning signs were everywhere: *flammable, explosive, poison.*

Calahan jumped out and checked his gun. He balked when I heaved my wheelchair onto the sidewalk. "*You're* not going in!"

I ignored him and swung myself into the chair, then raced over to the gate. "Chain's been cut," I said, examining it. "This is how he got in."

"*Get back in the car!*" snapped Calahan.

I pointed at the building. "There are five floors to search. We've got nine minutes,"

"The FBI are coming," he said stubbornly.

"From all the way downtown. Do *you* want to wait?" I checked my phone. "*Eight* minutes!"

Calahan cursed, glaring at me. I lifted my jaw, not backing down. I could see the battle playing out on his face. All he wanted to do was protect me...but he couldn't let a kid die. Scowling and shaking his head, he stomped back to the car and grabbed the spare gun from the glove box, then slapped it into my palm. "If you see him, you point this at him and you *holler for me!* Okay?"

I nodded quickly. And we raced through the gate.

The main doors were ajar and we crept inside. It was much darker than I'd expected. Most of the windows had been boarded over and the only light came in tiny slivers and pinpricks lancing down from above. The linoleum was so dried out, it had shattered into shards. Where it was missing, you could see the timbers underneath, stained black with chemicals and in places so shot through with woodworm that it split and crumbled under my wheels. Rusted metal drums were stacked high around the walls, leaking God-knows what. You could smell the chemicals in the air, a cocktail that burned the inside of my nose and made my chest ache when I breathed. The whole place was a death trap.

Calahan put his lips to my ear. "Check down here," he said. "I'll start on the second floor and work up."

I nodded. He squeezed my shoulder, gave me one last, worried look..., and ran.

I started along the hallway. The whole place was eerily quiet and the chair's rubber tires made me almost silent. The loudest sound was my own rapid breathing as I crept along, checking each doorway I came to. *Maybe Calahan was right. What the hell am I doing? I'm not a cop!*

I passed offices and storerooms, all empty. I stopped as I reached a huge, open space: the whole rest of this floor was one big room, packed with pipes and tanks. And as soon as I entered it, I had that sense of *wrongness* again, just as I had at the other crime scenes.

He was here.

I looked down at the gun resting in my lap. I needed both hands to work the wheels. If I saw him, would I have time to snatch it up?

I crept up to a tank the size of an SUV and peeked around the corner. Nothing. I started along its length, giving the wheels short, hard shoves and then lifting my hands as I glided along, ready to grab the gun—

Something shot across my vision with a screech. For a second, it pressed right up against my face, soft and warm, *alive.* I was so scared, the scream choked in my throat. I slewed to a stop, almost tipping over—

The pigeon flapped across the room, its beating wings shockingly loud in the silent room, and then settled on a rafter, glaring at me for disturbing it. I sat there panting, my heart hammering. *Just a bird. Just a bird.*

And then I heard a footstep, down at the end of the room.

I looked frantically. Equipment racks ran the length of the room, forming a partition with a narrow hallway beyond it. I raced over to them and skidded to a stop behind the nearest rack.

Another footstep and another, coming closer. I knew it was him. The footsteps were the opposite of Calahan's big, honest clumps. They were careful and measured, as if he'd thought through exactly where to put his weight. And they were unhurried, as if he wasn't scared that someone had found him. As if he wasn't scared of anything.

Closer. Closer. He was walking the length of the floor, checking to see what made the noise. Would he check behind the racks? *Why didn't I stay with Calahan?!*

He stopped, no more than six feet from me, on the far side of the racks. I could feel his eyes sweeping the room. I held my breath—

He moved on down the room. I had to force myself not to let out a sigh of relief. I peeked out from behind the racks and my throat tightened. It was him: the same long, dark hair and leather jacket I'd seen when he took Harry.

Harry! He must be down at the end of this floor, where the killer came from. I started forward, as fast as I dared. I only had until the killer searched the other end and came back.

At the end of the room, I had to pick my way through a dense forest of pipes and tanks. I rounded the final corner and there, on the floor—

I let out a low moan of panic and raced over to Harry. He looked so tiny, in the middle of all this. His wrists were trapped behind his back with a zip-tie and his skin was pale. Had the killer already bled him? I reached out and touched his cheek. Was he already—?

His eyes opened, bleary and unfocused. "*Loyanda?*" he slurred.

Something rose and swelled inside me, warm and powerful.

Something I'd been mercilessly suppressing for over a year. "Stay quiet," I whispered. "We're going for a ride."

I dropped the gun into the pocket behind my seat. Then I reached down with both hands, grabbed Harry's shoulders, and hauled him up. The angle was awkward and he was limp and floppy, a dead weight. But fear lent me strength and I managed to wrestle him onto my lap. Then I spun around and started through the forest of pipes again, going as fast as I dared. If I knocked a pipe with one of my footrests, the sound would echo through the whole room.

I finally got clear of the pipes and raced down the length of the room again, using the line of equipment racks to hide me. Long before I'd covered half the distance, I heard the killer go past, heading towards where he'd left Harry. *Shit!*

I tried to go faster, while still staying quiet. Any second, he'd discover what I'd done. *Just a little further, please....* I reached the end of the huge room and—

There was no shout. He didn't curse or scream. The footsteps just stopped for maybe a second. And then they were coming back towards me, this time at a full sprint.

I abandoned stealth and went all out, racing down the hallway towards the exit, hands wrenching on the wheels as hard as I could, the walls becoming a blur. I'm *fast*, in my chair. But I was weighed down with Harry, and he kept slithering down my body, forcing me to take one hand off the wheels and haul him back up onto my lap. The exit suddenly looked a long way away. And I could hear the killer's feet pounding on the linoleum behind me, gaining fast.

I wasn't going to make it.

"*Calahan!*" I screamed. I shot past storerooms and offices, the exit growing in front of me. But I could hear the killer's breathing now, only a step or two behind me, and I was going to have to stop to pull the door open....

I heard the metal stairs above me shake and clatter as Calahan raced down them. I reached the exit, grabbed the handle—

The world suddenly blurred and tilted as someone grabbed the back of my chair and *wrenched*, spinning me sickeningly fast through

HELENA NEWBURY

a hundred and eighty degrees. With one hand, I hugged Harry to my chest. With the other, I grabbed the gun.

We jolted to a stop. I slid the safety catch off and brought the gun up to point at—

My brother.

53

YOLANDA

W E STARED at each other for one breath, two. I could see the recognition in his eyes. It was him. *It's true. I'm not crazy. He's alive!* And then my stomach twisted. *Oh God, he—*

I could feel my face crumpling as shock and elation turned to raw horror. *He killed those people....*

Then two hundred pounds of pure protective fury slammed into Josh from the side. Calahan and my brother hit the floor and rolled. I just sat there staring.

Josh!

It had been a year since I'd seen him but he'd aged ten. He looked as if he'd been traveling, as if he hadn't stopped moving that entire time. He'd always been slim but now every scrap of fat had melted away to leave only lean hardness. His skin was that shade of brown you get from living rough, ground-in dirt and a deep tan. There were tattoos, too: those now-familiar black tendrils wrapped his biceps and peeked out of the neck of his tank top. His hair was greasy and brushing his shoulders and his jeans were so thick with dirt, I couldn't tell if they were originally black or blue. My heart ached. *What happened to him?*

Calahan was bigger, but Josh had become something quick and

vicious, almost feral. He had his legs wrapped around Calahan and was getting in three quick punches for every one of Calahan's big blows, biting and scratching and digging for Calahan's eyes with his thumbs.

"Get Harry out of here!" panted Calahan.

I hesitated for a split second, then hauled open the door and raced outside. He was right: we had to protect Harry. My mind was still whirling, trying to process Josh being alive. *What the hell do I do?*

As I reached the street, I could hear sirens in the distance: the FBI was finally on their way. All I had to do was wait with Harry.

But then I remembered what Calahan had said, when we were on the stakeout: he'd have to kill my brother to stop him. And my brother wouldn't let anything prevent him completing his plan.

One of them was going to kill the other. And I couldn't lose either of them.

Across the street, a woman was jogging. I shot across and skidded to a stop in front of her. "Take him!" I lifted the semi-conscious Harry and pressed him to her chest. "Just stay right here. The FBI will be here any minute."

"What?!" But she scooped up the boy.

I didn't want to let go of him. That deep, maternal instinct had kicked in full force. But Calahan and Josh both needed me. "Take care of him," I muttered in a choked voice. Then I turned and raced back into the chemical factory.

I burst through the door just in time to see Josh pound up the stairs with Calahan right behind him. I spat out a curse and looked for another way up.

Think! I raced around the first floor. There were elevators, of course, but the power had been off for decades—

There. Over in the corner, there was an open platform with ropes attached to its four corners, leading all the way up to a pulley in the roof. Probably the way they moved drums of chemicals between floors, before they installed the elevators. It looked like it might still work. But it wasn't designed for people, yet alone a wheelchair. There were no walls or railings, nothing to stop me falling off the sides.

They probably used to tie the chemical drums down, but there was nothing to tie *me* down.

Calahan and Josh were going higher and higher, the crashes of their feet echoing as they corkscrewed up the metal stairwell. I had no choice. I raced onto the platform, double-checked my brakes were set, and hauled as hard as I could on the rope.

With a lurch, the platform lifted a few inches off the floor and immediately swung to one side. My chair rocking sickeningly and I sucked in my breath in panic. But it was working. Thanks to the pulley system, I could lift myself, but it meant that for every heave on the rope, I only rose a few inches. I started pulling on it for all I was worth, the platform swaying and spinning as it ascended.

By the time I got to the third floor, I felt like I was gaining on them...and I no longer dared look down. By the fourth, I caught a glimpse of Calahan's heels. And as I reached the top floor, the fifth, I overtook them.

The platform jerked to a stop. I went to release my brakes...and froze. The platform was swaying and there was a three inch gap between it and the floor. Fine for workers loading drums, but I had to roll over it. If I went too slowly, my wheels would go down into the gap, the platform would swing back and I'd topple straight into the widening gulf and fall five floors.

Josh and Calahan burst out of the stairwell and onto the fifth floor. *Now or never.*

I took off my brakes and raced forward. My stomach lurched as my wheels hit the gap...and then I was onto solid floor. *Whew.*

My brother looked around, his eyes wild, and then took off for the far end of the building, with Calahan right behind him. I was exhausted but I gritted my teeth and hauled on the wheels, chasing after them.

This floor was in even worse shape than the rest of the factory. Rain had been coming in through holes in the roof and the wooden floorboards felt worryingly soft and crumbly. In a few places, I could see right through to the floor below. Chemical drums were everywhere, rusting and leaking. The whole place felt unsafe.

At the end of the building, my brother stopped dead. He must have been looking for an escape route: another stairwell, a fire escape, something...but there was nothing.

"Give it up," panted Calahan, slowing to a stop. "There's nowhere left to go,"

My brother slowly turned around to face him. I looked desperately into his eyes, praying I'd see something familiar. He looked as sharp as ever: I could see him calculating, weighing options. But there was something else in there, too.

I watched in horror as he picked up a rusted crowbar and took a step towards Calahan.

Calahan drew his gun. "*Don't,*" he warned. "Don't make me do it." But there was a sadness in his voice, like he already knew how this played out.

My brother took another step forward. Calahan's finger tightened on the trigger. It felt like someone was crushing my heart in their fist. I was going to lose my brother again: forever, this time. But I didn't know what to do or say.

Everything happened at once. My brother took two quick steps forward. Calahan cursed and brought his gun up to fire—

And I was moving, skidding around Calahan, putting myself between him and my brother. "*No!*" I sobbed.

The gun went off.

54

CALAHAN

I TRIED TO stop it but my brain had already sent the signal to my trigger finger. All I could do was try to wrench my outstretched arms to the side to throw the shot off.

The gun kicked. There was a flash, a boom, the stink of cordite.

I lowered the gun. *What did I hit?* Yolanda was sitting there in front of me, panting, the killer beyond her.

The killer threw down the crowbar and sprinted past me, unharmed. I didn't try to stop him. I was rooted to the spot, staring at Yolanda. Behind her, there was a *wumf* and a tongue of flame leapt up towards the roof. But I ignored it. I knew roughly where the bullet had gone. I could visualize it and my eyes were locked on her torso, on the fabric of her gray hooded top, waiting for the red to blossom through it. The nausea rose in my throat. *Jesus, no, please—*

Yolanda reached down and plucked at her hooded top. Just under her arm, there was a small, ragged hole in the loose fabric. But no blood. I'd missed her body by a half inch.

I ran over, fell to my knees, and hugged her to me. Behind me, I could hear the killer clattering down the metal stairs, floor after floor, heading for the doors and escape. I didn't care anymore. All I cared about was in my arms. I crushed her to my chest, wordlessly sobbing with relief. I could smell smoke and a harsh, chemical tang but I couldn't move. I needed to feel her heart beating against me for just a few more seconds, to know that she was safe.

I finally pushed her back into her chair and now the anger took over, the protective rage. "*What were you doing?!*" I yelled. "*I shot you!* You'd be dead except for dumb fucking luck!"

She'd started crying. Something she'd been bottling up was bursting loose and she was descending into wet-cheeked, ragged sobs. "I—He's—" She gave a halting gulp. "He's my b—My b—My brother."

I stood up.

I could see now that one of the drums was leaking chemicals across the floor, and the pool was alight, liquid fire spreading steadily. My bullet must have clipped the drum and ignited the contents. We had to get out of there. But....

Her *brother.*

I stared down at her, putting it all together. "At the shopping mall," I croaked. "At the hospital. You *knew!*"

"I wasn't sure! I hadn't seen his face until we got here!"

"We could have had an APB out—"

"I thought he was *dead!* I thought I was going crazy!"

We glared at each other, me accusing and her defensive. I was angrier than I'd ever been. She'd risked everyone. Worst of all, she'd risked herself. I wanted to scream at her. I wanted to grab her and hold her tight and never let go. And as she looked up at me, tearful and sorry and yet pouting and unrepentant—

My chest contracted as it hit me hard. *I love this woman.*

A sudden wave of heat made us both look up. The fire was spreading across the wooden floor and up wooden beams. The whole place was a tinderbox, the wood soaked in flammable chemicals. "Come on," I muttered, jerking my head.

She nodded and we hurried towards the stairs. But as the fire took hold, it started to outrun us. Burning wood fell from overhead. Flames shot along the stained floorboards, overtaking us. The air filled with roiling black smoke that burned our eyes and scoured our lungs. Yolanda was fast, in her chair, but she was lower to the ground, too, and as the flames rose around us, they started to lick at her face, her hands, her hair. She had to skirt round them, where I could step over them, and that slowed us down.

The floor under us gave a worrying creak. The boards had already been crumbling and now the fire was finishing them off.

We weren't going to make it in time. Yolanda realized it too, coming to a sudden stop, her face pale. She looked up at me.

"Sam?" she said querulously. "Pick me up."

I looked into her eyes and I saw something release. For the first time, she was leaning on me, putting her faith in me in a way she wouldn't with anyone else. Something rose and swelled in my chest, stealing my breath, and—

I bent and scooped her up, one arm under her shoulders and one under her legs, cradling her against my chest. The whole of this floor was ablaze now and the fire was spreading downward as burning debris fell and set light to the floors below. But the stairs were just ahead, a solid metal escape route that couldn't burn. I started to run, floorboards creaking and splintering under my shoes, flames licking up my ankles.

We were only thirty feet away when I felt the floor start to sink. Yolanda threw her arms around my neck, looking back over my shoulder. "*Hurry!*"

"*I'm hurrying!*" I pushed myself to go faster, stumbling and coughing. The floor was collapsing. I could hear the crashes behind me as boards fell to the floor below. The stairs were getting closer, but not fast enough.

"*Calahan!*" squealed Yolanda in terror.

We still weren't going to make it.

I made a decision. I changed my grip on Yolanda, swinging her back a little. Getting ready.

She looked up at me, confused. Then her expression changed as she realized what I was about to do. "*No!*" she croaked, her eyes huge. "No! Don't you—"

The floorboards started to feel loose under my feet. The collapse was catching up with us and the stairs were still ten feet away. "It's okay," I panted. I swung her further back—

"*No!*" she sobbed.

A sort of peace came over me. Ever since Becky died, I'd been asking why. *Why not me?* Maybe this was the reason. Because I'd been needed here, now. To do this.

As the floor collapsed under me, I swung Yolanda forward and threw her as hard as I could. She sailed through the air, flailing.

I had time to see her land on the metal stairwell, bruised and scared but safe. And then there was nothing below my feet and I was falling.

55

YOLANDA

I SCREAMED HIS NAME but it was lost in the noise. A cloud boiled up through the hole, dust and smoke mixed together to form something that looked almost solid, impenetrable gray shot through with burning embers. It engulfed me, blasting into my lungs and making my eyes burn and tear, and I flattened myself against the floor. All around me, the flames were roaring, coming closer and closer, but I couldn't move until I could see....

The cloud slowly cleared and I dragged myself on my stomach to the jagged edge of the hole. It was immense: pretty much the whole floor had given way.

I forced myself to look down.

The floor below was a mess of broken floorboards and other debris. Several fires had started, the flames spreading and joining. And right in the middle of it all lay Calahan.

He wasn't moving.

I yelled *Calahan*. Then, tears in my eyes, I tried *Sam*. No response. He'd fallen at least twenty feet. His back could be broken. His skull could be cracked.

I had to get to him.

At that moment, an explosion rocked the building. What was left of the floor bucked under me and the metal stairwell gave a tortured groan. *The drums.* They were catching fire and exploding, one setting off another in a chain reaction. I thought of the first floor, of all the drums stacked there. When the fire reached them, the whole building would explode. I had to go down a floor, get to Calahan and get him out before that happened.

Easy. If I had working legs.

I looked down through the hole again and saw my wheelchair amongst the debris. Until I got down there, I was going to be crawling.

I twisted around and belly-crawled back to the stairs, digging my fingers into the gaps between the floorboards and hauling myself forward. *Grab and pull. Grab and pull.*

I may not get out much, but when I'm thinking, I pace around the apartment in the wheelchair. I probably cover three or four miles a day and all of that wheeling around is done with my arms. I also lift myself in and out of the chair a lot, and lean over to get things. Because I can't use my legs to stabilize me, I have to use my core. So I've wound up with arms much stronger than average and well-toned abs.

But dragging myself all that way damn near killed me. Progress was painfully slow and the air was filling with choking smoke, making it difficult to get my breath.

At last, I felt metal under my palms. But it was uncomfortably hot. The fire was already blazing down below and the metal stairs were soaking up the heat. I started to slither down headfirst and now at least gravity helped me a little, but it was almost too much: my useless legs kept sliding to the side and threatening to send me into a roll. If I wasn't careful, I'd roll straight under the handrail and fall off the stairs into the fire below. I had to use my core to stay straight and my abs were screaming by the time I reached the floor below.

Just as I got there, another explosion rocked the building, bigger than before. The walls shook and bricks fell from the roof, one of them bouncing off my sneaker and another smashing into the floor a foot from Calahan's head. The whole metal stairwell groaned and shook...and then tilted drunkenly. *Shit!* I had to get down to ground level *now,* if I wanted to get out.

I looked at Calahan. No way was I leaving him.

I started to belly-crawl across the floor to him. This was much, much harder than upstairs. I was crawling over mounds of debris and it slid and shifted under my hands, making it impossible to get any traction. Nails and broken wood snagged my clothes and held me back. I felt like I was moving an inch for every *grab and pull.* And the fire was all around me, the air so hot that taking a breath was like gulping lava. I was crying, from fear and from the pain in my aching arms and shoulders. The heat was so intense, I could feel the wetness drying instantly on my cheeks.

It was fifty feet to Calahan but it felt like fifty miles. Every few minutes, I'd look up and he wouldn't be any closer. *Why couldn't he be with someone with a working freakin' body who could do this?!* I put my hand out to grab again and snatched it back, hissing in pain: I'd touched a piece of red hot metal. The world disappeared behind a haze of tears. It was useless. I wasn't going to reach him in time.

But I couldn't give up. Not when it was Calahan.

I reached out blindly, dug my fingers into the debris, and pulled. And again. And again. I became a machine. *Grab and pull. Grab and pull. Grab and—*

I felt cloth. I drew in a shuddering breath and looked up. I had hold of Calahan's jacket. I hauled my way along his body, grabbed his shirt, and shook him. "Sam!"

He didn't wake. But his chest was moving. I felt a tiny glimmer of hope. If I could just get him downstairs....

But when I looked over my shoulder, my hope evaporated. The fire was already between us and the stairs. Maybe if I'd been able to stand, I could have run through the flames. But crawling through them on my belly, I'd be burned to death.

Could I use my wheelchair somehow? It was lying in the debris, not far from Calahan. I grabbed the footrest and tipped it upright...and groaned. One wheel was bent almost ninety degrees. *Please! There has to be another way!*

And then, as the smoke cleared for a second, I saw something outside the open window, something that didn't match the rest of the building. Bright orange and new, amidst all the decay. I had no idea if it would work. But it was our only chance.

Pulling myself across the floor had been exhausting. Hauling Calahan's not-inconsiderable weight as well was almost impossible. I had to take it inch by inch: pull me, then pull him. The window was only about six feet away: any more, and I wouldn't have made it. By the time we arrived, my clothes were soaked through with sweat.

Fortunately, the windows ran almost down to the floor and the demolition workers had removed the glass when they'd started to clear the place out. They'd wanted a nice, big hole to throw stuff through. Out of the window and into the big, orange garbage tube that snaked down to the ground.

In theory, the tube would slow our fall as it snaked around, like a water slide. Except water slides were nowhere near this steep. And you didn't go down them headfirst, or without working legs.

I heaved Calahan's head and shoulders up over the brink and then inched him forward, pouring him into the tube. "Sorry," I muttered as I gave him a final push and gravity took over. He slithered in, a dead weight, and disappeared from view worryingly fast. I cursed, not sure what sort of landing he'd have.

Then it was my turn. Already, I could hear the explosions starting down on the second floor: any second, the first floor would go and it would all be over. I used the last of my strength to haul myself over to the rim of the tube and looked down. All I could see was blackness. God knows what was at the bottom: a pile of rusty metal, waiting to impale us, for all I knew. But we were out of options. I heaved...and suddenly, I was slithering in, *falling,* not sliding, the sides of the tube flashing past me. My arm hit a join in the tube and I cried out in pain. Then my head hit one and I saw stars and then—

I shot out of the tube and landed on something big and warm and solid. Calahan was on his back, on a pile of rubble, and I was lying face-down on him. I knew we needed to move: we were still way too close to the building. But I was *done*. Every part of me ached and throbbed and I was so utterly exhausted, I couldn't even lift my head.

Running footsteps, coming around the corner of the building. A muttered curse in a voice I thought I recognized. Then Calahan's body started to move, with me on it. We'd slid twenty feet before I finally managed to look up.

Alison. She was dragging us clear. "Keep going," I rasped. "Building's going to—"

A wall of sound and force smacked into us, knocking Alison on her ass. I saw our shadows for a second, a false sun of red and orange lighting us up from behind. Alison scrambled to her feet and dragged us even faster as debris began to rain down around us. Then there was a rumble that turned into a deafening roar as the building collapsed. A cloud of dust blew over us and Alison finally staggered to a stop, panting.

Calahan groaned. I took his face between my hands and slapped at his cheeks. "Sam? *Sam?*"

Those gorgeous blue eyes opened and blinked up at the two of us. "What happened?"

I let myself collapse on his chest and just lay there. "I saved your life," I mumbled. "It was awesome." I stayed there for a moment, just enjoying the feel of him. Then I remembered something and lifted myself up just enough to punch him in the arm.

"*Ow!* What was that for?!"

"That was for that *sacrifice yourself to save me* bullshit," I told him. "Don't ever do that again!"

And then I leaned down and kissed him long and hard. Out of the corner of my eye, I saw Alison grinning.

"And what was *that* for?" he asked when we came up for air.

"Same thing."

56

YOLANDA

CARRIE TOOK one look at us and said that our debrief could wait until tomorrow, and that we should get ourselves to the hospital. We didn't argue.

The emergency room was packed and we had to wait in chairs to be seen. Every so often, I'd look across and find Calahan gazing at me, determined and urgent. He'd draw in his breath, then glance at the people surrounding us, scowl and go silent. There was something he needed to say, something we needed to be alone for. I gulped.

When the doctor finally saw us, we discovered we'd gotten off lightly. We'd both picked up some bruises—Calahan several more than me—and some superficial burns, and Calahan had a mild concussion, but we were otherwise okay.

When the doctor told him how lucky he'd been, Calahan rubbed at the lump on his scalp and grinned. "I got a hard head." But as soon as the doctor moved away, he was back to gazing at me. All that stubborn, determined focus he applied to his cases was one hundred percent focused on *me*.

He drove me home and, as we pulled into my apartment building's garage, it hit me: no wheelchair. It was like a physical ache, like I'd lost a part of me. Calahan came around to my side, stooped, and held his arms out. I hesitated. This wasn't like in the chemical factory. That had been an emergency. I wasn't sure how I felt about—

He looked me in the eye and nodded firmly.

I tentatively reached up and put an arm around his neck. A big hand slid palm-up under my thighs and hooked under my butt. He leaned in and—

Suddenly, I was flying, lifted effortlessly, and cradled close, my body pressed against his. And it didn't feel like he was treating me like a child. I didn't feel weak, or helpless.

He brushed a lock of hair off my face. "Hey you," he rumbled.

"Hey you." It came out as a tight little whisper. One arm was hooked around his neck, my hand on his back, and I was suddenly aware of the hot solidness of him, the muscles under my fingers. Without willing it, my other hand went to his bicep, tracing the shape of it through his suit, feeling how hard it had gone as he hefted me. I looked around the garage. "What now?" I asked. "I mean...how long can you hold me?"

"As long as you need me to." And then he was walking to the elevator and I was rocking against his chest, cradled protectively to his big pecs in a way that made me want to cuddle in even closer.

So I did. And it felt amazing. *Why didn't I do this sooner?*

Because I'd never met anyone I trusted this much, before.

He carried me all the way up in the elevator, all the way into my apartment. There, he set me gently down on the couch. And then he knelt down in front of me and took my hands in his.

He shook his head and scowled at the ground for a moment. Then he slowly looked up and I caught my breath when I saw the force of the emotion in his eyes.

"There's some stuff you need to know," he began. "Stuff I don't tell anybody. I've been...*scared*." He spat the word out in disgust. "Scared that if you knew, you wouldn't want me. But when I nearly lost you, I realized...I need you in my life. You're the most amazing woman I've ever met. And I can't be with you, *really* with you, if I'm keeping this from you. So I need to tell you, and if you hate me, if you don't want to see me again...then that's how it is."

I gaped down at him. *Hate him?* I could never hate him. But I nodded mutely.

He took another deep breath, preparing himself. And he told me.

57

YOLANDA

"Five years ago," he said, "I'm leaving work, walking to my car, when a guy in a dark suit steps out of the shadows and asks me to come with him. He shows me his badge and he's Secret fucking Service. He takes me to an unmarked car and four hours later we're driving through the back gate of the White House. The Secret Service sneak me in a side door and I'm shown straight into the Oval Office: all off the record, no one knows I'm there. And then they leave the room and in walks The President."

I just stared at him.

"I knew Jake Matthews back when he was a senator," said Calahan. "But we hadn't talked since he became president. I had no clue why I was there. He sits me down, tells me I'm going to need a drink, and gives me a bourbon. Tells me he has this problem, something the previous president warned him about. A cult."

I blinked. A *cult?*

He shook his head. "Not like any sort of cult you've heard of. No white robes, no UFOs. These people can full-on *reprogram* you: you forget about your friends, your family, you become utterly loyal to them. They're smart, they're well-organized and well-funded and no one knows exactly what they're planning. And the reason they've flown under the radar for so long is that they've already recruited anyone who might try to go against them: police chiefs, judges, politicians...they can shut down any investigation that starts. Shut it down or worse. The President tells me that he's already seen a DA and a woman from the State Department die in 'accidents' because they looked into the cult. He looks me in the eye and he tells me I could be next, if I investigate. But he knows they've already infiltrated the intelligence agencies. I'm the only one he knows he can trust."

I nodded. I had no trouble imagining that part. If I didn't know who I could trust, Calahan would be my first call.

Calahan looked at the floor. "I should have told him *no*. I should have walked away. He offered me that, encouraged it, even. But...."

"But you knew if you didn't do it, no one else would," I said quietly.

He looked me in the eye and nodded. "So I go back to New York and I start looking into it. Quietly, off the record. And soon, I realize I'm out of my depth. This thing is *huge*. At first, I think it's going to be just a few hundred people but it's more like thousands, spread all across the country. Six months in, I'm sitting in my apartment at two in the morning, cross-referencing phone records...and I realize my boss at the FBI is one of them. This was before Carrie, a guy called Fontana. A guy I'd known and respected for eight years." He sighed and rubbed at his stubble. "That should have been enough. I should have dropped it. But because I'm a stupid son-of-a-bitch, I kept going."

Not stupid, I thought fiercely. I squeezed his hands and listened.

"I'd already been keeping my investigation under wraps but now I have to be even more careful. If my boss finds out what I'm doing, I'm dead. So I'm working FBI cases during the day, looking into the cult at night, coffee to keep me going and booze to let me sleep. I'm burning out. I know it's only a matter of time until I make a mistake, until someone at the cult finds out I'm onto them. But I can't quit."

"So one night, it's late, I've been staring at financial records for hours, trying to figure out how the cult moves its money, and I'm getting nowhere. I'm too wired to sleep so I head to a local bar. And they have a band on, some folk group, and...there's this woman. Becky."

I knew that I should feel jealous. But the grief in his eyes made that impossible.

"She's the singer. Complete opposite of me in every way. I'm this dumb flatfoot, up to his neck in the scum of society. And she's *light*. Airy. She sings these amazing old songs, and it's like she's brought them back from some other place. Another world." He sighed. "Am I making any kind of sense?"

I nodded. I could imagine her.

"From the first second I lay eyes on her...." Calahan shook his head. "Never known anything like it before or since. Not until I met you."

I flushed.

"I stay there until they finish their set. Try to talk to her, but she disappears backstage. I basically become that band's stalker, I go to every gig, even the ones way out of town, just to catch another glimpse of her. And finally, I ask her out. And—"

His voice suddenly broke. He was normally so strong, I wasn't ready for it. When he restarted, it was like he was having to pull the words like from deep within himself, jagged metal from a wound. "And it's *good*. She's like the antidote to everything I see, at the FBI. She doesn't have a cruel bone in her body, she wants to see the good in everyone." He sighed. "See, what people don't understand—" He broke off and glared at the floor. "What they don't *get*—" He went quiet, his lips pressed into a tight line.

I squeezed his hands. Reassuring him that it was okay to say it.

"We were only together a few weeks," he said. "But we spent just about every moment together. We'd both found—" He looked up at me. "It *worked*. I think we were...."

I nodded. I knew what he was saying. And I knew that now, I *should* be jealous. But I still couldn't be, not knowing how this story ended.

"And right at the same time, I start to really make some progress with the cult. I identify a couple of senators, the CEO of a big company. I start to see how it fits together. But it's getting harder and harder to keep my investigation under the radar. Someone's going to get wind of it. I talk to the President again and he warns me off. Tells me it's not worth it, he doesn't want to lose me. But I'm too stubborn. Too proud. I keep going."

"A few days later..." He closed his eyes, drew in his breath. When he spoke again, his voice was much slower. "I wake up. I'm lying there in bed and I'm in that warm, sleepy haze where you can't really be bothered to do anything. Becky's asleep next to me, her hair spread out across the pillow. And my mouth is kinda dry, and I can see the glass of water I always keep on the nightstand. But I can't reach for it because Becky's lying on my arm." His voice slowed even more. "I lie there looking at it for a while, getting thirstier and thirstier. And finally, I decide I'm going to have to wake Becky up so I can grab it. I know she'll be grumpy about it because she's not a morning person but I figure I'll make it up to her by making pancakes...."

He paused. His eyes opened.

And my stomach dropped through the floor because suddenly, I knew why he'd slowed down so much. He'd slowed down because he didn't want to get to the end.

"So I shake her, just gently. I say *Becky.* But she doesn't wake up. So I shake her again, and that's when I feel how cold she is. I panic. I roll her onto her back so I can do CPR but her eyes are open and she's just staring up at me."

I could feel my eyes going hot. I'd known she was dead but not *this.* I couldn't even imagine how it must have felt. And then I thought about how it must have been for him, holding me in his arms when I was having my bad trip, thinking he'd lost me, too. *Oh God....*

I couldn't take it anymore. I dropped his hands, leaned forward, and pulled him into a hug. Kneeling, he was about the same height as me sitting and I cradled his head on my shoulder, his stubble rough against my cheek. He wrapped his arms around me and clutched me tight. But after just a few seconds, he pushed back from me, shaking his head.

My stomach flipped over. *There's more?*

"I call it in," said Calahan. "The paramedics arrive, then the cops. They can't tell how she died, so it's treated as suspicious. My apartment becomes a crime scene. You'd think I'd be used to it: hell, I know some of the cops who show up. But—"

I bit my lip. I could picture him sitting on his bed, answering question after question while they wheeled Becky's body away, having to defend himself instead of being able to grieve.

"They do an autopsy. Discover she had a heart attack: she must have had some condition she didn't know about. I'm in pieces. I drink myself into a stupor. The next morning, I wake up...*alone.* And even with my hangover, I can feel that something's not right, in my apartment. Drives me crazy, for hours, but I finally figure it out. My water glass is missing. I *know* it was on the nightstand because I reached for it, just before I found Becky dead. But it's gone. I find it in the kitchen, washed up. Someone moved it, when the cops and the coroner were in my apartment. That makes no sense, you don't move something in an active crime scene. Not unless you're trying to cover something up."

"I take a real good look at the nightstand and there are a couple of drops of something, some liquid that's dripped there and dried. I scrape some off and give a sample to a buddy in the FBI lab, off the record. And you know what it was?" He took a deep, shaky breath. "Insulin, super-concentrated." He looked me right in the eye. "Insulin will kill you, if you're dosed with enough of it. Looks like a heart attack, if the coroner doesn't know what to look for."

"Someone poisoned her," I breathed. "Who? Did you find out—"

I stopped. His eyes were shining with tears.

And suddenly, I got it. I understood the guilt that ate at him, every minute of every day. I understood the self-loathing in his voice, that night at the bar. I understood why he'd kept pushing me away. *Oh Jesus, no.....* The heat in my eyes started to spill over. I wanted to be wrong. "It wasn't her they were trying to poison."

"I'd gotten too close to the cult," said Calahan. "I'd tipped them off, somehow. So they'd tried to get rid of me quietly. They snuck in, dosed my glass. But sometime in the night, Becky must have woken up, taken a swig from my water glass.... She died because I was too fucking stubborn to quit."

"Sam...." I said, horrified. But before I could find the words, he went on.

"I couldn't even tell anyone. I couldn't tell them it was my fault because anyone I told about the cult would be at risk, too. I had to break the news to her parents, tell them I was her boyfriend and that she'd had a heart attack. They were...*nice* to me. Told me they were glad she'd found someone. And the whole time I'm sitting there wanting to scream at them that *it's my fault. It's my fault your daughter's dead!*"

Silent tears began to roll down my cheeks. This was the reason for the cold cases in his apartment, for working himself into the ground. He thought he'd failed to protect her, so now he had to protect the whole city. "Sam—" I started. But again, he cut me off.

"And Carrie, and Alison, and Hailey, and everyone else I work with...I can't tell them the truth because then *they'll* be at risk. Everyone's consoling me, trying to help me through it, but they don't understand that *I don't deserve any of it!* I don't deserve to feel good, or be happy, because *I killed her!*"

Oh God. None of his friends knew. So he'd never had anyone tell him—"*Sam!*"

He looked at me, his face contorted with anger and guilt.

"You didn't kill her." I wiped at my face but the tears wouldn't stop coming. "They did. The cult."

He shook his head. "I shouldn't have gone after them. I don't know when to quit."

"Sam," I said, "That's what makes you, you. Do you remember what you told me, when we first met? *There's a woman in trouble and I'm not leaving until you help!* That woman would be dead, now, if you knew when to quit. Clara McConnell, too. And Harry. What happened to Becky...nothing I can say can make that easier but *it's not on you.*"

He glared at me. Those blue eyes drilled right to my core, searching for any hint of a lie.

But I stared right back at him, unafraid. Because I knew all he'd see was the truth.

"It's not on you," I said again. "It wasn't your fault."

He scowled at me, demanding that I back down. He wanted me to be lying because that would almost be easier. Torturing himself was what he knew.

But I held his gaze, tears running down my cheeks. I wasn't going to let him carry this weight any more. "*It wasn't your fault,*" I whispered.

And at last, I saw him crumble...and then break. It was like a dam giving way, years of pain finally released. He leaned forward and swept me up in his arms, crushing me to him. I locked my arms around his back and we held each other like that for a long time. I could feel his body gradually relax as the poison that had been inside him for so long was let out. He was still wounded. But now he could finally start to heal.

When we gently moved back, I looked into his eyes and my chest lifted and swelled. He looked *peaceful.* Still focused, still determined, still with that stubborn need for justice. But he wasn't tearing himself apart, anymore.

He slid his palm over my cheek, then rubbed his thumb gently across my cheekbone. He gave a wry little chuckle and showed me: his thumb had come away black with soot. I looked down and for the first time I registered the singe marks on my jeans where they'd been licked by the flames and the hole in my hooded top where he'd shot me. His suit was covered in brick dust, his shirt was torn and both of us reeked of smoke and chemicals.

Calahan caught my eye and shook his head, half in wonder, half in fear. *We survived that.* And then he wrapped me into his arms again, holding me so close I could feel each beat of his heart.

"We should probably get cleaned up," he murmured. We were pressed together so tight, I felt the words twice, as a low vibration against my chest and as hot little kisses of air against my neck. I wriggled in delight...but at the same time, my heart sank because it meant letting go of him.

I sat back, feeling myself pout. "Okay. You go first. Towels are in the bathroom cupboard."

He grinned at my expression and shook his head. "Not what I had in mind."

And then he scooped me up in his arms and carried me towards the bathroom.

58

YOLANDA

F OR A FEW seconds I just sat there cradled in his arms, gaping up at him as I bounced gently against his pecs with each step. Then he grinned at me again, wolfishly, this time. A *filthy* grin. A grin that said, *oh, the things we're going to do.* He was free.

And I loved it.

I pressed my palms to his chest and smoothed them outward over his pecs, delighting in the hot hardness of him. For days, I'd been wound up tighter than I'd ever been. Now it was finally over: we'd saved Harry, stopping the fourth and final murder. My brother was still out there, *alive,* and that was going to take me a while to wrap my head around. But we'd catch him. No one else was going to die. The FBI investigation into Calahan's conduct was still ongoing but now that Harry was safely back with his parents, a lot of the heat would go out of it.

And to cap it off, Calahan had finally opened up. *Everything was going to be okay* and all that stress I'd been carrying was suddenly being released, the energy flooding me and making me heady and wild. As I ran my hands over Calahan's chest, the energy started to coalesce into a slow corkscrew, twisting down towards my groin like a building hurricane. And Calahan was looking down at me, watching as my breathing got faster and my eyes got bigger, and the more turned on *I* got, the more turned on *he* got.

Within a few steps, he was leaning down to kiss me. Quick and teasing at first and then it turned open-mouthed and hungry. My hands were roving all over his chest, under his jacket. My thumbs circled his nipples and he groaned through the kiss. We slumped against the wall, too busy kissing for him to walk, and I laid kisses on his jaw and down his neck, while he kissed his way up my throat to the sensitive spot behind my ear. I squirmed against him and panted. One big hand squeezed my ass and I squirmed more.

He backed up against the bathroom door and tried to push the handle with his elbow, but missed. I glanced over his shoulder and guided him between kisses. "Down a little." *Kiss.* "Left." Kiss. "Your *other* left."

The door swung open and he backed in, then turned around, and pinned me against the wall. Using one arm and the wall to support me, he started stripping my clothes off and I helped, wriggling out of my hooded top. I started on the buttons of my jeans but it was awkward, dangling in mid-air. After the first two attempts, he got impatient. I yelped as he suddenly ripped them open. A brass button went pinging and bouncing across the tiles.

"It's all going in the damn trash anyway," he growled.

He had a point. As he wrenched open the last few buttons, I started doing the same to his shirt, grinding against him unconsciously as more and more tanned muscle came into view. When I had it fully open, he shrugged his jacket and shirt off his arms, dumping them on the floor in one tangled mass. Then he was topless, the hard ridges of his abs brushing my stomach.

He pulled my vest top up and over my head and tossed it away. I felt his cock harden against my groin. "God, I love your breasts," he murmured. He lifted them in the bra, rubbing at my nipples through the cups. And then, unable to hold back any longer, he pulled me forward against him, unhooked my bra and pulled it off me.

He pushed me back against the wall, his hands already full of my soft flesh. I moaned and flattened myself against the tiles, arching my head back as his thumbs circled and rubbed my nipples to aching hardness. Then his hot mouth was enveloping them and I ground myself against the wall, writhing, trapped between the cool tiles and the heat of his tongue and lips. The pleasure built and built, twisting in on itself and glowing hotter until I had to move, had to do something. I groped for his belt and tugged at the buckle while his tongue drew *Os* around one nipple, his fingers lightly plucking at the other.

I got his pants unbuttoned and they fell partway down his thighs. He kissed me again, long and deep, working my jeans down over my hips. But he couldn't get them off my legs while still supporting me. He cursed, panting. Stopped and thought for a second.

Then he lifted me and threw me over his shoulder, my naked upper body dangling down his back, my groin grinding against the hard muscle of his shoulder. I yelped again and he slapped me playfully on the rump. Then he hauled my jeans down my legs and, a second later, my panties were gone, too. Two thumps as my sneakers hit the tiles and then I was naked.

He kept me there for a moment while he kicked off his pants, boxers, shoes and socks. Then he let me down, sliding my naked body against his until my toes were just clear of the floor. He wrapped an arm around me, just above my breasts, to support me, and then he stepped into the shower and turned on the water.

I closed my eyes as the hot spray hit us, sluicing down our bodies, and washing away the smell of burning. Both of us just stood there for a while, enjoying it. He kept a few inches of space between us so that the water could reach my front but I could sense his body there, hard and naked and just *waiting*. And even though we had our eyes closed, I knew he could sense me there, too, because I could feel his cock brushing me as it stiffened and rose.

I heard him pick up the soap and then the hardness of it was pressing into my back, massaging my aching muscles as he rubbed it all over me. One soapy hand came up and gently washed the soot from my face. *But how's he going to do my front?* We were too close for him to fit an arm between us—

He suddenly spun me around and then pulled me hard against him. My back was pressed to his front, all the way from shoulder to groin and it felt fantastic, so warm and solid. He leaned back and I reached up and wrapped my arms around his neck, draping myself down his body.

Keeping one arm wrapped around me to hold me up, he began to soap my front with the other. He started with my shoulders and then teasingly skipped my chest, soaping up my stomach and hips. I ground back against him, feeling his cock straining against my ass, and he gave in and soaped my breasts, lifting and squeezing them, letting my pebble-hard nipples scrape against his palm. The pleasure was rolling down my body in shuddering waves and when it reached my groin it coiled and tightened into a needful ache.

He soaped down the top of one thigh. Up the top of the other thigh. Deliberately missing what lay between them. I was leaning right back, now, my head resting on his shoulder, and I ground it there, panting, feeling myself getting wetter and wetter. His fingers teased closer, closer....

"Ah, that's clean enough," he growled. He hurled down the soap and suddenly two thick fingers were stroking down the lips of my sex and I was gasping and grinding against them, riding them as they rubbed slowly, firmly, *up...*and *down.* With each stroke, I could feel the pleasure cinching tight and turning to hot slickness. Then he brought his thumb into play, gliding it over my throbbing clit, and I went crazy, twisting and rocking the back of my head against his shoulder so hard, the water from my soaked hair was squeezed out and ran down his back.

His fingertips teased my lips and I could feel myself swelling, opening. At the same time, he leaned down and kissed me hard and I moaned and flowered open under him. His tongue slipped into my mouth just as two thick fingers slid up into my sex, and suddenly I was bucking and shuddering against him. My back arched and my shoulders and ass pressed into his hard body as I spasmed around his moving fingers.

I rode the orgasm on and on, long enough that when I finally came back to reality, I started to worry about how long he'd been supporting my weight. I'd helped him out by putting my arms around his neck and leaning back, but he was still doing most of the work. He gently nudged my arms from his neck, carried me out of the spray and crouched, cradling me across his knees. A deep pang of guilt went through me: *he's exhausted! He needs to put me down!*

He used one hand to grab his pants and take something from the pocket. Then he stood, bringing me with him, and stepped back under the water, turning me to face him. He slid both hands under my ass and lifted me, pressing my back against the wall and using his body to pin me there. Then I saw what he'd taken from his pocket.

Oh. That was his plan.

A rush of heat went through me as I watched him roll on the condom. I ran my fingertips over his wetly shining pecs in wonder, all my fears melting away. He wasn't tired, he looked like he could happily do this all day, lifting me and tossing me and pushing me up against walls like I weighed nothing. The thought made me go weak.

He used his forearms to hook my legs up and slid his body between my raised thighs. His straining cock brushed my inner thigh, then nestled against my damp lips, and I got the trembles. He looked deep into my eyes, savoring the moment...and then he pushed forward and slid into me in one long, slow stroke. Our bodies pressed together, wet skin on wet skin. He shuffled forward and my arms went around his shoulders, fingers digging into the hard muscles of his back as he went deep...*deeper.* My breasts pillowed against his chest, our bodies crushing closer, closer...both of us moaned as the base of him ground against my clit. We stayed like that for a moment, the water coursing down our joined bodies, as close as two people can be.

Then he began to move, his hips drawing back and then pumping forward in a smooth, slow rhythm. Each thrust was a long, pink rush of pleasure with that incredible silver-edged stretch at the end, that satisfying, addictive sensation of being completely filled. Each time he drew back, my fingers tightened on his shoulders and I panted faster against his neck, wanting him to return *now, immediately.* But he kept it maddeningly slow and steady, teasing me. At the end of every stroke, though, I could feel a little flutter as his muscles tensed. He was fighting the urge to go fast and each time he drove into me, he came a little closer to losing the battle.

He drew it out for long minutes, until the pleasure had tightened and concentrated into a glowing, heated core I had to release. He could have probably kept it going. But I wasn't going to just sit there passively: that wasn't in my nature.

My lips were right at his ear. The water crashing over us made it feel even more private: there was no possibility anyone would hear. That gave me just enough confidence to start whispering to him. My face went hot as I told him how much I loved it, how I wanted it harder, faster. But with every word, I felt him getting more turned on, his muscles hardening, his cock twitching. He tried to resist, but his thrusts lost their smoothness: he was on the edge. And as my confidence built, it all started to pour out of me in a scalding rush: all the fantasies and dreams I'd been bottling up, not just in the last year but even before. I whispered every filthy thing I wanted him to do to me and he growled and finally began to pound me, his hips pumping hard between my thighs, his big hands holding me pinned against the tiles as he slammed into me.

My whispers became pants and then wordless grunts, my fingers clutching at his back, my ass and shoulders trying to climb the wall as he gave me exactly what I'd begged for. The rushes of pleasure became one continuous chain and the glowing core inside me expanded, filling me, and then contracted *tight*—

He bit the side of my neck and growled, every muscle in his body going like rock—

I cried out as the orgasm ripped through me, pressing my cheek to his wet shoulder as I rode it out. He pushed deep one last time, his cock seemed to swell...,and then I felt him shoot inside me in long, hot bursts.

We stayed like that for a long time, our wet bodies pressed

together, as the sensations slowly ebbed away. He found my lips with his and kissed me, long and slow and tender. Then he turned off the water and walked us, still dripping wet, to my bedroom, stopping only to grab a couple of towels and toss them on the bed. He stretched us out on them and we lay there, limbs entangled, until we fell asleep.

59

YOLANDA

I WOKE TO DARKNESS. Our bodies had dried and at some point Calahan must have tugged the comforter out from under my sleeping body because it was now on top of us. He was spooning me from behind, an arm wrapped protectively around my chest. I could feel his slow breathing against the top of my head. I could feel the hardness of his pecs against my shoulders. I could feel the thick weight of his cock, warm and half-hard, against my ass—

And that was it. I knew there must be more, I knew he must be in contact with me right down the back of my legs, but I couldn't feel it. That wasn't exactly a revelation, I was used to not feeling anything in my legs. And it didn't take away from how good him spooning me felt. But it was a reminder that things were never going to be totally the same as if he was with some other woman. And that thought started a chain reaction in my mind, worries releasing worries until they reached the one I've tried to keep locked down tight, right at the center of my soul, ever since the accident. It had been thrashing harder and harder against its chains ever since I'd met Harry and now it was finally free, bouncing off the walls of my mind, screaming, drowning out all other thoughts.

Sleep was impossible. Normally, I'd go to the bike and sweat out the stress but getting up might wake him and then there'd be questions. I lay there staring determinedly into the darkness. I'd stay like that until morning, if that's what it took. I wasn't going to let him know anything was wr—

"What's wrong?"

I jumped so hard, I think my whole body left the bed. Then I lay there calling him every name under the sun, my heart racing. "I thought you were asleep," I muttered.

"I can't sleep if you can't sleep." Not an accusation. A sworn oath that made me light up inside. Without consciously willing it, I hugged his arm tighter around me. "What's wrong?" he asked again. This time, there was a little more steel in his voice, a little more of the FBI agent. He would be gentle, he would be patient...but he *would* find out the truth. He'd protect me...even from my own demons.

I took a deep breath. I was going to build up to it, talking about *us* and the future and that I knew it was too early to talk about this but he'd asked what was wrong and.... But as soon as I opened my mouth, it was like a seal broke inside me and it just came out, my voice cracking on the last word. "I can't be a mom."

I was never an athlete. I never even *liked* running. The real impact of the accident wasn't stopping me doing things I loved, it was stopping me doing things I'd never done. It took away my future, not my past. "I m—mean, everything *works*. I could physically have a baby. But I can't look after one, I can't raise a kid. And I just wanted you to know because I—I understand if it means this can't be...you know, serious."

The arm around me tightened. His other arm slid underneath me, wrapped around me and pulled me hard against him. "For starters," he growled, "the *serious* boat already sailed."

A big, hot, throb of emotion went *boom* in my chest.

"Secondly," he said. "So we're going to have problems. All parents do. We've got each other: not everyone's that lucky."

"Sam, I can't *be a mom*. I can't push a stroller."

"You built a *drone*. I'm pretty sure you can figure out a way to make a stroller that attaches to your chair."

"That's not what I mean! You know what people are like! Every time I go out, everyone's going to be looking at me, judging me. If *one thing* goes wrong, *ever*, they'll all be thinking it's my fault. '*What the hell was she thinking, having a child?*'"

Strong arms turned me around. I stared into blue eyes, calm and fiercely protective.

"Firstly, I'm pretty sure that's the same fear all moms have. Secondly, if anyone gives you a hard time, ever, they're going to be answering to me."

"What if she runs into traffic and I can't chase her?" I asked, my eyes filling with tears.

"Are you kidding? You're faster than me, in that thing."

"What if she's—she's choosing prom dresses and I can't—"—my voice hitched—"I can't even get into the shop because there's a step and all the other moms are in there helping *their* kids and she's embarrassed by her c—*cripple mom*—"

A thumb touched my lips and I went silent. Then his lips pressed to my forehead in a kiss that lasted several seconds. He moved back just enough that he could look me in the eye. "Yolanda," he said firmly. "I will be there for the steps."

I let it go. I let it all go, all of the fears I'd had about becoming a mom. And that part of me I'd been crushing down inside ever since the accident, the part that had woken when I'd met Harry...it came to tentative, hopeful life. I threw my arms around him and hugged him close. Tears ran down my cheeks and plopped onto his neck.

"You crying?" he asked.

"Only in a good way."

60

CALAHAN

I WOKE FIRST and lay there watching her sleep. She looked so peaceful: sleep seemed to be the one time that big brain of hers actually spun down and came to rest. There'd be moments, though: her brow would furrow, her eyes would tighten and her lips would silently move as she came up against some problem in her dreams. Then her face would relax as she solved it. A big swell of protective love swept through me. I could have watched her for hours.

I slipped out of bed without waking her, hit the shower and then went in search of coffee. The penthouse felt absurdly huge: I was used to waking up and having all four walls of my apartment almost within touching distance. And the low counters in the kitchen still made me feel big and clumsy. But I found a couple of mugs and then poked at the coffee machine like a caveman trying to figure out a laptop, until it finally spat and gurgled into life.

Outside, dawn was breaking. It was time to get back to work. I had to find Josh...and that presented a problem. I looked uneasily down the hall towards where Yolanda slept.

There was a knock at the door. *At this time in the morning?* It turned out to be a delivery guy, with a brand new wheelchair for Yolanda. She must have ordered it right after we escaped the chemical factory, before we'd even had our wounds looked at, and had it rush-shipped overnight. I wheeled it through to the bedroom for her, along with her mug of coffee, and woke her with a kiss. She came awake slowly, clearly not a morning person, her nose twitching like a bunny's as she smelled the coffee. She levered herself upright, drank half the coffee, and only then did she fully open her eyes. Despite what was weighing on my mind, I couldn't help but grin at her. "Hey you," I said softly.

She smiled shyly back and glugged the rest of the coffee. Then she pulled on a nightshirt, slid into the new chair, and tried a few experimental moves. "How is it?" I asked.

She gave a non-committal shrug and wriggled her ass further into the seat. "Okay. Weird. I'd had the old one a long time. It's like trying to get used to new shoes." She frowned and turned an adjustment knob a fraction of an inch.

There was another knock at the door. This time, it was a package for me: a big, soft one. I tore open the wrapping, frowning in confusion.

A brand new suit, shirt and tie. Yolanda had been busy.

"I got your sizes from your old one," she said. "Try it on."

I did, enjoying the feeling of new fabric against my skin. I couldn't remember when I'd last bought a new suit. "How do I look?" I asked, pulling on the jacket.

She smiled. "Great. But rumpled. As it should be."

I began doing up my tie. "I'm going to go track down your brother."

Out of the corner of my eye, I saw her nod. "Yep. Let me just take a shower."

I kept my eyes on my tie knot. "You went through a lot, yesterday. Rest up, I can handle this."

"*I* went through a lot? You fell through a floor! I'm coming."

Dammit. I focused *very intently* on the knot. "Maybe you should sit this one out." I tried to keep my voice light, as if it wasn't a big deal either way.

That utterly failed. "What are you talking about?" asked Yolanda. "He's my brother!"

I finally lifted my eyes and looked at her.

As soon as she saw my expression, her face twisted. Shock, then anger. "What is this?"

I laid my hands gently on her shoulders. "I have to do this on my own," I told her.

"What? No, no way!"

"He's dangerous," I said firmly. "I'm not letting him near you again."

"He's my *brother!*"

"He's not...himself. You saw that."

And then she saw something in my eyes and she went pale. "You think you might have to shoot him," she said slowly. "That's why I can't be there." My silence was all the confirmation she needed. "*No!*"

"If it does come to that, I can't have you there," I told her. "Last time, I almost shot *you!*"

"If I'm there, I can talk him down!" she said desperately. "I can get through to him!"

I sighed and squeezed her shoulders. I hated fighting with her but I had to protect her. "When he's in cuffs in an interrogation room, I promise you can talk to him as much as you want. But until then, it's too dangerous." I pulled her into a hug but she was stiff, staring at me in disbelief. I felt like a piece of shit, but there was no other way. If Yolanda was there, she was at risk: Josh would hurt her to get to me, or she'd get hurt trying to save him from me, or she'd watch me kill him. I couldn't let any of those things happen.

I turned around and headed for the door. But before I'd gone two steps, I heard the hiss of tires. "Tough," she said. "I'm coming with you, even if I have to come in a goddamn nightshirt."

As I left the apartment, she caught up with me and wheeled herself down the hallway beside me. I shook my head in despair. *What the hell am I going to do?* Her determination was one of the many things I loved about her. But right now, it could get her killed.

We reached the elevator and she hit the button to call it, then looked up at me, defiant. *Dammit!* I remembered how she'd wheeled herself through dark, rain-soaked streets to find me in that bar. There was no stopping this woman, not once she'd decided she was going somewhere.

And then, as I watched the elevator's floor indicator climb, it hit me. There *was* something I could do. But it made my stomach churn. *Aw, hell no, I can't....*

The elevator arrived and the doors opened.

I had to make a split-second decision. I imagined her getting in front of my gun again, blood soaking her nightshirt. Or her brother, coming at her with a gun or a knife. Or her watching as I ended her brother's life—

I had to do this to protect her. Even if it meant the end of us.

I leaned inside the elevator and hit the button for the first floor, then quickly pulled my arm back. The doors closed and the elevator started to descend. Yolanda frowned at me, mystified.

Oh God, I don't want to do this. But there was no other way.

I took a deep breath...and opened the emergency exit door next to the elevator. The one she never used.

The one that led to the stairwell.

I heard an intake of breath behind me as she realized what I was about to do. "No. No, wait!"

I was already running down the stairs. The elevator had to go all the way to the first floor and then she'd have to call it all the way back up again and *then* ride it down. I'd be out of the building and gone before she caught up. It was a good plan.

But it was a shitty thing to do.

"*Sam!*" I heard from above me. "Sam, *please!*"

I kept going.

"Calahan, you son of a bitch!" she yelled, her voice cracking. As I reached the thirty-eighth floor, I heard the tears start. "If you do this, we're through!"

I stumbled to a stop, looked up, and saw her leaning over the handrail. I'll never forget her expression: absolute, horrified disappointment.

I hated myself. But it was the only way.

I started down the stairs again, as fast as I could. I told myself it was because I needed to make sure she didn't beat me downstairs. The real reason was, I wanted to escape her pleas. But it didn't work. They echoed down the stairwell, following me all the way to the bottom.

I burst out of the stairwell, legs burning, and staggered out into the street. The sky was darkening as a storm rolled in: it almost felt as if dawn was reversing back into night. I stood at the edge of the sidewalk, waiting for a gap in the traffic so I could cross to my car. I kept telling myself that I was doing the right thing. *I'm keeping her safe.* That was worth it, even if it meant we were finished.

A gap appeared. I started to jog across the street.

I'm doing the right thing. But I kept seeing her expression, when she'd looked down at me on the stairs. I'd seen that look once before: the very first time I'd met her, when I'd seen the wheelchair and I'd reacted with shock. She'd been disappointed then, too.

I slowed to a stop in the middle of the street and looked back at Yolanda's building. I'd just proven everything she'd first thought about me. It had been a split-second decision and I'd been trying to protect her but...*what was I thinking?!* I'd utterly fallen for this woman. I couldn't do this to her.

Horns reminded me that I was still in the middle of the street. I sighed, turned around and trudged back towards Yolanda's building. I had no idea what I was going to say to her, or what I was going to do about her brother. I only knew I couldn't leave things like this.

61

YOLANDA

I ROLLED BACK to my apartment at walking pace. It had hit me on three levels: first, the sharp, humiliating pain of what he'd done, like a slap in the face. *How could he do that to me?* Second, the crushing loss: we'd had something, something *great,* and it was gone. And third, the mocking voices in my head, the ones that had quietened down since Calahan entered my life, were back and louder than ever, telling me I'd been stupid to think he wanted to be with me.

I reached my apartment and rolled inside, slamming the door behind me. The place was a mess, paper still strewn around the floor and hanging from the ceiling and walls, but I ignored it. I wheeled myself over to my chalkboards: the exact place I'd been sitting, when I first heard his knock at my door. *It's like it never happened. It's like I'm back where I started.* Isolated. Scared to come out. Utterly alone.

I leaned forward in the chair as the wracking sobs began. It hurt. It hurt *so bad.* It wasn't just the loss of *us,* the romantic *us.* I'd thought that we were friends. *Partners.* I'd thought we were a team. What he'd done violated all of that. I put my elbows on the chair's armrests, laid my face in my hands and just let it pour out.

There was a knock at my door.

My head lifted slowly, suspiciously. Then I drew in my breath.

He came back.

I started to roll towards the door, slowly at first but picking up speed. He'd realized he was wrong. He wanted to apologize. *He came back.*

My hands hauled at the wheels, hurrying, now. Maybe...maybe there was still hope. Maybe we could talk about it and figure it out. The important thing was, he came back. My chest lifted and filled. *He came back, he came back, he came back!*

I grabbed the door handle and threw it wide open.

"Don't fight," said Josh.

And he stepped forward and plunged the syringe into my neck.

62

CALAHAN

eird. I'd reached the lobby and headed for the elevator, but it
was already on its way back up to Yolanda's apartment. Had
she called it? That made no sense. If she was going to chase after me,
she would have done it as soon as I'd headed down the stairs. The
elevator reached the penthouse and then stubbornly stayed there, no
matter how many times I pressed the button. Was this her way of
pulling up the drawbridge, so I couldn't come back?

I scowled at my reflection in the elevator doors. Well, fine. I
deserved that, and more. But a few stairs weren't going to stop me.

By the time I'd climbed twenty floors, I was a cursing, sweating
mess. Thirty, and my legs were ready to quit...but I wasn't. I'd messed
this up. I'd put it right.

As I passed the thirty-fifth floor, I heard the elevator rattle into
life. *Shit!* Was she heading down? I forced myself into a run,
pounding up the last five floors, and burst out of the stairwell panting
and groaning.

The first thing I saw was a metal door wedge, beside the elevator
doors. Someone had wedged them open: that's why I hadn't been
able to call the elevator from downstairs.

Then I looked down the hallway and saw the door to Yolanda's apartment standing wide open. And inside, her new wheelchair...on its side.

My exhaustion suddenly wasn't relevant. Raw fear took over and I covered the distance to her door at a dead sprint. *"YOLANDA!"* I yelled as I burst in.

Nothing. Dead silence. But the wheelchair told me all I needed to know. There's no way she'd leave her apartment without it.

The elevator! I raced back to it: it was already down to the twentieth floor. *She's in there!*

And there was only one person who could have taken her. *Oh Jesus.* He must have walked into her apartment seconds after I walked out. *This is all my fault!* I'd tried to protect her and instead I'd left her alone, right when she needed me.

I pounded down the stairs for the second time. Adrenaline was flooding my veins: I didn't feel the pain in my legs, anymore. But I couldn't overtake the elevator. When it reached the first floor, I still had ten to go. *Come on! Come on!*

I burst out into the lobby and looked wildly around. The doors to the street were still swinging and I raced outside. *There!* Across the street, a beige sedan with its passenger door open. I could see Yolanda inside, slumped as if half asleep. And Josh was standing beside the car, fastening her safety belt. *Shit!*

I started forward across the street...and had to jump back as a truck missed me by inches. Josh glanced up, saw me, and calmly walked around to the driver's side of the car. I raced forward again...and almost went under an SUV. *Fuck!* I pulled out my FBI badge and held it up, showing it to the oncoming traffic. A few drivers slowed down and I dodged between the lanes. But I could see Josh starting the engine....

I reached Yolanda's door. Grabbed the handle.

Locked.

Yolanda turned to me. Her eyes were glazed. *God, he must have drugged her.* But she was lucid enough to recognize me. Her lips formed my name.

I clawed uselessly at the window, almost hysterical. *Yolanda!*

The car roared away.

For a second, I just froze. Then I turned and raced to my car—thank God, I'd parked only a few yards away. As I threw myself behind the wheel, Josh's car was halfway down the block. I started the engine, hit the gas and pulled out—

The car spun sideways as someone slammed into my rear fender. Then two more crashes as cars piled into *that* car in a chain reaction. I hadn't thought to check my mirror.

I jumped out of my car. One of the rear wheels was bent almost sideways: I wasn't going anywhere. Behind me, a woman in an SUV was looking pale-faced at her crumpled hood. No one seemed to be hurt, but—

I jumped up onto the hood of my car and just managed to spot Josh's car as it reached the end of the block. He turned right...and was gone. No way would I catch him on foot. Even if I could commandeer a car, by the time I got to the end of the block he'd have made more turns. I'd never find them.

I've lost her. Oh Jesus, I've lost her. Josh was taking her God-knows where and from the way he'd drugged her and abducted her...she was going to be his next victim.

The despair hit me. My legs, worn out from racing up and down stairs, buckled and I half-sat, half-fell on the hood. Part of me refused to believe it was over. She was still so close, probably only a block or two away. But I didn't know where, and she was slipping deeper into the maze of streets each second. I'd gotten a good look at the car, a crappy beige sedan. I'd know it if I saw it again. But there was no way to search every damn street.

I froze. Unless there was.

63

YOLANDA

WHATEVER DRUG he'd given me was gradually wearing off. When he'd zip tied my hands and slung me over his shoulder in my apartment, I'd been a dead weight, barely conscious. By the time he'd carried me down in the elevator and loaded me into his car, I was beginning to stir. And when Calahan ran up to my window, I managed to turn my head and look at him. I saw the regret on his face. The fear. This was exactly what he'd been afraid of, what he'd been trying to prevent when he insisted on going it alone. *It's not your fault,* I wanted to tell him.

And then the car roared away.

Now, a few minutes on, things were starting to work again. I could move my jaw and lips but forming words still felt awkward and clumsy. I focused on Josh, taking in the long, greasy hair, the tattoos, the dirt that was ground into his skin and his clothes. Ever since I first saw him in the chemical works, I'd been struggling to process him being alive...and being so completely different to the brother I remembered. "How?" I mumbled.

He kept his eyes on the traffic ahead but he spoke, his voice eerily calm. That was the scariest part of the change in him, that *calm.* It was as if all self-doubt had been taken away and he was utterly certain that he was doing the right thing. "They got you out," he told me. "And then the debris pile collapsed. I was buried, down near the bottom of the river. Pitch black, like before. Except this time, I was alone."

The way he was describing it was all wrong. His voice was as casual as if he was discussing what he'd eaten for lunch. "The new air pocket wasn't much bigger than a coffin," he said. "There was a slab of concrete a few millimeters from my eyes and lips, my nose was mashed up against it so I could barely breathe. It was..."—he considered and then, completely without emotion, "—*claustrophobic.* And my hand hurt. A slab had broken two of my fingers." He glanced down at his right hand and I saw how the first two fingers were lumpy and misshapen. "They didn't heal right. Had to learn how to write with my left hand."

My stomach knotted. *That's why I didn't recognize his handwriting.*

"I waited to die," he said. "I was glad you got out but I knew this was the end, for me. As the air started to run out, I didn't want to die in panic and fear so I went *deep.* Figured I'd pass out while I was solving some equation and that didn't seem like a bad way to go. But I was scared that my body would pull me out of it when I started to gasp for air so I went even deeper. Deeper than I'd ever gone before."

For the first time, he took his eyes from the traffic and turned to me. The beatific grin he gave me was the most unsettling thing I'd ever seen, more disturbing than even the crime scenes but with that same sense of *wrongness.* "I found things," he told me. "Things no one knows exist. I understood it all. And I saw the flaw."

I could feel my heart breaking. His mind had snapped. Trapped and alone in the blackness, minutes from death, his brain starved of oxygen, he'd hallucinated God-knows what. That's what had changed him, that's what had started him on this path. That's what had made my brother capable of killing.

But all I said was, "The flaw?"

He nodded and grinned again, glad that I understood. "But it's okay. Because I'm going to put it right." He turned his attention to the traffic again. "I just need your blood to do it," he said matter-of-factly.

I went quiet and sat there as the fear crept up my body, inch by freezing inch. He was going to kill me. My brother was going to kill me.

Calahan, I pleaded silently, *where are you?*

64

CALAHAN

I BURST INTO the dove loft and grabbed the VR goggles from the desk, wasting precious seconds because the straps needed adjusting to fit my bigger head. There was a disorienting shift as the goggles lit up and I started seeing from the camera on the nose of the drone: there was the wall of the loft and—Jesus, there was *me*, stumbling around a few feet away.

Will this even work? It felt wrong, being up in the dove loft when I should be out there, on the streets, looking for her. But in a city the size of New York, I'd have no hope. This was the only chance I had.

I fumbled around until I found the big red button...and pressed it. There was a hiss of air from behind me and my vision leapt forward so fast I overbalanced and fell on my ass. But I barely registered the pain because *I was flying.*

It was incredible: I was floating over the tops of buildings, swiveling my head to look in all directions. I was *there*. The whole city was laid out beneath me like a map, the cars like toys and the people ants. Now I saw why Yolanda loved this so much. *It's like being God.*

I got to my feet and got my hands on the controls, then tried to get my bearings. *That* was her building, so over *there* was the street Josh had driven along. I fumbled with the controls and managed to turn.

Too fast. A building loomed up in front of me, a sea of gleaming glass reflecting the slate-gray sky—

I veered the other way, went into a spin, and had to fight the controls to level out. My heart was racing. If I crashed the thing, Yolanda had no hope at all.

Very, very carefully, I flew along the street I'd last seen Josh on. By now, they could have taken a few more turns: the search area was growing by the second. *Okay, okay, don't panic.* What would Yolanda do?

Math. She'd do math. I looked down at the traffic below me. The traffic was moving at maybe a block every three minutes. It had taken me about six minutes to get up here. They had to be within a two block radius.

I began to fly back and forth in a rough grid, searching the traffic for beige sedans. There were plenty, but most were too shiny. I finally found an old, beat-up one but when I got closer, the license plate didn't match. I was about to give up hope when I spotted a beat-up beige car turning into a side street. I lost them for a second behind a building but then they reappeared and I swooped in closer for a better look. I thought I recognized the dents, the shape of the hood...*yes!* The license plate was a match!

I slowed, keeping pace with them. Now I could call Carrie and tell her to intercept them. I fumbled for my phone, brought it to my ear—

Shit! I caught the edge of it on the VR headset and the thing slipped through my fingers. Worse, I heard it bounce off the metal grate that formed the floor and then clatter deep into the steam catapult machinery beneath *that.* Maybe if I climbed down there and dug around with a flashlight, I could find it. But I couldn't take off the headset or I'd lose them.

I was on my own.

65

YOLANDA

THE DRUG he'd given me had almost worn off. I could move freely, now...but that didn't mean I could escape. My wrists were zip-tied together and with the seatbelt holding me back against my seat, I couldn't lurch forward with any momentum to attack Josh, or reach the button for the central locking. If only my legs worked, I could have brought them up and kicked him in the face, or kicked out the windscreen or something. But I was trapped.

Josh suddenly slammed on the brakes and the car slewed to a stop, even though the street ahead was clear. Horns honked behind us. Josh ignored them and just sat staring through the windshield, panting in fear. *What does he see?*

Then I saw it. Ahead of us, a construction truck carrying a load of fine, black gravel was pulled up by the side of the road. The wind was whipping up the black dust and drawing it out into long, dark tendrils, just like the ones at the first crime scene.

Josh nervously hit the gas and we moved off again. "I thought that was *them*," he muttered. "Angry because I'm slow."

"Them?" I asked.

"The dark things."

I thought of the creatures I'd seen when I was tripping on LSD.

The things with tentacles, leathery wings and spider legs, the things he'd drawn at the crime scenes. *Hallucinations,* I told myself fiercely. *That's all this is.* He saw them during the bridge collapse because his mind was gone and now because he was suffering from some sort of PTSD, and maybe acid flashbacks. And I'd seen them when I'd taken LSD. That's all.

So why was my skin crawling? Why was cold sweat trickling down my spine?

I shook it off. I had to try to get through to him. This was my *brother.* Something terrible had happened to him, down in the darkness, but it wasn't his fault. If I'd spent another few hours in the darkness, I'd probably be in the same state. "How did you get out?" I asked.

"The debris pile shifted," he said. "The water rushed in and I was carried away by the river. I didn't know which way was up, it was just *black.* When I finally surfaced, the current had swept me downstream." He glanced at me. "They saved me," he explained. "So that I could put things right." He glanced in the mirror, back towards the cloud of dark grit, and there was real terror on his face. The eerie calm dissolved if he even thought about disobeying them. In his mind, these *dark things* had been his saviors, but they were also his masters.

I went quiet and thought: I didn't dare push him too hard and I could figure out some of the rest for myself. Everyone had thought he was dead so he would have had to stay off the grid. Probably, he'd slept on the streets: that explained his appearance. He'd learned about superstitions and witchcraft, planned all four rituals and completed three of them. He'd probably spent a lot of the time *deep,* figuring out all those equations, and the rest of the time on LSD, thinking he was communicating with these...*dark things.* I shuddered. Just a few days working on the equations had been enough to burn me out. Josh had been working like that for a whole year: no wonder he looked like he'd aged a decade.

But he was still *him.* He was still in there, somewhere. I had to try to talk him down. I thought of how I used to calm him, when he was a child and he'd awaken from a night terror. While eating the Toffee Cores, we'd play a game. "125,222," I said.

For a moment, there was nothing. Then he said, "27,750."

The game was to take the answer the other person gave you, split it into thousands and units and multiply the two together, as fast as you could, like a mental game of catch. 27 x 750.... "20,250," I threw back to him.

"5,000," he threw back almost instantly. Which ended the game because the next answer would be zero. It always worked that way: that's the beauty of math. So he started again. "192,764."

"146,888," I said. The math felt like a child's comfort blanket. My mind could nestle in it.

And the same was happening to him. "129,648," he said. And for the first time, I saw him relax. A little part of him slipped out of the delusion's grip and came back to me.

"Josh," I said gently. "This stuff, the dark things. I know it seems real...."

He went quiet. Was I getting through to him, or making him mad? I tried a different tack and showed him my zip-tied wrists. "These things hurt," I told him. "I know you don't want to hurt me."

He glanced across at me. And for a second, he looked uncertain, as if the eerie calm surface was being disturbed by a ripple of memory.

"I know you don't want to hurt me," I said again, desperate, now.

He frowned. I could see the indecision on his face. It was working, I was getting through to him—

Then he looked at the street ahead and had to stamp on the brakes before hauling the wheel hard over: he'd almost missed our turn. That seemed to annoy him. He shook his head as if to clear it and, when he pulled over a moment later, the uncertainty in his voice was gone. "We're here," he told me.

66

CALAHAN

THEY STOPPED in a quiet side street. I circled and then swooped in low. I saw Josh pull Yolanda from the car and start to drag her towards a metal door. She was struggling and yelling for help, pulling at her bound wrists. I flew lower, a hot rush of fury soaking through me, and reached out to grab Josh's throat. *Get away from my woman you—*

My hand closed on thin air and I swept past them.

I ripped off the goggles and swayed as a sickening disorientation grabbed hold of me. I'd been *right there*, close enough to touch them, but the whole time I'd still been here, in the dove loft, miles away. I stared at the goggles in horror. Jesus, you got *lost* in those things. No wonder Yolanda had such a comedown, every time she took them off.

I raced out of the dove loft and onto the roof, heading for the elevator. The first heavy drops of rain were just starting to fall, a slow patter building rapidly into a constant hiss. I was halfway across the roof when I remembered my phone.

Cursing, I ran back into the dove loft, dropped to my knees and looked down into the maze of pistons and pipes beneath my feet. It was down there...somewhere. But finding it would take time I didn't have. Backup would have to wait.

I ran.

67

YOLANDA

W E WERE going down, down, *down*. Josh was dragging me by the arms down flight after flight of concrete steps. I had no idea what this place was, but it was old: the mortar holding together the cinderblock walls was crumbling away and the only light came from small camping lanterns placed at intervals: Josh must have put them there when he discovered this place and broke in.

Five floors down, the stairs started to become damp. Then slick. Then actually wet. Josh slipped a few times and each time, my heart jumped into my mouth. If he fell and lost his grip on me, I'd go sliding straight down to the bottom of the next flight and the first thing to hit the concrete would be my head.

We finally reached the bottom ten stories down, and he dragged me through a hallway that was ankle-deep in foul, stagnant water. He had to lift me over a strange metal outcropping on the floor and it was only when we were past it, looking back, that I saw what it was: the seal for a huge, metal, pressurized door, like you get on a submarine. The door itself was brown with rust and looked as if it had been left open for a decade or more.

The first room we passed through was full of rusting metal frames: it took me a while to identify them as bunk beds, enough to sleep fifty people. The next room was a cafeteria: long tables and scattered plastic chairs. Then a kitchen, then a room filled with computers so old they had big magnetic tape reels. *What the hell is this place?* We passed through a series of storerooms and then we finally stopped and Josh put me down on my back. I immediately rolled over onto my side, desperate to find a way to escape...and screamed. I was rolling into a bottomless, black drop.

Josh caught my shoulder an instant before I rolled over the edge. *"Careful!"*

I lay there panting with fear. I was on the edge of a precipice, a jagged crack in the floor that must have been eight feet across. I couldn't even see the bottom. It just plunged down and down into blackness.

I looked up. There was a matching crack across the ceiling, Water was dripping down from it and falling into the precipice below. I suddenly realized what this place was, and what had happened here.

It was a fallout shelter, built back in the 1950s. They'd dug ten stories down and then tunneled out a long chain of rooms for government officials to shelter in. Except at some point, one of the city's massive storm drains had cracked, and the water had found its way down here and broken through the ceiling of this room, and then, over the years, eaten away at the cheap concrete that made the floor, forming the precipice and hollowing out a cave beneath it.

That's why everything was wet. Every time it rained, this place filled up with water. My stomach twisted in fear. We were a long way underground. Without a wheelchair, it would take me hours to crawl back to the surface.

Josh took a plank that was leaning against the wall and laid it across the precipice. Then he threw me over his shoulder and walked carefully across. The plank creaked under our weight. I held my breath, staring down at the dark drop and not daring to struggle.

On the far side, he laid me down and cut the zip tie binding my wrists. Then he walked back to the other side and removed the plank. I looked around. This storeroom was the final room in the complex, a dead end. There were walls with empty steel shelves on three sides of me and the precipice on the other. I was trapped.

Josh started to walk away. I looked around, my breathing going tight with panic. The room was only lit by a camping lantern and I was terrified to think about how dark it would be if it went out. More than anything, I didn't want to be left on my own. I could feel the weight of all that earth above me pressing down, crushing me. We were so far underground, it almost felt like....

Like we were closer to *them*. The creatures Josh had drawn, the ones I'd hallucinated when I'd taken the LSD. Was that why he'd picked this place?

"Josh, wait!" I yelled.

He stopped and looked back over his shoulder...

"W—Why?" I asked, my voice cracking. "Why do you want me?"

His voice had that calmness again. "There have to be four rituals. One for each of the four dimensions. But you stopped the fourth and I can't just redo it: I missed the time. But I can still put things right, if I have powerful enough blood." He gave me that eerie, beatific grin. "Our blood is more powerful than any of the special people. Don't you understand?"

And suddenly, sickeningly, I did. In his mind, math was magic. So as mathematicians, we were essentially magicians. And what could be more powerful than the blood of a magician? He was going to sacrifice me to complete his crazy plan, and what I couldn't understand was that he still didn't seem to see anything wrong in any of this. The Josh I knew would never be able to justify killing someone. "Josh—" I began.

But he cut me off. "I need to go and set things up. I'll be back for you when I'm ready."

And he left me there on the floor.

68

CALAHAN

I SCREECHED to a stop right behind the beige sedan. The street was so wet that I actually skidded a little and smacked into its bumper. The rain was really coming down, now, thick gray sheets that plastered my hair to my head and made it difficult to see. My suit was soaked in seconds.

I pulled my gun and ducked inside the door I'd seen them enter. *Dammit*...concrete stairs, leading down into darkness. A really good place for an ambush. Josh would hear and see me coming long before I saw him.

But I didn't have a choice. Yolanda was down there, somewhere.

I started down the stairs.

69

YOLANDA

Think! I had to get out of there. It wouldn't take Josh long to prep the blood thinners and other blood-taking equipment. I was lucky he hadn't already anesthetized me: I was guessing he was running low on supplies, since he'd only been planning on four rituals.

Think!

I pulled experimentally at the shelves. *Maybe I could use them as a bridge.* But they were bolted to the wall.

A bitter little voice pointed out that I could take a run up and maybe jump the precipice...if I had working legs.

I wanted to scream in frustration. I'd never felt so powerless. And what really tore me apart wasn't the thought of dying. It was that Josh would be the one to kill me. I still couldn't understand how he'd lost his moral compass so completely.

Think!

But there was nothing. My brain wasn't going to get me out of this one.

I let myself flop back on the floor and stared up at the ceiling. The rain outside must have been getting harder because the drips of water had turned into a steady stream, thickening as I watched into a waterfall a foot wide. My stomach lurched. How big was the cave below us? How long before the water filled it up...and then filled up the whole bunker?

And then I saw something on the ceiling and frowned.

Bare bulbs had been placed at intervals to light the rooms. They were all dark: there was no power and the wiring was probably fried by the water long ago. But I wasn't looking at the bulbs themselves. I was looking at the thick bundle of wiring they hung from. It ran along the ceiling for the whole length of the room...including over the precipice.

I looked down into the darkness. It was so deep, I couldn't even see the bottom. If I fell, I was dead. *No. No way.*

But then I heard something. A tiny noise, maybe a footstep. It came from right down at the other end of the complex, where the stairs were, but sound carried a long way in that silent, echoey space. *Calahan!* There was no one else it could be. Somehow, he'd found me!

I froze as I heard more footsteps, closer by. Through the storeroom's open door, I saw Josh creeping away from me, heading for the stairs. *He's going to ambush him. He's going to ambush Calahan!*

I looked at the dark precipice one more time...then I set my jaw, grabbed hold of the metal shelves and started to pull myself up to standing.

70

CALAHAN

I REACHED the bottom of the stairs and cursed. I knew Josh could be lying in wait for me. I knew I should go slow, searching every corner. But there was no time. What if he was already bleeding her? What if the life was draining out of her *right now?*

I hurried forward and—

I didn't even see him. The only thing I registered was the crowbar swinging down towards me and then the crack of bone as it hit my arm. I cried out in pain and my gun went skittering across the floor. I backed away, cradling my injured arm. *Shit.*

Josh advanced, the crowbar raised.

71

YOLANDA

I'D USED the metal shelves to haul myself upright. Now it got hard. Grunting, I started to climb, my legs dangling uselessly beneath me. The shelves were smooth metal, difficult to get a grip on, and their edges cut into my hands.

But he needed me.

I levered myself up onto the top shelf and dangled there, my arms wrapped around the shelving. Now I was high enough to reach up and grab the cable bundle, but I had no idea if it would take my weight.

I gripped it with one hand. The wires were so old, their rubber casings sloughed away into dusty shreds under my fingers and soon I was touching bare metal. *The power's disconnected, right?* I had no choice. I just had to hope it was.

I let go of the shelf and grabbed the wires with both hands. Now I was dangling from the ceiling, my feet a few feet above the floor. My momentum swung me like a pendulum, threatening to tear my grip loose, and my stomach churned. But I held grimly on.

And then, as the swinging slowed, I started to shimmy across the room.

If I hadn't built up my arms hauling on the wheels of my

wheelchair and lifting myself in and out of it, I never would have even got off the ground. Even so, my whole bodyweight was dangling from my hands and I could feel my grip weakening by the second.

By the time I reached the edge of the precipice, I was sweating and panting. I looked down at the approaching blackness and it seemed insane. *Go back! Go back before you fall!*

But I could hear a fight, echoing through the complex. My man was in trouble.

I gritted my teeth and pulled myself along: one hand, then the other. I stopped looking down but I could feel the sudden chill of cold air when I swung out over the precipice. *Oh Jesus.* I stared straight ahead, at the far side and safety. The temptation was to go fast, before I lost my grip, but going fast made my body swing, and that made it harder to cling on. My arm muscles were burning, now. *Left hand. Right hand. Left hand—*

And then, to my horror, the sound of the water pouring into the room changed. The rain outside must have intensified because the waterfall widened and thickened. It had been coming through just one end of the crack but now it spread right along its length, blocking my path in a translucent curtain.

I was going to have to go through it.

I didn't allow myself time to be scared. If I hung there thinking about it, I was going to lose my grip and fall. I kept going, bracing myself—

The water was ice-cold. It soaked me instantly, hammering down on my scalp and freezing my brain, forcing my eyes shut and making it impossible to breathe. All I could do was keep going but the wires were slippery and my hands were quickly going numb. *Left hand. Right ha—*

I slipped.

There was a white flash of pain in my left arm as it took all my weight. I don't know how I managed to keep my grip: my left hand had locked down like a vice on the wires. I dangled there sobbing. The water was blasting my face and I couldn't breathe or see. I heaved myself up and grabbed with my right hand. Missed. Missed again. I couldn't get high enough and my left hand was slipping, slipping—

I heaved myself up a third time and found the wires. Another grab with my left hand and I was out of the water. Spluttering and panting, I carried on: left and right and left and right, but my muscles were on fire, now. My fingers refused to grip and my palms were wet and slippery. I grabbed again—

And this time both hands slipped. I fell....

And landed hard on the floor, a few inches beyond the precipice. All I wanted to do was collapse in relief. But I rolled onto my stomach, got myself turned towards the door and started to haul myself towards it.

72

CALAHAN

JOSH SWUNG the crowbar again. I managed to stumble to the side and it whistled past my head. The next one, though, connected, and I thought I felt a rib break. It was only a matter of time, now. I was bigger than him but I was unarmed and with a broken arm it was no contest at all.

He swung at me again. I ducked but the crowbar glanced off my scalp and the world exploded into red-edged pain. I tottered sideways and fell to my knees. I'd failed. Failed to protect her.

Josh raised the crowbar over his head....

"*Stop!*"

Both of us froze and turned.

Yolanda was lying on her stomach, halfway through the door. My gun was clutched in her hands: she must have found it on the floor. And the barrel was pointed right at Josh.

Josh's face darkened. His knuckles whitened where they gripped the crowbar. He didn't think she'd do it.

"*Stop!*" yelled Yolanda again. "Josh, don't!"

The crowbar twitched. I wanted to throw up with fear. I wasn't scared of the pain, when the crowbar finally came down. I was terrified of what it would do to Yolanda, if I died because she didn't pull the trigger. Or even worse, what it would do to her if she *did* pull the trigger and killed her own brother. I honestly didn't know which would be worse. I tried to struggle to my feet but my legs were like wet paper and the world spun and blurred. *Goddammit....*

Josh looked at me. Looked at Yolanda. He seemed to come to a decision.

"Don't!" she yelled, but it was almost a sob. Her voice broke and my heart broke along with it. This was going to destroy her.

Josh swung the crowbar.

He'd reached the same conclusion I had: she wouldn't shoot her own brother. I closed my eyes. *I don't blame you,* I thought. I wouldn't have been able to do it, either.

I felt the gust of air against my scalp as the crowbar descended.

Then a gunshot split the air, deafening in the confined space.

73

YOLANDA

OR A SECOND, I thought the gun had exploded in my hand. It kicked upward so hard, it nearly tore itself out of my grip and there was a flash of fire and smoke that blinded me and stung my nostrils. Josh fell backwards and sprawled on the floor. The crowbar clattered across the concrete. *Oh God. Oh Jesus, what have I done?*

Josh groaned and gripped his leg. I took a shuddering breath and crawled over to him. Blood was welling up between his fingers from a wound on his upper thigh, but....

Calahan crawled over to us and pulled Josh's hands away from the wound so he could look. "You didn't hit an artery," he said after a moment. "He needs a hospital but he'll live."

I let out a huge sigh of relief and threw an arm around Calahan's neck. He lifted me, but he grunted in pain and I saw he was favoring his left arm. "You okay?"

He scowled. "I've had better days."

Then he crushed me against his chest as if he hadn't seen me for weeks. *That* made him wince, too. Had he cracked a rib? "That hurts?" I asked, worried.

"Worth it," he muttered. Then, "Sorry. That thing with the stairs...I was just trying to keep you safe."

I stretched up and nuzzled my cheek against his stubbled jaw and that warm, hard scratchiness against my softness was the most reassuring thing in the world. "You won't ever pull something like that again?"

"No."

"Because partners don't leave partners behind."

"Got it."

I kissed him quickly on the lips. Then I turned to Josh. "What are you *doing?* You were going to kill him! You killed Daniel Grier and Sharon Kubiak. You tried to kill Clara, you were going to kill a *kid!*"

I guess maybe I thought being shot would bring him to his senses, snap him back to being the Josh I knew, who'd never hurt anyone. But he just shook his head, unrepentant. "It'll all be okay," he said firmly. He clambered to his feet, taking all his weight on his uninjured leg.

I just gawped at him. *"Okay?"* I broke off as water started flowing into the room. Just as I'd predicted, the whole place was steadily filling up. *We better get out of here.* I shook my head bitterly. "How can it possibly be okay?"

Josh cocked his head to the side and frowned at me. "You don't— Wait...." he said doubtfully. "Have you not figured out what the spell *does?*"

I glared at him, my cheeks coloring. But he wasn't trying to make me feel stupid. He genuinely thought I knew.

"Yolanda," he said slowly, spreading his arms wide, "This...*all* this...is to fix one tiny thing. To correct a flaw way back in the past."

What?! "What...*flaw?*"

"The flaw in the bridge," he said calmly. "So that it never collapses. It *won't have happened,* Yolanda. The bridge will still be standing. Over three hundred people who died that day will be alive. I won't have been trapped in the dark. And you won't be injured." He gave me a gentle smile. "Yolanda...I did all this for you."

74

YOLANDA

I T WAS AS IF all the blood in my body turned to freezing, slimy oil. I went woozy, swaying in Calahan's grasp. *No. No, it can't be—*

From the beginning, I'd been horrified by this case. I hadn't been able to comprehend how anyone could do what the killer did to Daniel Grier, or how they could kidnap an innocent child. I hadn't been able to believe that my brother was involved in something this twisted and dark.

And the whole time...*it was my fault. He did it all for me.*

The water was up to Calahan's ankles, now. I knew we had to get up, get moving, get out of there but—"How?" I croaked. "How could you possibly think you could—"

"The bridge only fell because of one miscalculation," said Josh. "All we have to do is reach back through time to correct that one detail and then everything will play out differently. I figured it out after you were rescued, when I was trapped in the dark. Then I spent a year refining the equations until I had it exactly right." He looked between Calahan and me and his eyes gleamed, just as they had back in college when he'd solved a problem no one else could. "And because the bridge won't collapse, I'll never do any of this. The spell will self-delete from history. None of this will ever have happened. It's so elegant!"

I let out a groan of horror. That was the other part that had never made sense: how he'd killed with such a lack of regret. Now I got it. " The people you killed, Daniel Grier and Sharon Kubiak...."

He smiled, happy that I finally understood. "They'll all be alive again because none of this will ever have happened.

I felt sick. In his mind, it didn't matter how many people had to die to complete the spell because everything would be undone. No one would be dead and hundreds of people who'd died in the bridge collapse would be saved. *Oh God.* For the first time, I really accepted it: my brother was a murderer. Not because he'd turned evil but because he believed he was being a hero. I wanted to weep. It wasn't his fault. He'd lost his mind, down there in the dark. But that didn't change what he'd done. My brother was going to jail, or to a secure psychiatric ward.

I shook my head. "No. Josh, no...." I looked down. The water was up to Calahan's knees. "Josh, it's not real."

He stubbornly shook his head. I sighed. I didn't even know where to begin trying to convince him. There was no time, we had to go—

"Look at me," said Josh quietly. "Look me in the eye."

My heart breaking, I looked.

He stared right at me. "I'm right about this," he said firmly.

And the strange thing was...his eyes didn't look crazy. They were clear and focused.

A tiny thread of doubt whispered into life, as insignificant as a single candle in a vast cathedral but impossible to ignore.

I'd been assuming that his eerie calm was because his delusions had hold of him so completely. But...what if there was another possibility?

The whole world seemed to slip sideways.

What if he was right?

"Yolanda?" asked Calahan, sounding worried.

I couldn't answer him. My mind was spinning. My brother was the smartest person I'd ever met. People can do incredible things under intense stress. What if, *what if,* down there in the darkness, he really had discovered something new? If there was anyone who could figure out something as crazy as changing the past, it was him. He *did* have the background in theoretical astrophysics. He understood wormholes, and black holes, and all that stuff.

But what about the rest? The black magic, the 'dark things' he'd drawn at the crime scenes, the evil that supposedly powered the spell...that was pure superstition, right?

Except...I was remembering how creeped out I'd felt, just reading the equations on my computer, long before I knew they were a spell. There was something discordant and wrong about them. And at the crime scenes.... I glanced up at Calahan. He was scowling, trying to look as if didn't believe a word of it, but he couldn't hide his unease. He'd felt it at the crime scenes, too, the shadow of something truly *bad,* something that didn't belong in our world. Maybe the LSD really *had* opened Josh's mind. And that, together with his incredible brain, had let him make contact with something evil and very, very powerful?

What if—the hairs on the back of my neck rose and prickled— what if all of it was real? What if there really was a chance to undo everything? I'd have my legs, my job, my *life* back. Wasn't that exactly what I'd been wishing for, ever since the accident?

"Yolanda?" Calahan's voice was hoarse with fear.

If we undid the last year...God, he'd knock on my door that first time and I'd run—*run!*—to the door to open it. He'd meet the *before* me, just like I'd always wanted. My kids could have a mom who could dance with them and play tag and—

All I had to do was let my brother complete the spell. He could bleed me and write the fourth set of equations and it would be over. I'd die, like Daniel and Sharon, but when the spell worked I'd be alive again and everything would be fixed. All those people would be alive. My brother wouldn't be a murderer. We wouldn't even remember this whole nightmare because none of it would have happened.

I looked into Josh's eyes again.

"You can't seriously be buying into this," spat Calahan. "Yolanda, he's—" He broke off, not wanting to say *crazy.*

"You don't have to trust me," said Josh. "Just trust the math."

I closed my eyes and thought of the equations. By now, I knew whole chunks of them by heart. And now I knew what the spell did, I could decipher the final parts. I was silent for long minutes, studying the equations as a whole for the first time. However many times I checked and double-checked, I came to the same conclusion.

My whole life, I'd put my faith in numbers. And the numbers said Josh was right.

I opened my eyes. "Okay," I whispered.

There was an intake of breath above me. I looked up into Calahan's terrified eyes. "He's *nuts,*" Calahan growled.

"I'm not so sure he is," I told him.

"I'm not letting him kill you because he *might* be right!"

My eyes went hot. "I'm not letting three hundred people stay dead because I'm scared to take a chance. Remember Daniel Grier's family? We can give him back to them! Remember Sharon Kubiak, lying there in that empty house? We can undo that!"

"You *seriously* believe this shit?!"

"The math checks out. I believe *enough.*" I gripped his arm. "It's worth the risk. It's worth risking...me." I hung my head, unable to look at him. "I was ready to kill myself, just a couple of weeks ago. My life's not precious."

Calahan put his finger under my chin and lifted my head. He stared into my eyes, actually shaking with anger. "It's *fucking precious to me!*" he spat.

I could feel tears starting to trickle down my cheeks. "I have to try. I couldn't live with myself if I didn't."

"This stuff is bullshit!" he yelled. "It's based on LSD trips and *psychosis!* How can you—"

"Sam, its *three hundred people.*"

He stared down at me, that strong chest swelling against me with each heavy, enraged breath. He tried to speak but the words died in his throat. I'd never seen him so torn apart. He couldn't bear to let anything happen to me but, just like me, he couldn't just discount hundreds of lives. He'd been there, that day on the bridge. He'd seen the bodies, the grieving families. He ran a hand through his hair. "Let's get above ground," he muttered. "You can figure all this out up there."

"No," said Josh. "We're running out of time. We need to do this *now*." He pointed to a doorway marked *Command Center*. "I have everything set up. The Command Centre is a few floors up. It'll be hours before that part of the complex floods. We have time to finish the spell."

Calahan looked at the stairs doubtfully. "Is there another way out, up there?"

Josh shook his head. "We'd have to come back through here."

Calahan looked around in dismay. The water was already up to our thighs. I knew what he was thinking: if this didn't work, there'd be no way out for us because these rooms would be underwater. We'd be trapped and then drowned as the upper levels flooded.

But then he caught my eye and shook his head, dismissing it. If this worked, history would change and we'd all be safe in our new, bright futures. And if it didn't work, I'd be dead. And if I was dead, he didn't care what happened to him. I threw my arms around him and hugged him tight, burying my face in his chest.

Josh led the way, limping and holding onto Calahan's shoulder when he needed to. He led us up two flights of stairs, through a set of double doors and we emerged in a large room filled with desks. A map of the United States filled one wall. I gazed around for a few seconds before it really hit home: this is where New York's officials —or what was left of them—would have worked, in the aftermath of a nuclear war. Huddled deep beneath a radioactive wasteland, trying to organize what was left of society. A shudder went down my spine.

Josh had pushed four desks together in the center of the room to form a makeshift table. He patted it: God, that was where I was going to lie, while he.... I swallowed and nodded to Calahan.

Calahan sat me down on the edge of the table and put his hands on my shoulders, squeezing gently. "Yolanda," he whispered, "there's still time. We can still get out."

I shook my head. "I have to do this. I have to try."

His hands tightened on my shoulders. He couldn't speak for a second and when he did, his voice was rough and throaty with pain. "*I need you.* I need you like I've never needed anyone. Don't...."

Don't leave me. If this didn't work, he'd be holding my body in his arms, just like he'd held Becky's. It would utterly destroy him. And then he'd die a slow, terrifying death as this part of the complex filled with water....

"You could go," I said, my voice trembling. "You *should* go. It makes no sense for you to be here. You could go now and still make it out. Just...in case it doesn't work."

His eyes hardened. "If you're doing this," he said. "I'm staying right here."

I stared at him a beat longer, my eyes filling with tears. Then I grabbed him and pulled him into the tightest hug ever, as if I was trying to imprint his soul onto mine. We sat there shaking, locked together, until I couldn't bear it anymore, until I knew I'd chicken out if I didn't do it *right now.* Then I reluctantly let him go and lay back on the table.

"I can give you blood thinners," said Josh. "But I'm out of anesthetic. It shouldn't hurt, though. It'll just feel like going to sleep."

I closed my eyes and tried to breathe slowly, to control my rising panic. *Trust the numbers.* The math was right.

I felt the coldness of an alcohol wipe on my arm, then a sharp scratch as Josh inserted the needle. I kept my eyes shut, imagining the blood starting to flow. All I had to do was lie there and let it happen.

Trust the numbers. The math was right.

I began to feel light-headed and wondered if that was just my imagination, or if I'd already lost that much blood. *Don't panic. This is what's meant to happen. Just let yourself fall asleep.* I gradually felt my body going heavy. I thought about opening my eyes so that I could see Calahan one last time. But he was only just restraining himself as it was. If I looked at him, he might just snap and run forward and stop this whole thing. I kept my eyes closed. But I couldn't stop tears welling up at the thought that I might have seen him for the last time. They escaped my closed eyes and trickled down my cheeks, and I heard Calahan mutter a curse and step forward—

"It's okay," I said quickly. "I'm okay."

He stopped. I could tell he was right by my side, looking down at me, and from the way his breath was shaking, he was in pieces, a hair's breadth from pulling the needle out of my arm. *Calahan!*

Trust the numbers, I told myself again, repeating it like a mantra. The math was right.

But...something else wasn't.

My whole life, I'd cozied up to hard, reliable things. Numbers, facts, science. I'd never been much good at the softer things: people and relationships and feelings.

But since I met Calahan, things had started to change. That night when I'd gone to find him in the bar, I'd felt that he needed me. When I'd found the candy wrapper and gone to the grocery store, I'd been following a hunch. I was starting to trust my gut.

Something was wrong. Not the math. Something else. I was definitely starting to go light-headed, now, and that made it difficult to think. But in a weird way, my dreamy state made it easier to feel. And there was a feeling of...unfairness. No, not unfairness. I didn't know what it was but it scared me, the fear spreading like dark ink through water, turning me cold. *What is it? What's wrong?*

It felt like this whole thing was mis-weighted. Slumped to one side. I fought to think. God, I was so sleepy. I just wanted to drift off....

And then I suddenly sat bolt upright and my eyes snapped open. *"It's imbalanced,"* I yelled.

A lot of things happened very quickly. First of all, the room spun like a carousel and went dark around the edges: sitting up suddenly when you've lost—I looked down to my side—two full pints of blood isn't a good idea. Secondly, Calahan grabbed me and held me, his eyes wild with anger and worry. He pinched the tube that led from my arm, stopping the flow of blood. *"What?"*

Josh looked shaken but was trying to stay calm. "The equations all work out perfectly," he said gently.

I tried to shake my head but that made the room spin more. "No, that isn't what I mean. The *whole thing* is imbalanced. It's *too* perfect. All those people on the bridge come back to life, right? And the people you killed, even *they* come back to life. So there's no... *cost*. And everything has a cost."

"No such thing as a free lunch," muttered Calahan. He sounded beyond relieved: finally, something he understood. Maybe understood better than me. He turned to Josh, scrunching up his brow. "She's right. This whole deal is one-sided. These...*forces* you're messing with—"

"The dark things," said Yolanda.

"The dark things. What's in it for them?"

Josh hesitated. He tried to brazen it out. "I'm not sure that.... Maybe it doesn't work that way...." But for the first time, the certainty in his eyes flickered.

I closed my eyes and started to hunt through the equations. Thanks to Calahan, I now knew what I was looking for. Something that stood on the other side of the scales, to balance out everything good the spell asked for. There seemed to be nothing and I was on the point of giving up and telling Calahan I'd been wrong.

And then I found it. The innocent little thread of equations that wound around the main part like a vine growing up a tree. It made use of some of the same math, all about bending space and connecting places together, but it was much simpler. When I figured out what it must be, I gave a guttural moan. My eyes flew open and I stared at Calahan in dread horror, my heart crashing against my chest.

"What?" he asked, grabbing my upper arms. "*What?*"

I tried to speak but I couldn't. I'd never known fear like it, not even at the crime scenes, or when I'd had the bad trip. *Oh God. Oh Jesus, we nearly—*

"Yolanda," said Calahan desperately, "what does it do?"

I was sweating, my whole body damp with it, but I felt colder than ice. "To work, the spell has to open a doorway, between *now* and the past. But..." I swallowed. "But that isn't the only doorway it opens."

Calahan and Josh went sheet white. I knew what they were imagining because I was imagining it, too. The dark things, not just seen in drawings or glimpsed in acid trips but here.

We nearly let them in.

Josh sucked in his breath as the implications hit him. We couldn't complete the spell, now. And that meant everything he'd done, the people he killed...it wouldn't be undone. "Oh God," he whispered. He looked at me, utterly lost. *What have I done?!*

I lifted my arms and he ran to me, clutching me tight. The cool, collected mathematician was gone and in his place was the terrified boy I used to comfort in the middle of the night. This time, the nightmare he'd woken from had lasted an entire year.

There was a sudden, sharp pain in my arm. I looked around and saw that Calahan had pulled the needle from my arm. He pulled off his tie, wrapped it around my arm, and tied it tight, using his one working arm and his teeth. Then he scooped me up into his arms. I looked up into his eyes and the love and protective fury I saw there made me melt.

"Let's get the *fuck* out of here," he growled.

75

CALAHAN

I was *mad*. I don't think I've ever been angrier. I was mad at Josh for risking her life, mad at Yolanda for agreeing to it. I was mad at the spell and the way it had seduced both of them with visions of a better life. I was mad at geniuses. I was mad at math.

Mostly, though, I was mad at myself for letting things go this far. I'd felt powerless. I didn't understand the math so I'd had to watch from the sidelines. Now, we were back in a world I recognized. She was in danger. I needed to get her above ground. *That* I could do.

My head was still throbbing and my right arm hurt like hell. I had Yolanda snuggled into the left side of my chest, my left arm under her butt to take her weight and my right one just loosely wrapped around her to hold her against me. But even so, every step bounced my arm around and made things move and scrape inside it. Just walking hurt and anything faster was agony.

I ran, spitting curses with every step. Through the double doors, down two floors to—

Shit.

In the time we'd been up in the command center, the lowest floor had filled up to neck height. Most of the emergency lanterns Josh had spread around had failed so the room was almost dark. The few lanterns that were still working were flickering fitfully as they floated around, turning the place into a confusing mass of moving shadows. And over it all, the roar of the water as more and more of it flooded into the complex. Yolanda moaned in fear and I heard Josh curse behind me.

I waded in, hauling Yolanda higher so that her head was right up near mine. But it was slow going: the water resisted my movements and because I couldn't use my arms, I was unbalanced. The current made it even worse: water was pouring into the room from behind us, rushing towards the exit. In theory, that made it easier but it also made it more dangerous: my feet kept wanting to go out from under me. And all the time, I was fighting to keep Yolanda safe and secure against my chest, despite my left arm tiring and my right arm throbbing with pain.

I got halfway across the room with slow, steady steps. But slow and steady wasn't cutting it: the water was rising too fast. It climbed my chin and I had to crane my head back to keep my mouth above water. We had to get out *now*. I waded faster—

And slipped. My feet went out from under me and I fell full-length on my back.

I inhaled water and started to cough and choke, precious life bubbling up towards the surface. But all my focus was on Yolanda. She was underwater, helpless, and I had to save her. But I couldn't get her above water until I had a firm footing myself and I was still falling in slow motion towards the bottom, Yolanda pressing me down from above. My feet skittered and slid on the floor but I couldn't get them under me. I needed to use my arms to push myself up to standing but my arms were holding her.

I had to let her go or we were *both* dead.

I glimpsed her face in the confusion, her hair billowing out in a black cloud around her head, her eyes huge with panic. I let go of her and she tried to claw her way towards the surface. But with her legs weighing her down, she just hung there, suspended, running out of air. I scrambled to get to my feet but I only had one working arm to push with—

A dark shape above us. Then Yolanda shot towards the surface. I stumbled to my feet a moment later, coughing water, and found her being held by Josh. The poor guy was barely able to stand, with his leg wound, so carrying her must have hurt like hell. He was a little shorter than me, too, so his mouth was only just out of the water. I still didn't trust him. Hell, I still hated him for what he'd done, even if I understood why. But he was trying to make it right. I grabbed Yolanda from him and he gasped in relief.

"We're going to have to swim," I panted.

76

YOLANDA

I FELT THE PANIC rise to claim me as he turned me onto my back and lay back in the water, lifesaver-style, so that I was lying on his stomach. Before, I'd at least been able to hang onto him but now I was utterly passive: all I could do was lie there and try not to move. The water was only a foot from the ceiling, now, which meant my face was almost brushing the plaster. I was utterly reliant on Calahan: one slip, one fumble, and I'd plunge to the bottom, unable to stop myself—

But then his voice was in my ear, panting and tight with pain but determined. "It's okay," he said. "I'm going to get you out of here."

And I believed him, because Calahan never bullshitted. And I felt the warm solidness of him under me, the warmth of his chest against my soaked back, and it was okay because I wasn't alone.

We reached the cafeteria and Josh had to take the lead, clearing the way for us through a forest of floating plastic chairs. Calahan picked up speed as we reached the bunk room: once through that, we'd be at the stairs and then we were home free. But halfway across the room, he looked over his shoulder and muttered a curse. "What?" I asked.

"The door's closed." We slowed as he waited for Josh to open it.

But nothing happened, just some grunting. "What's going on?" I asked, frightened. I couldn't see anything except the ceiling.

"It's jammed," said Calahan, and he couldn't hide the fear in his voice. "Or locked."

What? The door had been open when we came through. There was no one else down here who could have locked it. "Put me down," I said.

The bunk frames went right up to the ceiling. He swam over to one and I grabbed a metal strut and dangled, taking my weight on my arms. Now I could turn around and see, Josh was tugging on the door's handle but it didn't budge. *That makes no sense.* Then I saw the slot cut in the door, one of those things with a sliding metal cover, so that you can see who's outside before you open the door. Water was rushing through it.

Suddenly, the problem was clear. And terrifying.

"It's not jammed," I told them, my chest going tight. "It's the pressure. There's no water on the other side. The water must have swung the door closed and it's built up on this side like a dam. The weight of the water's holding the door closed."

Calahan joined Josh and together, they hauled on the door handle. This time, it opened a fraction of an inch. Water started rushing through the gap but the flow wasn't enough to relieve the pressure: the room was filling up too fast behind us.

The two men got their feet against the wall and used their legs to push. The door creaked wider, wider.... But as soon as Calahan let go to come and get me, the pressure of the water slammed the door shut again. He and Josh looked at each other, white-faced and panting.

"I could hold it for a couple of seconds," said Josh. "While you two go through."

There was silence for a second as the implications sank in. Then, "*No!*" I yelled. "No, you're not—*No!*" Calahan was shaking his head, too.

"Someone has to hold it," Josh said. He looked at Calahan. "*You* can't, I busted your arm."

I started to haul myself hand-over-hand along the bunks towards him. The water was rising fast: to keep my mouth above the water, I was having to press the top of my head against the ceiling. "I'm not leaving you here to die!" I told him.

"I'm the reason we're down here!" Josh snapped. The words echoed off the bare walls and in the aftermath there was silence. "I have to. If I don't, we all die."

I looked at Calahan. He looked as horrified as me. But then he looked at the door, at the rising water...and reluctantly nodded his head.

Hot tears prickled my eyes. I shook my head in denial. "No. There has to be another way!" Josh shook his head. "No. *I just got you back!*"

Josh swam over to me and hugged me close. The water was lapping at our lower lips and we had to tilt our heads back to breathe. "I fucked up. I've *killed people*. Let me do one thing right," he said.

The tears slid down my cheeks as he moved away. *No. No no no!* There was so much I needed to say to him. But there was no time: in another minute, we'd drown.

Calahan and Josh looked at each other and something passed between them. The anger in Calahan's eyes faded.

"Be good to her," Josh told him. Then he got hold of the door again and braced his legs. Calahan did the same and they heaved the door open again. It was even harder, this time. They had to fight for every inch, grunting and panting, muscles straining. All of us had our mouths brushing the ceiling, gulping from the last sliver of air in the room. They got it open just over a foot, barely enough for Calahan's big frame to fit through.

"Go," hissed Josh.

Calahan let go of the door and it swung closed a full inch before Josh managed to catch it and hold it. He swam over to me, I gulped down a big breath—

And then he was pulling me underwater to the door. I glimpsed Josh, up near the ceiling, the veins on his neck standing out as he put everything he had into holding the door open. Then Calahan was pushing me through the opening and I was grabbing and pulling with my hands to help. I slid through and floated on the other side, looking back towards the gap. Calahan's head emerged. His chest barely fit and he had to wriggle and kick, squirming through inch by inch. Then suddenly he was past the widest part and he came through in a rush. As his legs slithered through the opening, I could see the door starting to close: Josh's muscles must have given way. Calahan kicked frantically, drawing his legs up...and the door slammed closed an inch behind his foot.

He grabbed me under the arms and kicked for the surface. We burst into the air gasping and spluttering. The water wasn't as high, here, and it wasn't rising as fast because it could only flood in through the narrow slot in the door.

I grabbed hold of a pipe so that Calahan could free his arms. Immediately, he swam back to the door and heaved at it: maybe we could push it open from this side and let Josh through. But however hard he pushed, the door didn't budge. I climbed hand-over-hand along the pipes until I reached the door and then joined him, dangling from one hand while I pushed with the other. But the pressure on the other side was just too high. We looked at each other helplessly. Then I stared at the door, imagining Josh running out of air on the other side.

Calahan slipped an arm around my waist to support me. "There's nothing you can do," he said gently.

I could feel the hot tears running down my cheeks. *Josh!* Then I pressed myself close to the door and felt underwater for the slot. When I found it, I slipped my hand through.

There was one thing I *could* do. He didn't have to die alone.

At first, I thought it was too late. Then I felt Josh grab my hand and squeeze tight, and I squeezed back. I screwed my eyes shut, sobs wracking my body. Calahan said nothing, just held me close and curled his body around mine, his lips pressed to the top of my head.

Josh's hand gripped mine tighter and tighter. *It's okay,* I thought. *I'm not letting go.* I'd left him once, when I was rescued and he wasn't. I wasn't leaving him again.

Josh gripped me so tight it hurt. I welcomed it, wished I could take all his pain and fear. His hand trembled....

And then his fingers slowly uncurled and he was gone.

I let out a wail and Calahan pulled me even tighter against his body. Then he was pulling me across the room to the stairs, swimming and then wading and then finally climbing, carrying me up out of the dark towards the light.

EPILOGUE

Yolanda

CALAHAN CARRIED ME up the final flight of stairs from the bunker and we emerged, soaked and shivering, onto the street. His legs shaking from carrying me up ten floors, he carried me to his car, set me carefully down on the passenger seat...and then slumped down on the sidewalk next to me, utterly exhausted, his head nestled in my lap like a dog,

We sat like that for a good fifteen minutes before Calahan got up the strength to move. And as I sat there stroking his hair, I thought.

My brother had done awful things. But he'd done them because his mind had snapped, down in the dark of the bridge wreckage. The person who'd killed Daniel Grier and Sharon Kubiak...that wasn't *him,* not really. The guy who'd given his life to save us, *that* was my brother. But he'd be remembered as a murderer. Unless....

No one except Calahan and I knew that Josh was the killer. Calahan hadn't told Carrie yet. Josh had never been arrested so his fingerprints and DNA weren't in the FBI database. He'd been living off the grid for a year, using false identities, so I knew they wouldn't find Josh's driver's license or any other ID on his body. The killer would never be identified. The families of Daniel Grier and Sharon Kubiak would still get closure: the killer was dead, drowned in the bunker after kidnapping and trying to kill me. And my parents wouldn't have their memories of their son torn apart and have their lives ruined by TV reporters hungry for a story.

All we had to do was keep quiet.

Calahan finally managed to clamber to his feet and went down the street to the nearest store to call the FBI. When he returned, I tentatively put the plan to him. I thought he'd be against it. More than anything, he was a crusader for the truth, for people getting justice. And he *was* an FBI agent. He sat there brooding for a long time and I was sure the answer was going to be *no.* "I want you to know," I said awkwardly, "If you need to tell them...I understand."

He sighed. I could hear sirens approaching: we only had a few minutes before the FBI showed up. "I remember what you were like, when I came to your apartment and you'd been writing those equations all day. It was like you weren't *you,* anymore."

I remembered that, too. How I'd actually been eager to get rid of him. I'd been addicted.

"Josh was around that stuff for a whole *year,*" said Calahan. "I'm not saying I believe in this shit. Maybe it was something controlling him, maybe he was just in some kind of psychosis. But I know he wasn't *him,* just like you weren't *you.*" He rubbed at his stubble. "I don't think it does anyone any good for him to be remembered that way. So I'll go along with it. But you gotta promise to do one thing for me, when all this is over."

The sirens were only a few streets away, now. "Name it."

He leaned close and whispered in my ear.

I hesitated. And then I nodded.

Calahan

One Week Later

When Carrie, Alison and the others had shown up at the bunker, we'd told them a story that was mostly the truth, leaving out only the identity of the killer. Yes, he was dead, drowned while pursuing us through the complex as it flooded. No, we had no idea what his ultimate plan had been.

We'd had a few days of holding our breath but as we'd hoped, Josh's fingerprints and DNA weren't in the database and the case was closed with the killer as a John Doe. That just left Yolanda's promise to me.

"This feels wrong," she said, staring at the chalkboards. "We're destroying something we can never get back. The FBI doesn't have the bits I recreated when I was on LSD. This is the only full record of all the equations. The only one in the world."

"It's the right thing to do," I told her, and pressed a wet rag into her hand.

She stared at it, going rapidly pale. I knew she thought I didn't understand, but I did. The equations were literally a work of genius. Beautiful, compelling...*addictive*. I could see the way she was drawn to them, even now. That's exactly why they had to go. "You promised," I reminded her.

She nodded. Gulped. She actually looked ill at the thought of doing this. She took a deep breath...and swept a big arc of shiny wetness across the board. As soon as it was done, she stiffened: *God, what have I done?* I saw her eyes go to a piece of chalk: she was wondering if she could grab it and recreate them from memory, before she forgot them—

She closed her eyes, gathering her courage. Then she opened them and quickly wiped the rest of the board. With every number that disappeared, she relaxed a little. When the board was clean, she started on the next one. Then she wheeled herself into the bathroom and scrubbed the marker pen from the tiles. Then together, we fed all her paper notes into a shredder. And finally, she wiped all the photos from her laptop's hard drive.

When it was done, she blinked and looked around in amazement. I felt it, too: something had lifted from the place.

I told myself it was just because the equations were creepy. And I told myself that, down in the bunker, when it had seemed like maybe this stuff might be real, that had just been our minds playing tricks on us. All of us had been under incredible stress, Josh had been in the grip of psychosis, Yolanda had only just surfaced from a bad acid trip and none of us had slept properly in days. We'd all wanted to undo the bridge disaster—who wouldn't? And combined, that had been enough for us to buy into Josh's delusion, just for a few minutes. It didn't mean any of it was real.

I told myself all that. But I wasn't a hundred percent sure. All I knew was, I was glad the equations were gone.

I bent, slipped my arms around Yolanda and lifted her, crushing her to my chest. My arm was still in a cast and I wasn't really meant to do things like that yet, but when did I ever follow the rules? I loved her, dammit.

"Well done," I growled in her ear. "Now grab your stuff. I got a surprise for you."

Yolanda

It was amazing. I was light as a feather, soaring high on rising warm air and then swooping down to glide effortlessly over fields and forests.

"You're a natural," said the instructor from behind me. "You *sure* you haven't flown a glider before?"

I shook my head. I figured it would be a bad idea to mention I'd been illegally flying a drone around downtown New York. And this was so much better! There was no VR headset, no jarring shock when I had to take it off. This was real: I was here, up in the sky. Free.

The gliding lesson had been Calahan's surprise. We'd driven way out into the country to reach the place and when I'd seen the gliders ahead of us, sleek and white and graceful, Calahan said my face had lit up like it was Christmas. I'd just never considered flying a glider before. It was something that had to be done out here, in the real world, and that had been off limits to me...until I'd met him.

"How you doing?" asked Calahan on my headset. He was in another gilder, with his own instructor.

"Incredible," I breathed, and pulled a steep turn, standing the glider almost on its wingtip. I was already going through my calendar in my head, figuring out when I could have another lesson. "You?"

"Yeah," he muttered. "Great." And then a thermal caught his glider and he unleashed a stream of curses as the ground dropped away from him.

When we landed, Calahan did everything short of kissing the ground. We reached an unspoken agreement in that moment: gliding was going to be a hobby for just me.

We climbed into my new car and set off, but not back to the city. We had something else planned, that afternoon. Our diaries were filling up fast: I wanted to try all the things I'd been missing out on. There was a place not too far away that offered horse riding for people with injuries like mine, and I wanted to try a shooting range too. Plus my folks had been to visit and would be coming again soon. They'd loved Calahan, who'd shocked me by smartening up for the day and calling my mom *ma'am*. He was reassuringly disheveled again an hour after they left.

Calahan gripped the dash as we sped over a hill, catching a little air. He still complained I drove too fast. "Carrie's been making noises about you helping us out on a few cases," he said.

I thought about it. It was good that Calahan was back in Carrie's good books. They'd closed the investigation into his conduct, finding no wrongdoing. And there were probably a lot of times the FBI needed something decrypted, or hacked. But me, work for the FBI? I'd have to play by the rules.... "Only if I can have a red flashing light for my car," I told him at last.

He nodded and we drove in companionable silence. I loved that we could do that. Neither of us were exactly people persons but together, we worked. He balanced me, grounding me and stopping me going too deep into my own head, and he said I cleansed him, after a day at the FBI seeing the worst of humanity. What we had was deeper than love. I was pretty sure I'd found my soulmate.

We came over the brow of a hill and our destination crept into view ahead of us. I drew in my breath and unconsciously slowed the car a little, the nerves spiraling up from the pit of my stomach.

Calahan leaned over and covered my hand with his big, warm one. "It's time," he told me.

And he was right. It was high time I did this. I'd realized something, after the bunker. Whether the spell was real or not, I'd believed in it because I wanted it to be real. I'd wanted to turn back the clock and undo my injury just as much as Josh. It was all I'd been wishing for, since the accident.

It wasn't like I was suddenly overjoyed with what had happened to me. But maybe I'd reached what that counselor had called acceptance. All I knew was, my wishes now were all about the future, not the past.

I floored the gas and the car leapt forward. A few minutes later, we arrived at a quaint little inn tucked away by a bend in a river. The car was almost silent as it pulled up but someone inside had good ears because I'd barely got out and into my chair before I was slammed into from both sides and became the filling in a hyper-excited female sandwich, garnished with a lot of *squees*.

They finally moved back...and for the first time ever I was looking at the other two Sisters of Invidia, *live*.

"You're shorter in person," Lilywhite deadpanned.

I hadn't wanted the wheelchair to be a shock but I hadn't known how to broach it so I'd wound up putting off telling them until the very last minute. Lilywhite was literally about to leave to get her flight when I finally messaged both of them in our private chatroom, feeling sick to my stomach, and just spat it out.

yolanda> Look, I use a wheelchair
lilywhite> Okay

diamondjack> OK

And then we'd started discussing which in-flight movie Lilywhite should watch. I'd sat back from the screen, blinking. *Is that it?!*

I made the introductions. The woman in the jeans and plaid shirt who'd just flown in from Montana was Lilywhite, who'd used to be known as Lily before she went into witness protection and was forced to change her name. She went by Mary, now. And the huge cowboy with his arm around her waist was Bull, now rechristened Luke. Calahan and Lily went way back and he gave her a huge hug, then was almost crushed by Bull, who lifted him clear off the ground.

The woman with the soft, dark hair in sweater and jeans was Gabriella—diamondjack. And that meant that the tall guy with the Russian accent had to be Alexei. He gave us all European-style double-cheek kisses, but regarded Calahan with more than a little suspicion. To be fair, he was former Russian mafia and Calahan had spent a lot of time trying to bring down one of the big Russian crime bosses: there were always going to be trust issues.

After all the rain, spring finally seemed to have arrived and it was comfortably warm. "Is this place okay?" I asked Lily as we all moved to the table the inn had set out for us in the garden. "It's a long way from the city, but...." I looked nervously over my shoulder. There was no one else around but I knew the risk she was taking, coming back to New York. There were people in New York who'd kill her on sight, hence the new life in Montana.

"It's perfect," said Lily as she sat down. "Thank you for organizing it."

"I booked out the whole place," I said seriously. "Just to be sure."

She pulled me into a hug. "You're the best."

Since we were the only guests, the inn had really pulled out all the stops for us. The table was decorated with spring blossoms and there were pitchers of cocktails, an ice bucket with cans of coldly sweating beer, platters of cheeses and cold meats, freshly-baked bread and olives. Fairy lights were looped overhead, ready for when they served dinner that evening. We weren't going to have to move all night.

"How's teaching?" I asked Lily. It was strange, talking to her face-to-face after all this time, almost as if a movie star had climbed down off the screen. But it was feeling more normal with each passing second.

"I hate it," she said. "And love it. Part time seems to be working: I hack, and that's great, but after a few hours it starts to feel pretty lonely. And that's about the time I need to go teach class, and the kids are a nice relief. And then by the end of the day, I'm ready to kill them and all I want to do is disappear into some code and be anti-social...so it balances, you know?"

I nodded and looked thoughtfully at Calahan. Maybe that was another reason to accept Carrie's offer and do some work for the FBI. I had enjoyed being part of a team.

"And Bull just made sergeant in the sheriff's department," said Lily, squeezing Bull's huge forearm. He grinned as if embarrassed.

Alexei rolled his eyes and muttered something in Russian, but it sounded good-natured. Probably something about being surrounded by law enforcement.

"And what about you two?" I asked Gabriella. "What have you been doing?"

She told us about how they'd been to Russia to visit some of Alexei's family, and how Luka Malakov and Konstantin Gulyev, the two big Russian crime bosses in New York, had both tried to tempt Alexei to rejoin the mafia and come and work for them. "I think once one of them heard the other was after Alexei, it almost became a competition," said Gabriella, her eyes huge. "It was like, *what do you want? Do you want money? A sports car?*"

"But I said no," said Alexei, bringing his fist down dramatically on the table. "No more trouble." He turned to Gabriella and looked at her with absolute adoration. "Have all trouble I can handle, right here." And he kissed her tenderly.

Lily leaned forward. "We, um...have something to tell you," she began.

And then she took Bull's hand and squeezed it in a *very particular way.*

My jaw dropped. *Oh God, are they—*

Lily showed us her left hand, which she'd been carefully hiding under the table until now. The diamond caught the setting sun and glowed like fire. Gabriella and I *shrieked,* and I'm not someone who shrieks often. We immediately wanted to know *when, where, how?* Which she told us was yesterday, when they were camping out in the wilds, as they were watching the sunrise.

Lily looked at Gabriella and me. "If it's okay, I'd like you two to be my maids of honor."

I gawped at her. "Of course it's okay! But...don't you want...you know, your real life friends for that?"

Lily put her hand on mine. "You idiot," she told me. "You *are* my real life friends."

~

Lily, Gabriella and I spent the rest of the evening talking dresses, table layouts and bands. The three men huddled together at the far end of the table with the bucket of beer. By the time the yawns became infectious and we all agreed we should continue the planning over breakfast, it was after two in the morning. Alexei seemed to have gotten over his suspicions and was laughing and joking with Calahan and Bull as they said goodnight. I rolled over to my man and we wandered together towards the inn and bed.

As we reached the top of the path that led down to the rooms, we stopped. The stars were out and we were far enough from New York that we could see the Milky Way stretched across the sky, a million glittering pinpricks in a deep blue blanket.

A few weeks ago, I'd felt like there was nothing in my future. A big, fat, dark zero. Now, all I could see ahead were possibilities. Some short term, like teaching Calahan how to make decent coffee and him teaching me how to cook. Some long term, like...well, I didn't want to jinx things by thinking about it too directly, but...I looked at Lily and Bull as they walked hand-in-hand. *That.* Even the idea of a little

Calahan junior running around was starting to seem not totally crazy, off in the far future.

The temperature was finally starting to drop and despite my sweater I gave a little shiver. Calahan pressed in close behind me and wrapped his arms around me, shielding me from the breeze. I snuggled my cheek against his and just sat there for a while, soaking in his warmth, utterly satisfied.

At last he stood, stretched, and walked around in front of me. He looked down at me and rubbed at his stubble. "What?" I asked.

"Figure this is a good time to remind you that I'm crazy about you."

Hearing that still made a hot bomb detonate in my chest. I flushed, fumbled for words and couldn't find any. But when I looked up at him, I think my expression did all the talking because he smiled.

"And I want to say something," he said. "We're good together. And I don't just mean...."

And those big blue eyes crinkled and he goddamn *smoldered* at me.

I drew in a shuddering breath as electricity crackled down inside me from my flushed skin, setting my heart thumping against my ribs and then turning dark and hot as it moved down towards my groin. This man did it to me every single time.

My hands tightened on the chair's wheels and I rocked forward like a racehorse waiting for the off. Eight seconds, I estimated. We could be in our room, on the bed, in eight seconds. Maybe seven.

But he wasn't done. "I mean everything. Talking to you. Spending time with you. We even work well together. I trust you more than a lot of the people at the FBI."

"Mm-hmm," I murmured, looking up at him. I felt drunk and heady. My fingers were itching with the need to dive under his shirt and slide across his chest.

"What I'm trying to say is, when you put us together, we're more than the sum of our parts."

"Enough math," I told him breathlessly. "Get down here and kiss me."

And he did.

The End

Thank you for reading!

Agent Calahan first appeared in *Texas Kissing* (which is also Lily's story) and then in *The Double*. The story of how hacker Gabriella met Russian hitman Alexei is told in *Kissing My Killer*.

Find all my books at helenanewbury.com.